MUDMAN

A Tale of a Texas Swamp

John D. Parfait, Jr.

ISBN: 978-1-916770-58-4

Dedications:

To my wife, Judy, who understands and tolerates me, even while being blatantly ignored when my attention is focused elsewhere.

To my mother, who thought I was special. I was not. She was.

About The Author

John is the type of man who is alone in a crowd and unless you engage him in conversation, he will remain immersed in his own thoughts, oblivious to the crowd. The fact he was there in the first place is unlikely to be remembered, so do not be offended if you are not remembered the next time you meet, because he was never there.

However, should you have a conversation with the man, neither of you will forget the other.

Table of Contents

Mudman
Prologue

In this world, the particular reality in which we exist, we live in ignorance. Apparently everyone is ignorant to some degree, meaning that some are less ignorant than others. Someone once wrote, "Ignorance is bliss." I suppose that statement is, on some level, true; however, I don't like it, because a blissfully ignorant populace is the boon of the powerful. In other words, when one's cattle and sheep are happy, his purse and stomach are secure.

Mudman told me that when I was very young. I did not understand at that time what he meant, but a "blissfully ignorant populace" just sounded bad. I now understand. The way to control a collective is to convince it that its best interests are served by obeying authority, which is accomplished by rewarding the herd for following and punishing it for straying. An intelligent, free populace cannot be successfully herded so, you manage that populace by dumbing it down, which is accomplished by controlling its education and information while, at the same time, convincing it of the necessity of your leadership; all accomplished with the power of the media which, of course, you control. Concluding that, you have yourself a herd, with tremendous wealth and power to boot, all in the best interests of the herd, of course. Wink, wink!

This is a story that should probably not be written and yet, here am I, beginning to do just that. It is my umpteenth effort at 'beginning' the story of Mudman over very many years so, the likelihood of it being torn up and gently discarded into the trash is high. Then again, I may finish the book this time and you, after reading it, may wish I had thrown it into the trash.

I began keeping a journal of my Mudman experience at 12 years of age and continued for almost four years. This journal has never been seen or read by anyone and is hardly legible anymore as pencils were my writing devices at the time and much of what is written is light or smeared. I can decipher it though, because I wrote it.

Why have I kept this journal a secret? After you read this book, you will understand. I should use the word 'if' in place of 'after' as few people read books anymore and who will be attracted to a book titled "Mudman" among the millions of books published every year, anyway? Understand this, "Mudman" is not being written for the collective of humans; rather, it is written for you.

Morals and ethics demand full disclosure. I have no idea if "Mudman" will be an entertaining read, as it is not being written for such and is being written into existence at this moment, in this now. "Mudman" will be my third book and, if finished, may be my last. I am 81 years of age and not a professional writer. Full disclosure requires that I tell you this: Mudman, is. The swamp, is. So is truth, such as it is.

Read "Mudman". You will see yourself herein, and everyone else you have ever met, heard about, or will in some now. And try not to attack the messenger, for that is a path of least resistance and you know where that leads, or soon will.

Chapter 1 - Home By the Swamp

We first met in 1952. I don't remember the month, but it was a warm day and school was out for the summer. I was 10 years old and spending time wading in the water at the edge of the swamp, looking for tadpoles. I had a pet catfish that liked them. The swamp water looked black, but that was an illusion caused by the dark mud on the bottom. Swamp water was clear. I liked the mud and the way it squished between my toes when wading and the way it was sometimes cool and sometimes warm. I didn't understand why, I just liked it. A little water snake was swimming just ahead of me and I tried to catch it, but it got away.

"A little water snake?" you exclaim! "What is a 10 year old kid doing in a swamp by himself, chasing snakes?" That's a fair question; I'll try to explain.

Our family bought and moved to a house close to that swamp just before my 7th birthday. I had two younger brothers and that home was perfect for us, we loved it. It was an old two story wood house, with an outdoor toilet and no bath facilities. We bathed in a metal tub. Primitive? Of course, but it was at least two steps up the social ladder from where we were living before. And the swamp began about 50 yards from the house and was thick with trees. Totally fascinating to me! The day we moved in, I found two turtles in the back yard; I was in heaven!

Momma wasn't that enthusiastic. She had three young boys to care for and to her, that swamp was a problem. Snakes, alligators, leeches, and quicksand were dangerous and just waiting to prey on her boys. In addition, the woods were full of dangerous animals. I was the oldest and she banned me from going into the swamp. My two brothers didn't have to be told to stay out of those spooky woods, they didn't like the looks of it. Mom got to where she sometimes would take me for walks along the swamp looking for turtles and frogs, but going by myself was not an option. Seven-year-olds had no business going anywhere by themselves anyway and I pretty much always obeyed my momma. . . pretty much.

Listen now, I don't have to tell you about young boys. 'Explore' is their middle name. At seven years old, I was an explorer of the unknown and to me, that swamp was the most mysterious and exciting place in the world. Besides, no one ever seemed to go there, which was perfect for me. I would sit in the back yard in the day and watch little birds and big birds fly into and out of the swamp. There were always bird calls and strange sounds coming from there. At night, I would lay by the open window next to my bed and listen to the night sounds, imagining the different creatures making them.

Anyway, the point I am trying to make is that I started roaming the edge of that swamp at eight years old, learning about fish, frogs, snakes, and a whole lot of other critters I never knew existed. If I didn't mention it before, I'll say it now, I loved that place. By the time I was ten, the swamp was my comfort zone. So this 10 year old boy wading the swamp and chasing snakes was a normal occurrence. I even had a snake and turtle collection. I kept the snakes in home-made rabbit cages and the turtles in a wooden box. Momma didn't know about the snakes; she didn't abide snakes.

Chapter 2 - Rex

Oh, I have to tell you about the dog. The mudman story can wait a while longer. We had lived there next to the swamp for several months and were settling in like most folks do when getting used to new surroundings. I had not yet gone into the woods by myself, but I thought about it. Momma wouldn't have it, Seven-year-olds stay in the house and the yard. So, I dreamed and pretended a lot. Daddy brought home a huge cardboard box from work in which he intended to store things, but to me and my brothers that box was a pirate ship on the ocean and sometimes a tank in a war or a secret cave. I would drag it under a big pine tree at the end the yard and pretend I lived there. Needless to say, daddy didn't get to use that box for storage.

Sometimes momma would make a sack lunch, give it to me and say, "Go play in your box, Johnny."

"Momma, it's not a box!" I would say, indignantly. "It's a fort!"

She would laugh and say, "Oh yeah, I forgot about that."

I think momma liked to dream a little bit too, cause there were times when she would come outside, get in the fort with us three boys and read while we played.

Well, about the dog. One morning when I went outside to get in my fort, a dog came out of it, jumped on me, knocked me down and began licking my face. I was laughing and wrestling with him when momma came outside and called for me to come in for breakfast. As soon as the dog heard her voice, he ran back into my fort. I looked in and he was laying down in a corner looking at me and wagging his tail, or what there was of it. He had a real short tail. I didn't know where he came from, but I never had a dog before and always wanted one. It was love at first sight; he was my dog, we belonged together, and that was that. Uh, except for momma. How was I going to tell her about that?

I left him there in the box, ran in to the house and went in to eat breakfast. Momma had made pancakes and sausage. I ate as fast as I could without drawing attention to myself and asked momma if I could take some food out to my fort. She fixed me several more pancakes, some sausage, and sent me on my way. The dog was still in the box when I got there, so I gave him the pancakes and sausage and he wolfed them down. He was hungry! I was so happy; I had a dog now! I named him Rex. Now I had to introduce him to the family. Rex followed me as I walked back to the house. Grandma Cora was sitting in a rocking chair on the porch. She was old, in her seventies, and was my momma's grandma, making her my great grandma and she lived with us. Grandma noticed me walking up, with Rex following and said, "Whatcha got der, Johnny?"

"This is my dog, grandma. His name is Rex." I proudly stated.

Grandma smiled at me. "He's got the markings of a terrier." she said and commented, "Those are good dogs. Where didja git him?"

"He was in my fort this morning." I answered. Rex went up on the porch and laid down next to her rocker.

She reached down, patted his head and said, "Well, you know he just might b'long to sum'un else." Grandma thought about those things.

I stated firmly, "No, he's mine."

"Does yur momma know?" she asked.

"Not yet." I said.

Grandma thought a moment, then gave me some advice, "Why don't cha wait 'til yur dad gits home and tell 'em both at de same time? Yur dad laks dogs 'n if yur mom balks, he'll likely talk 'er into keeping it." Sounded like a good plan to me, but no matter what, Rex was my dog. Somehow, I just knew it. I took Rex back to the fort.

Strange, isn't it, how things work out sometimes? Daddy came home from work and surprise, surprise! He got out of the truck holding a black puppy. Said he found it wandering along the road on the way home and had already named it Blackie. I ran back to my fort, called Rex to follow me and promptly introduced him to the family. Little brother Rocky was holding Blackie and Ricky was laughing and started wrestling with Rex, who was licking his face. Momma was a bit exasperated. What could she do? She turned around and said, "Supper's almost ready. Y'all wash up and get to the table." Then she added, "And leave them damn dogs outside, I'm not havin' them in the house!"

That was great! We were all a family now! Momma was only puttin' on. She came to love those two dogs, 'specially Rex. He won her over in no time and followed me everywhere. I was a happy seven year old boy. I had a dog!

Chapter 3 - Mudman

I could tell a bunch of stories about me and Rex, but let's get back to where I left off. I was ten and wading slowly along the edge of the swamp and stopped to look at my reflection in the water. Rex was investigating a crawfish at the edge of the water. While standing there looking down, I could see the mud bottom through the clear water. Suddenly two eyes opened up in the mud and looked at me. It was startling! I was familiar with a lot of strange things in the swamp, but this was new and curious. "Uhh, hello?" I stammered. The eyes closed and the mud bottom returned to normal. What was that? I didn't know, but it kinda scared me. I grabbed my clothes and me and Rex ran home.

Now up to age ten, I never went more than knee deep into the swamp and never out of calling distance from home. I had already earned more than a few whippings for not answering when momma or daddy called, so staying in range was a "must". Anyway, there is more to see and learn four feet from shore than most people know. You can only imagine how many strange and beautiful bugs and lizards lived there for me to catch and examine in that small section of swamp that I considered mine.

After seeing those eyes in the mud and running home, I had a bit of a dilemma, in that I couldn't tell my parents about being in the swamp or the eyes looking at me. Punishment of some sort always followed rule-breaking in my home. Now I'm not trying to give the impression that my parents were mean or abusive. They weren't like that at all, but we kids had rules that were laid down and expected to be obeyed or else. "Or else" usually meant extra chores, loss of privileges, or a whipping. I know this is going sound like self aggrandizement, but I was not often punished because, for the most part, I was a good boy. I really loved my momma and daddy, sought their approval, and obeyed their family rules. Like I said, "for the most part". My brothers? Not so much but, because they were so young, they got away with a lot. Anyway, I didn't tell anyone about the "eyes in the mud". I was very curious, though and had to check out the mystery.

Not having to go to school, I was up early the next morning to go and investigate "the eyes" in the mud. Couldn't go right away, though 'cause momma had chores for me to do that takes up time. According to momma, I had to eat breakfast and wash my plate afterwards. Breakfast was a necessary part of the morning. I had to take out the garbage and feed the dogs. If the clothes were washed, I had to hang them on the clothesline to dry. I gotta say, being the oldest child was loaded with responsibility. On top of all that, I had to have a good story about my plans and promise to check in often. As always, momma's last order to me was, "Stay out of the swamp." Okay, maybe I wasn't all that good, but remember, I qualified my statement with, "for the most part".

So I headed for the swamp and upon arriving, I changed into my swamp clothes. One of the first things to be learned about playing in a swamp is that you are going to get dirty, wet, and probably even tear your clothes once in a while. There are long thorns and broken limbs that seem to reach out and grab a passerby occasionally. We kids were expected to take good care of our clothes and shoes, because clothes were hard to make and the store bought clothes were expensive. An old pair of pants and a tee shirt served as my "swamp clothes". They were kept in a toe-sack and hidden in a hollow log. When I said earlier that I "grabbed my clothes and ran home", that is exactly what I did. No time to take changing back into my regulars; I just scooped them up and took off. Later that fall, I had to find a new hiding place for my clothes. During a heavy rain period (it rained a lot in Beaumont), the swamp water rose and covered up my hollow log. After the water receded, I went to look and the log and swamp clothes had disappeared. I wasn't too upset with losing the clothes, they were easy to replace, but I really liked that hollow log and the toe-sack.

You're going to notice, while reading this book, that I talk a lot about my momma. She was the most important person in my life, more so in those early years, and I was, without a doubt, a momma's boy. She seemed to understand me and my insatiable desire for adventure. She fed my interest in books by telling me stories about Sherlock Holmes, Tarzan, James Bowie, Noah and Moses. She made a bookworm out of me. One of the things often quoted was, "When God closes a door in your life, He opens another one specifically for you." Well, that is what happened when I lost my hiding place. While walking back to the house, I found another one, a better one: a hollow tree. That tree had been there all along, but the hollow opening was facing the swamp and I never noticed it before! I cut out the opening with my "Popsicle Pete" hatchet and made it big enough to crawl inside. I built a fire inside and put wet leaves on it to smoke it out. A lot of small creatures hang around in hollow trees you don't want to mess with. Some of 'em bite and some sting, making them necessary to remove. They don't like smoke and an hour's treatment took care of them. That became my hiding place and no one ever found it for as long as we lived there. Many of my boyhood treasures remained in that hollow tree when we moved away. I still dream about them sometimes.

There I go, wandering away from the story to tell another story, something that is common for me to this day. Anyway, I put on my swamp clothes and waded to where the eyes appeared and watched as the stirred up mud settled down. The water cleared and like yesterday, I stared intently at the mud bottom, but today I was looking for something specific, eyes. I stood there for at least three minutes, watching. Nothing! It was beginning to cross my mind that maybe nothing was ever there. I reached into the water to the bottom, pinched some mud and put a streak beneath each of my eyes. That was something I often did as a symbol to make me look like an Indian or an army commando, depending on my mood at the time. While gathering more mud and smearing it on my arms to enhance my camouflage, I heard his voice for the first time!

"So you like playing in the mud, do you?" Startled, I turned quickly and saw it for the first time. A lot of "firsts" in that first meeting. It looked tall to me and had mud all over it. In fact it **was** mud! It was standing on the ground next to the water about ten feet from me. I backed farther into the swamp than was normal for me, afraid and unsure what to do. The thought was running through my head, "Momma told me not to go into the swamp today." I had never seen anything like it, nor had anyone else.

I was above knee deep in the swamp and couldn't run, so I acted brave and answered, "Yeah, I like the mud. So what?"

"Why?" it asked and stepped into the water toward me.

I backed up a few steps more and said, "I dunno. I uh, I like the way it feels, I guess."

"How does it feel? Why do you put mud on yourself?" it asked and glided forward a little more.

I was really scared now. This thing didn't walk in the water, it glided through the water! And it didn't have a face or a mouth that I could see, and it talked! Yeah, I was real nervous. "What do you want?" I said with defiance, trying not to panic.

"I want an answer to my question." it said and the eyes I had seen yesterday opened and looked directly at me. Strangely, seeing those eyes come open kinda made me calm down a little. Talking to a plain mud head was spooky.

"I smear mud on my arms because it makes me feel like I'm part of my swamp." I stammered.

"Your swamp?" It said and glided a little closer.

I replied, "Well, not the whole swamp, just this little part here. This is where I play." While backing up more, the cool water against my stomach was a warning that I was in trouble. Going deeper into the swamp was really unknown territory for me.

"What do you want, anyway?" I asked it. I just wanted to get out of there and go home.

"Nothing really important." it said. "I just wanted to talk with you. You interest me. I have been watching you for a long time. You seem to have no fear of this swamp."

"That's because I like it here, the swamp is my safe place." I said.

"Safe place?" it questioned.

I answered, "Yes."

Then it calmly said, "Look behind you."

Being suspicious and wanting to keep an eye on the mud creature, I turned for a quick glance and what I saw took my breath away, causing me to begin backing out of the swamp and towards the mud thing. All of the water behind me was covered with snakes! They were everywhere, all over each other and steadily slithering around. I couldn't cry out, my throat was too dry. They were all sizes and different colors. Some were falling out of the trees into the water and crawling back into the trees they fell from. I stumbled backwards and fell in the water at the feet of the creature. Two long black snakes were swimming at me and I couldn't get up. Suddenly, I was lifted up and out of the water by the creature.

He turned me around in his big hands, smeared some mud on my face, laughed and said, "The swamp is not really a safe place, Little Muddy, but I am sure you will be alright here."

Then he put me down. Up close like that, he had a face and a mouth and the appearance of a man. I turned to look at the swamp; the snakes were gone, except for a few that were always seen swimming there.

He pointed to me and said, "Wash yourself, put on your clothes, and go home, Little Muddy. Your mother will be calling soon and you should not be late. We will talk again." I couldn't say anything and just nodded my head. Then he turned, glided into the deep water, and melted into the swamp.

I wondered, "Why did he call me 'Little Muddy?" I didn't know it then, but that nickname would follow me forever in the swamp.

After that, I never referred to him as "it" or "creature" again. He was Mudman. More than that, I thought, "I like him and he seems to like me. We're gonna be friends."

I had no idea then of the influence Mudman was going to have on my life, but even at ten years old, I knew things were already different.

Chapter 4 - The Monster Story

Back at home, momma was upset with me. My two little brothers, Ricky and Rocky, had trashed their rooms and left the kitchen in a mess. I was late getting home at the prescribed time and she had to leave to get some groceries for supper. Momma was only gone for 30 minutes, but that was enough time for two young boys to do their thing. Apparently they made peanut butter and jelly sandwiches, getting jelly all over them and the kitchen. In addition, they indulged in a pillow fight in our bedroom, tore a pillow (by accident of course) and spread feathers all over the room. I was ready to go back to the swamp with the snakes. Of course it was all my fault. I was the oldest and going to get the blame. Truth is, had I been home to supervise, the mess would not have happened. Telling momma about my episode in the swamp was out of the question, so I apologized for being late and cleaned up the mess.

That night was revenge time. I told my brothers a horror story about a hairy monster in the woods who came into people's houses at night, stole their little children, and took them to the swamp to feed the alligators. It was a good story, especially the part about how only I knew how to keep him away. I filled that story with all kinds of terrible things the monster did to people and told them how it was always watching and looking for bad little kids to throw in the swamp. He liked hearing them scream when the gators showed up. Ricky and Rocky begged me to keep the monster away, so we made a pact about how little brothers are supposed to behave and it worked out real well, for a while anyway.

As it happened, Rocky told momma about the story because he was too scared to sleep by himself, which led to a lecture from momma, reminding me that I was the oldest and had responsibilities, one of which was to help and care for my brothers. Telling them scary stories that made them afraid in their own home was hurting and not helping them. After momma's talk, I actually felt a little bad about scaring my brothers so much. She wanted me to admit to them that my story wasn't true and I had made it up, but I wasn't ready to go that far. My brothers were unruly sometimes and often in my way, digging into my stuff and all. That's how it is with little brothers, being a nuisance seems to be their job and my brothers were real good at it. So, when Ricky or Rocky would start acting up to the point of being unbearable, all I had to do was remind them that the monster was watching, waiting, and looking for them because he liked seeing the alligators eating bad kids and listening to their screams. Worked for me. Problem is, my story didn't stop there, it multiplied.

Turned out that my brothers told all their little friends up on the street the story about a monster in the woods who fed children to alligators and, of course, their friends told the story to their friends and so on, until it ultimately reached the parents, who wanted to know why their children were afraid to sleep alone at night. The next thing I knew, people in our part of Beaumont were talking about a hairy creature in the woods that was terrorizing campers and hunters and carrying them away to who knows where. There were even a few articles in the newspapers about the creature. People were apparently spotting the horrifying beast everywhere! Hunters were banding together and going into the woods to find and kill it. Beaumont is near the Big Thicket section of Texas and many monster legends already existed in that area. (those legends exist today). The point is, there was a lot of woods to search; so, no monster was ever caught or killed.

I didn't know what to think. It seemed that my story had grown a life of its own. People didn't buy the story of a monster though, they reasoned that there was some sort of dangerous, primitive human-like beast in the woods of which they were seriously afraid. I began thinking that maybe someone saw Mudman in the woods. After all, people were reporting seeing a monster and Mudman would qualify as a monster to them! But what they were describing was not Mudman. They were talking about my made-up monster!

Daddy heard the story at work, came home and told us boys about the report of a dangerous creature in the woods and said we should stay away from there until we had more information. Rocky and Ricky told daddy that they heard about the monster too, but I interrupted and stopped them from telling that they heard it from me. I should have told daddy about my story right then, but I didn't. What the newspaper reports meant to me was, I didn't have to worry about anyone seeing me in the swamp. Everyone was afraid to go in the woods, much less the swamp.

Well, up on the street, where the civilized humans lived, the real cause of the original story was being investigated by parents asking their kids where they heard the story. The trail ultimately led back to me, but not before all little girls and boys in the area were horrified and scarred emotionally for life from my made-up story. There was even talk that some of those kids would scream and cry if their parents tried to take them for a walk in the woods.

"Wow!" I thought to myself, "That was a really great story!" But it occurred to me that my little brothers might have enhanced my story just a tad in their re-telling. They had that tendency.

Anyway, what was done couldn't be undone. Because of my monster tale and the subsequent effect on little kids, our house was not a place where parents brought their children to visit or allowed them to stay for a sleepover anymore. That lasted for a good while. Didn't hurt my feelings any. Momma said not to worry about it, that it would all blow over before long. Daddy said that from what he heard, my story was great and those parents should be ashamed of themselves for raising such a bunch of little crybabies. More parents agreed with him than anyone knew. Momma was right though, the uproar was over in a few months and the only punishment I received was getting a reputation as a storyteller. In some ways, that reputation worked to my advantage. No one would ever believe another story from me, particularly about something like a mudman living in the swamp.

An interesting thing to consider and think about is this: Stories of a "Bigfoot", "Boggy Creek Monster", "Wood Ape", "Sasquatch" and more still linger today in the area of Texas where I lived in the 1950's. If anything, those stories have magnified. From where did they come?

Chapter 5 - The Birds

Let's return to the day I came home from that encounter with the mudman. I thought about it much of the night and didn't get a lot of sleep. First, I liked the mudman. I didn't know his name or even if he had one, but the name I gave him,'Mudman' was fitting. I had so many questions. He seemed to know me and said we would talk again. I couldn't wait.

It would be weeks before I was free to go to the swamp again. Momma took me over to my cousin's house to stay for a week and when I got back, there were baseball games to play and Cub Scout meetings to attend. Momma was a "den mother", so that activity took up time as well. We boys were kept busy and, of course, me being the oldest, I caught babysitting duty when momma went to the store or just needed a break. It's not like I could tell anyone that I had better things to do than hang around the house and look after my little brothers. During that time, I read books. I loved reading books at that age, particularly mystery stories like The Hardy Boys and Nancy Drew. My favorite books were dog stories and biographies of American heroes like James Bowie, Davy Crockett, James Monroe and Thomas Jefferson. I read the biographies of all of the early American historical people. Everyone who reads has their favorite book or books. What is yours? Mine? I first read my favorite book when I was about 12 or 13 years old in the sixth grade and suspect that I have read "Shane" about 20 times or more since. Watched the movie more than a few times, too. Alan Ladd became one of my favorite actors because he was Shane in the movie. I don't know that I can explain why that story grabbed me like it did. But it did and still does. I remain an avid reader of books to this day.

Like I wrote before, get used to me wandering off the track occasionally and getting lost in another train of thought. Guess that means that I'm not a very 'disciplined' writer. I seem to be compelled to write things down as my memory brings them forward.

Anyway, after about three weeks of being away from home or otherwise occupied, I was anxious to get back to the swamp and relax in the stillness there. For the most part, there is no wind in the swamp. Truth is, there is little sunlight there as well. Beaumont doesn't get real cold or real hot in the various seasons, but it rains a lot and the humidity there, especially in the swamp, is unbearable for some as it makes breathing difficult for those with asthma and sinus or lung problems. At my young age, it was hardly noticed. When I arrived at my hollow tree, my swamp clothes were laid out for me, hanging on a limb.

Looking around and not seeing anyone, I said aloud, "How did you know?" to no one there. No answer. "He's not here yet.", I thought to myself. I changed clothes, waded into the shallow water and felt the familiar squishing of the mud between my toes.

Bird sounds filled the woods more than usual. I looked up into the trees and saw there were birds everywhere, thousands of birds in all the trees. That was new to me but not really surprising. At this time of year, thousands and thousands of birds in large flocks could be seen every day flying in aerial patterns to their own special rhythm. I had just never seen them land before and had no idea that they could make so much noise.

Another thing that caught my attention was that these birds in the trees were not all the same! There were many different colored birds up there. I always thought birds all hung around with their own kind and here, there were many different types of birds all singing together. Well not really singing, more like making noise together.

I started whistling, making noise along with them when a voice said, "Are you talking with birds now?"

Looking around quickly, I saw Mudman sitting on a stump with a redbird on his head. So far, each time I met Mudman, I had trouble knowing what to say. This time was no different. What does one say to a being with a cardinal sitting on his head? I was at a loss for words and just stood there in the water looking at him.

He pointed at me and said again, "Are you talking with birds now?"

I stammered, "Uh, no, not talking. I'm just whistling with them."

"Whistling?" he asked, almost as if he didn't know about whistling. I wondered if he knew that a bird was sitting on his head.

It was a little embarrassing, but I had to ask, "You do know there's a bird on your head, don't you?"

"I am interested why you do that." he said.

"Do what?" I asked.

"There, you did it again!" he said.

I was confused. "What did I do?" I asked.

"You answered my question with a question. Why did you do that?" he said.

I thought, "He's right!", so I explained, "Whistling is a thing that I do sometimes and just now I was whistling with the birds, not because I was talking with them, but because I felt like it."

Mudman replied, "I understand now and yes, I know about the bird." Then he asked me, "Any reason you think a bird should not sit on my head?" he asked.

"Well no, but it looks funny." I answered. I don't remember hearing the birds leave, but they were now gone and silence had settled on the swamp.

Mudman stood up and the cardinal flew away. Then he looked at me with a serious stare and asked, "Funny? Do you mean 'strange'? Do you think it funny or strange that snakes and turtles swim in this swamp?" He answered his question before I could, "Of course not, because that is natural here and so is it natural here for birds to land in the swamp." he said gently.

"But it was on your head!" I weakly argued, "and a bird landing in the swamp is not the same as as a bird landing and sitting on someone's head!"

Mudman smiled, walked into the water, looked back at me and said, "I am the swamp, Little Muddy." and glided into the shadows beyond the trees where he disappeared.

Once again, I was without words. I stood there in the water, wondering, "What does that even mean? I am the swamp?" I felt like something really special was going on in my young life, but I didn't have any idea what it was. I mean, Mudman talks with me, Johnny Parfait, and as far as anyone else knows, he doesn't even exist. And I didn't have anyone to talk to about it. I was frustrated. . . and a little lonely in my isolation.

Chapter 6 - I Need a Boat

After that day, I didn't see Mudman for over a year. Me and my dog Rex played in the woods and went craw-fishing several times a week. My family liked boiled crawfish, so that gave me an excuse to go into the swamp where they were easy to catch. I caught perch there too. Like I said, I didn't see Mudman for a long time, but I talked to him a lot. He didn't talk back, but that didn't matter 'cause I just knew he was there. Rex knew it too, I could tell by the way he acted sometimes.

Anyway, with school and all the other things going on, there really wasn't much time to think about anything else. Momma and daddy separated during that time and later on got divorced. I didn't really know what that meant, just that daddy left for some place up north called Chicago, leaving momma and us boys alone in the house next to the swamp.

Well, not really alone 'cause grandma was still living with us and was a big help around the house when it came to cooking and watching over my brothers. I suppose she looked after me too, not that I would admit it or anything. I could take care of myself. Yeah, right. It's easy to be independent when you have a safe place to live, eat, sleep, and feel loved. We had that, me and my brothers. Not everyone did.

So yeah, I talked to Mudman when I was playing or busy in the swamp. You wanna know something strange? It was a lot easier talking 'to' him than 'with' him. There was something odd about him that kept me off balance during those few times together. I didn't know how to explain the feeling, but it never seemed that I could get around to asking all the questions there were to be asked. He always veered our conversations off into something that I didn't understand.

There were times since our last meeting when I wondered if I would ever see Mudman again. A lot of thoughts went through my mind since then. You know how it is, after a while a person gets to thinking if something really happened or not. I mean, when you think about it, a man made of mud who lives in the swamp and talks like everyone else sounds a little bit "far fetched" as grandma would say. I was sure that if I told anyone else about him, they would think I had lost my mind. Worse yet, I had no evidence that proved Mudman even existed! But all that didn't matter, I might not know how or why Mudman existed, but was absolutely sure that he did and that was good enough.

I began getting more curious about the swamp. It was big, but I no idea just how big or far reaching it was and wanted to know more. I needed a boat, but momma darn sure wasn't going to allow that to happen. Fishing for crawfish and perch from the bank behind the house was bad enough, but paddling around in the swamp was out of the question. Eleven year old boys were not allowed to do that sort of thing.

Now, in defense of my momma's attitude about me or anyone going out there, you have to understand some things about this swamp. Virtually no one knew anything about it, other than it was dark, huge, thick with trees, and dangerous. It looked menacing from shore! Heck, even the woods between our house and the swamp looked dangerous and in some ways probably were. Of those up on the street where the civilized people lived, few dared to venture there. On top of that, talk was that men had gone into the swamp and never returned! Most recently, three duck hunters were still missing since last fall. It had been reported that alligators, snakes, poison plants and quicksand were in the swamp as well. Wouldn't that make anyone anxious about going in there, much less allowing their kids to do so? Absolutely!

The thing is, my momma didn't know about her son's ventures into the swamp. She had been to the edge of the bank to go craw-fishing with me and, even then, always carried a 22 rifle, but she knew nothing about my hollow tree or the cages containing my snakes or my safe place where I went wading and hunting. And she darn sure didn't know about Mudman. Why, we would have been packed up and gone from there in a week had she known about those things. So her eleven year old son paddling around in the swamp was unthinkable and not allowed.

I wanted a pirogue and couldn't have one. A pirogue is basically a small flat-bottom boat that is ideal for marshes, swamps, and bayous because it is mobile in shallow water and narrow enough to navigate close areas between trees. Perfect for exploring my swamp, but not attainable for me. I still needed something on which to float further into the swamp where I couldn't or wouldn't wade. I built a raft that might have been okay in a pond, but was useless for the swamp because it didn't float high enough. Momma threw away an old trunk that I recovered, removed the lid, and tried it out as a boat. Not good. It floated too far down in the water and tipped over easily. Certainly wasn't something I could fish from.

Then I had an idea. There were four empty metal barrels in the shed by our house that were just sitting there, not being used for anything. They would float good. So one day when momma was away visiting some neighbors up on the street, I rolled two barrels down to the levy and tied them together with a long roll of wire and pushed them into the water. They floated great! But there was a problem; when I got on, the two barrels moved up and down too much to make it useful as a boat. I needed help. There was an older boy on the street named Dorman that I knew because he was our paperboy. He was about two years ahead of me in school. I went to see him and told him what I was trying to do.

"You're not thinking of going out in the swamp, are you?" he asked. He was concerned about me.

Dorman, being two years older, looked after me when I went to play with other kids up on Idylwood Street. For some reason, three older rough kids from down the block didn't like me much and picked on me sometimes. They smoked cigarettes and were always acting tough. One afternoon they were teasing and calling me a 'swamp rat', and pushing me around, trying to start a fight. Dorman saw us, walked over and knocked down the biggest kid. He told them I was his friend and to leave me alone or else. Well, that didn't cause them to like me any better, but they quit teasing and calling me names.

I said, "No, Dorman, but I want to get a little ways away from shore to catch bigger fish." Our mothers were friends and I wanted to keep my exploring plans secret.

Dorman said, "What you need to do is build a frame for the barrels to hold them together. That way you will be sitting on the frame instead of the barrels and they won't move around on you."

Boy! That sounded good. I asked him if he would help and he said, "Sure, if I can borrow it sometimes. I'd like to catch some of those big fish too."

I agreed, and we framed in the barrels. Dorman did most of the work, but I helped where I could. The barrel boat floated great. It couldn't be paddled though, so I made a long pole to navigate with. We both got on to try it out and I poled about thirty feet from the levy and back. I thought to myself, "Heck, I can camp out on this thing." I was excited!

We had to wade in order to get the barrel boat into the water and then again when we took it out for the trial run. When we got back, Dorman had two leeches attached to one of his legs. He didn't like that at all. I showed him how to get 'em off and advised, "You probably shouldn't tell your mom about the leeches."

He said, "Don't worry about that Johnny, mom and dad have warned me a bunch of times not to go near the swamp. Where we went today is the only time I've been out there." Then he asked, "How come you didn't get any leeches on you?"

"I dunno." I answered, "Sometimes they get on you and sometimes they don't." and added, "Thanks Dorman, for helping me today. You're really good at building things."

I didn't tell him that leeches never seemed to get on me.

"Don't mention it." he said. Then he laughed and added, "and I really mean don't mention it."

Dorman never stepped on that barrel boat again. As far as I know, he never even came back down to the swamp.

Now, I had a boat and couldn't hardly wait to take it out, but momma had things for me to do, so the maiden voyage was delayed for two days. An eternity.

Chapter 7 - BB

My swamp ride was still there by the levy when I arrived that morning. I named him BB for Barrel Boat. I know, original, right? I had two peanut butter & jelly sandwiches, an apple, a jar of water, a fishing pole, a stringer, and a can of worms. I was set for the day. Here is a big truth, if there is such a thing: I learned a lot on that first outing, all of which I never forgot, even to this day. Here's a short list of the most important things to remember when entering a swamp:

1. The swamp is subject to tides.

2. Mark your trail when going into the swamp.

3. Take more than a jar of water.

4. Cottonmouth snakes like to hang around the bottom of trees in the swamp.

5. Take a hatchet and a knife with you.

6. Be prepared for rain.

7. Never panic in the swamp!

There are more, but those will do for now. I learned those seven in that one day. Allow me to tell you how I did it.

The swamp is subject to tides. I didn't know that. Remember I am eleven years old here, poling a square barrel boat. This particular swamp has many cypress trees growing there, some of them huge and tall. A cypress tree in the swamp grows very large at the bottom and gets slimmer the higher up the trunk you go. "So what?", you ask? Well, back to the tides. This cocky eleven year old went into the swamp when the tide was high and floated between trees with ease. I found what looked to be a good fishing spot, stopped and tied BB to a limb. It was beautiful out there, my heart was soaring from watching the rainbows through the trees and the color of the fish in the water. I never knew there were so many beautiful fish in the world.

Now think about this, I was maybe a hundred yards or more from where I left. But seeing where I left was not possible, that swamp forest was a jungle, the likes of which I had never seen before and every direction all around me looked the same. But that didn't bother me, I knew my way back. I was catching fish, all sun perch, and adding them to my stringer. Momma was going to be surprised. I ate my sandwiches about noon and drank most of my water. Soon after that, it got darker and began to rain. I decided it was time to return to the levy and go home. I reached to untie the boat rope from the limb and noticed that it was tighter than I remembered. The tide had gone out and BB was lower down than when I got there. The rope knot had tightened around the tree limb so tight that it was impossible to loosen it. The time may have been 1:00pm, but it was dark, thundering, lightning, and raining. I was soaked and tied to a tree in the swamp. I could have used a knife about then, but hadn't brought one. I looked to where the rope was attached to the boat and saw that it was not tied there but looped over a tie-down. When I sat to the opposite side of the boat from the tie down, that side of the boat tipped up and loosened the loop. I got my fishing pole, wound the line tight around the pole with the hook close to tip and hooked it through the loop. Then, holding the pole tight, I scooted to the other side of the boat and when the rope side went up, the loop loosened and I easily slipped it off the tie down. BB was free! I felt great.

Now, I had to get back to the levy, but where was it? The swamp looked the same everywhere I looked! I remembered that I was facing the limb when I tied to it and the tree was on my left. That meant that the way back was behind me. The rain had stopped and the sun was shining through again. A typical Beaumont thunder storm. I stood up with the rope behind me and the tree on my right, looked straight ahead, mapped out a trail to take in my mind, and began poling in that direction. The going was hard, because when the tide went out, the water level went down, causing the distance between trees to narrow, because the bottom part of the trees was wider. I could get through some of the openings by shifting my weight on the boat, but BB was a square boat and some openings were impossible to pass through. I had to pole around a lot of trees to find a way to get through.

BB got stuck when I tried to force my way between two trees. I reached down to push away from a big cypress knee at the bottom of the tree and a fat cottonmouth moccasin was arched back with its mouth wide open to strike. I was so startled that when I tried to push my self backward, my hand slipped and I fell forward, off the boat toward the snake instead. I was tumbling off the boat right into the curve of the tree with the big cottonmouth. Before I landed there, the snake lowered its head and slithered away into the water. I fell into the soft mud and water next to the tree, unharmed but for a cut on my shoulder where I hit the tree. I got up, slowly pushed my boat away from the cypress knees, got back on it and laid down. In that moment, all the confidence and cockiness in me had evaporated. I was just an exhausted, wet, and scared little boy about to cry.

"You should go home, Little Muddy." he said. "You can come back and get your boat later. It will be here."

I didn't say anything. I wasn't even sure I heard anything. Then I heard Rex barking and knew home was close by. I sat up and saw Rex standing on the levy, barking. He was maybe 50 yards away. I slipped into the chest high water and walked through the muddy bottom toward the levy without a single ounce of fear. I was being watched over today.

Rex was happy to see me and when I crawled up on the levy he began whining and licking my face as I laid down. I couldn't remember ever being that tired before and would have stayed there if it weren't for Rex. He kept whining and pulling on my shorts, almost like he was demanding me to get up. I think he just wanted to go home. He had waited for me on the levy, through the storm, refusing to go home until I returned and now wanted to get back to the house. So did I, and forced myself to get up. We slowly walked home while the thought about how stupid it was to go into the swamp unprepared was running through my mind. "I will be smarter next time." I told myself.

I couldn't get that voice out of my thoughts. I never saw anyone, but I know it was Mudman who caused that big cottonmouth to swim away instead of biting me. One bite from that thing and I would never have made it back to the levy, and they don't bite just once. But the truth is, I was tired and panicked at the time and couldn't be real sure that I actually heard anything. Anyway, I had not seen Mudman in over a year. Maybe I was imagining things, but when I heard his voice, all fear drained from me. Even now, it is hard to believe I walked over fifty yards to the levy, through that swamp in water up to my chest, without fear of anything, knowing I was safe. Mudman was there. I am sure of it! It's not like I could tell anyone, though. Besides, no one would believe me. I was learning to keep things to myself, a trait that would continue throughout my life.

At least a month passed before I took BB on another run to the deeper swamp. I floated around 40 feet from the levy behind our house most of the time, just fishing. Caught a few pretty good catfish too. I also learned more about the tide. The tide schedule was published in the newspaper, something I had never paid attention to before. I was always hoping to meet Mudman out there, but he wasn't predictable. Several of the boys from school would come over occasionally and ride on BB. I told momma about my barrel boat and to my surprise, she was okay with it. Didn't tell her about my adventure, though.

Chapter 8 - Howie, Bernard, & Bobby J

One day while I was floating a little way from shore, day dreaming, three boys dropped by to see me; the same three that were always picking on me before Dorman set them straight. They were interested in BB and indicated they wanted to take him out for a ride. I had met them a few times since the episode up on the street and always avoided them because they were mean. Everyone thought them to be brothers because they were always together, but they weren't related. Today, all three were smoking cigarettes and acting important.

Howie was the smallest of them and said to me, "It smells like shit around here, how can you stand it?"

I said, "Well, you know, it keeps the creeps away; I don't like creeps." I felt safe out and away from the bank.

He glanced at me and said, "You callin' me a creep?" Then he asked his friends, "Did he just call me a creep?"

I didn't like where this was going, so I asked, "What do y'all really want? I don't think that you want to ride on an old barrel boat in a smelly swamp."

Bobby J, the oldest, pointed his cigarette at me and in his high pitched voice said, "You callin' us liars now, Johnny? First you call Howie a creep and now you call us liars!"

"Yeah", said Bernard, "You think yur hotshit just 'cause you got a boat and we don't! Well, you ain't! You ain't nothing' but a stupid coonass swamp rat!"

It crossed my mind that this conversation is a lot like the ones I have with Mudman. One thing leads to another and goes off in a crazy direction. I looked over at Bobby J and exclaimed,

"Wow! 'hotshit, stupid coonass swamp rat'; I didn't know Bernard liked me that much."

Bobby J growled, "You're an asshole, Johnny, and you're gonna be sorry about not respecting us." Then ordered, "Come on guys, let's git out of this shithole." He defiantly flipped his cigarette out into the water toward me and they left. It was actually kind of impressive, the way he flipped that cigarette such a distance. I figured it took a lot of practice to learn to do that.

They never said what they wanted, but it must have had something to do with my boat, because two days later, I went to the levy and found BB destroyed. The frame was broken, the wires cut, and the barrels poked full of holes and sunk in the swamp.

Momma called the police and gave them the name of the boys. The police interviewed them and Howie confessed that they did it because I wouldn't sell them my boat. The boys were punished and their parents gave momma some money for the damage done. In any event, I didn't have a barrel boat anymore. Too bad, I really liked BB.

Cleaning up the swamp area where the barrels were sunk was a hard job. It was my thought that the punishment of the three boys should have included cleaning up the mess they made, but it was considered too dangerous for young boys to work in the swamp because of the dangers there. No one considered that the boys had to get into the swamp to destroy BB. As expected, cleaning up the mess came down to me. Removing the barrels was the hardest work, but I got it done in about four hours early one morning. All the small stuff was cleaned up by noon. It was apparent that the holes in the barrels were made by hatchets. The wires holding them together were cut by snips. The wood was chopped by hatchets too. The boys did all that while we were not at home, because the noise made must have been tremendous and we would have heard it.

Something interesting happened later on in school that is probably not all that unusual. I got involved in baseball and basketball and found myself playing alongside of Bernard; we were teammates and developed a friendship as a result, which caused me to realize that people are more likely to become friends when they have a common interest. Of course, all bets are off when that common interest is a girl; but that's another story.

Chapter 9 - Can't and Don't

I turned twelve in March of 1954. I hadn't seen or heard from Mudman in over a year. Schoolwork and social activities took a lot of my time. It got dark early and I only went to the swamp about twice a week, except on weekends. I talked to him all the time while crawfishing and hunting turtles there, mainly because it made me feel better to think he was close by. I kinda figured he was busy; the swamp seemed to be really big and he probably had things to do. Several weeks after my birthday, while sitting on a log at the edge of the swamp with my feet in the cool water, watching the minnows swim around, Mudman surprised me. It was a nice Saturday afternoon, probably in the 70's, but looking like it was gonna rain. He rose up out of the swamp, glided up and sat down beside me.

I don't know what it is about Mudman, but I just never know what to say to him. It has been almost two years since we last met, not counting my deep swamp event on BB, and here I am tongue-tied. Even though he looks a little spooky, I have no fear of him and actually feel safe in the swamp because of him. I think it is because of a feeling I have that he is always around. I don't know, maybe he didn't know what to say either because we sat there not talking for several minutes.

I decided to break the ice and asked, "Mudman, do you like me?"

He seemed to think for a few seconds and answered, "That is not the really the correct word, but yes."

I wondered why and then I asked him, "Why do you like me?"

"Well, aren't you the philosophical one today, Little Muddy." he stated and continued, "Because you are interesting and polite to me." and then he asked me, "Why do you wonder if I like you?"

"Because you and I are so different from each other." I answered, and continued, "and different types of people don't get along in my world outside the swamp. Heck, if people knew about you, they wouldn't like you because of how you look."

"How do I look, Little Muddy?", he asked.

I answered truthfully, "Well, you look different and you **are** different from other people! And people don't like or trust 'different'. I think they are uncomfortable with people who are different and don't want to be around them."

"Are you saying that I am a 'people'?" he asked.

I thought about that and replied, "No. I'm not sure what you are, but I'm pretty sure that you are not a human."

"Do you like me, Little Muddy?", he asked.

I quickly answered, "I sure do, I like you a lot!"

Mudman then asked, "Why do you like me if I'm not human and so different from you?"

He caught me by surprise with that question. I thought a moment and realized that I didn't know why I liked him, but I actually liked him a lot. I was still struggling with an answer, when he said, "Little Muddy?"

I answered the only way I could at that moment. "I don't know why," I replied, "it's just a way that I feel."

"A way that you feel." he said softly, and then asked, "What makes you so sure that others of your kind would not feel the same way about me as they do you?"

At this point in our talk, I began to believe that Mudman was 'yanking my chain' as my daddy would say. He had to know how people would react to him.

So I said, "Well, maybe if they took time to get to know you, humans would learn to like you, but you look so different that no one is going to take time to do that. Look at how people reacted to the monster seen in the woods around here, they wanted to kill it."

"Yes, that is true," he said, and then added, "but there was no monster, you invented it."

I had to change the subject. "Mudman, why can't humans get along with each other?"

He didn't answer right away, then softly replied, "My thought is that you are too young and ignorant for such a discussion."

Mudman was watching a whirlpool forming in the water in front of us.

I looked at the whirlpool, which was really interesting, and almost asked him why it was forming there, but I stopped myself, thinking, "This is one of Mudman's tricks to throw me off the subject." So I argued, "If I'm so ignorant, why not try to teach me to be more smart."

"Intelligent.", he said. "I cannot teach you to be more smart."

I replied, "Okay, more intelligent. Does that mean you will teach me?"

He looked away from the whirlpool, focused on me for a moment, and the water stilled itself.

"It means that I will try, but the subject you have chosen is difficult for many to understand, most of whom are far more educated than you."

"Do you understand it?" I asked, grateful that he was agreeing to teach me.

"Yes." he replied, "I understand." and then he warned me, "Such an understanding, should you achieve it, will make you unpopular among others if you tell." I nodded my head without saying anything, but didn't understand a thing he said.

Mudman stood up, turned and pointed at me. "Do you remember the question?"

"Why don't humans get along with each other?" I answered.

"That is not what you asked, Little Muddy." he said firmly, and then added, "Just what is it that you want to understand?"

Confused, I asked him, "What did I ask?"

Mudman, in a patient voice, explained, "You originally asked 'Why **can't** humans get along with each other?' and then you asked, 'Why **don't** humans get along with each other?' Two very different questions. Which is it, my young friend?"

Now I began to understand what Mudman meant when he stated that I was too ignorant for this discussion. I didn't even know the difference between "can't" and "don't". I wondered silently, "What grade do teachers start telling us that stuff in school?"

"I don't understand why the questions are different," I confessed, "and I would really like to know."

Mudman smiled, sat back down beside me, and explained, "Many are confused about 'can't' and 'don't' and believe their meanings to be the same, but they differ. A simple explanation is that 'don't' indicates an **unwillingness** to do something and 'can't' indicates an **inability** to do something. So, your two questions can be stated this way:

1. Why are humans unable to get along with each other?

2. Why are humans unwilling to get along with each other?

Each of your original questions will result in a long discussion and each answer is a beginning. Which one do you want to talk about?”

It was starting to rain and my mind was weary from thinking.

“I'm tired and need to think about it.” I said. “Can we talk about it later? It's raining anyway.”

“There is only now.” Little Muddy. “We will finish our discussion at another now.”

My mind was too tired to to even ask what he was talking about. I thanked him for teaching me, stood up from the log and started home. I looked back, watched him glide into the swamp and disappear beneath the water. It struck me how such a strange happening seemed so normal now.

“How does Mudman know so much?” I muttered under my breath. “No one would ever believe any of this.” I was worn down and headed home in the rain.

Chapter 10 - Created Diversity

What with schoolwork and all, I didn't meet with Mudman to continue our discussion until the next weekend. It was a wonderful day, with no rain in sight. You never can tell about Beaumont though, little showers come out of nowhere around here. Mudman was sitting on the log, watching me walk up and commented, "Little Muddy, you seem to be full of energy today."

Remember me saying that Mudman had a way of making me speechless? Well, he had another effect, too. I don't know if it's just in my head or not, but I seemed to be smarter around him. I don't mean like a genius or anything like that, but I noticed things more and used words that I normally don't use very often. I believe he inspired me somehow by making even the smallest things interesting.

Anyway, I was feeling good and looking forward to getting smarter today, uh, I mean more intelligent or as Bobby J might say, "more learned." and I chuckled about the thought.

Mudman noticed and said, "You really are feeling your oats today! Why are you laughing?"

"How does he know that phrase?" I thought. "I doubt he eats oatmeal for breakfast. Wonder what he does eat?" Those thoughts went leaping through my mind.

"Nothing important," I answered and sat down beside him. "I was just thinking a mean thought. You know, like 'the little moron jokes', they're mean, but funny."

"I see." said Mudman. Then he asked, "What is a moron, Little Muddy?"

I thought, "There he goes again, yanking my chain! Where is he going with this?" Sometimes his questions were a little aggravating.

I sat down next to him and answered, "A moron is a stupid person."

"Are there many morons among your people?" he asked.

I thought, "Sounds like a trick question." but replied, "I think so."

Mudman was quiet, thinking. Then he asked, "Are you a moron, Little Muddy?"

I thought, "Yep, it was a trick question alright!" Then I looked at Mudman and said, "Yeah, I'm starting to think so."

I'd never heard Mudman laugh before, but he was laughing now! Really laughing. I couldn't help but laugh with him. I got the point he was making, though. From then on, Little Moron jokes were not funny anymore.

Mudman was serious again and said, "I like your answer." and then got right down to business. "What is your question?"

"Why can't humans get along with each other?" I asked.

He thought a moment and asked, "How would you answer your question? It is a very good question. You know that, do you not?"

I answered, "No, not really. I always figured that there are good people and bad people in the world and good and bad don't mix, so they fight."

"Give me an example of people not getting along," he said.

"Well, momma and daddy don't get along and argued a lot and got divorced," I replied, "and now daddy's gone."

Mudman didn't say anything, but stood up, walked into the water and sat down facing me. I gotta say this, Mudman was odd and spooky sometimes. He just became part of the swamp! All I could see of him was his upper part from the chest up. He looked like one of those half statues that you see when you go to a museum. I kinda wanted to laugh, but he looked too serious to laugh at.

"Created diversity." he said.

"Huh?" was the only response that I had.

"Created Diversity is the reason humans cannot get along with each other." he stated.

I had no idea what that meant, or was, and didn't know what to say. Mudman's answer was 'two words simple' and filled my mind with question marks.

"Are you the only one in the world who knows what that means?" I asked him.

"Possibly, Little Muddy, but I am going to try changing that." then he said, "Listen closely and try to absorb this."

"Absorb?" I said. "Do you mean, learn?"

"No. Well, in a way." he said, "but that is not important now. 'Created diversity' is a simple way of stating the complex answer that your question requires."

"Well! Well. Well! That certainly clears everything up!" I thought, keeping the sarcasm to myself. I kept quiet and waited for an explanation.

"Remember this," he said, "to create means to bring something into existence and diversity means significant differences between things, or in the case of our subject here, humans." Then he continued, "When you create something, a thought or a thing, what exactly are you doing? Now, think about that, Little Muddy." Then he suddenly dissolved into the shallows.

"Johnny! What are you doing down here sitting on a log in the swamp?" It was momma. She had come looking for me. "Where are your shoes?" Then she slapped her arm and exclaimed, "The mosquitoes are going to eat you alive down here!"

"I was just thinking about things, momma, and I took off my shoes 'cause I didn't want to get 'em muddy." I explained.

"Well it might be best to do your thinking at home. Pick up your shoes; we're going to grandma and grandpa's. Hurry now, before these damn mosquitoes carry us both away!"

"Mosquitoes don't bother me much, momma." I said.

She slapped a mosquito on her leg and exclaimed, "Well, they're bothering me. C'mon, let's go!"

I got up and we walked home together.

Chapter 11 - Grandma's Chair

We went back to the house and the whole family got in the car and headed to grandma and grandpa's house. They lived at the edge of the Neches River across from the Beaumont Country Club. There used to be a ferry that took cars across, but it was gone now and grandpa would drive his boat across to pick us up. Momma would honk one long and two shorts on the horn so they would know it was us. That was our signal to tell them we were there.

The side of the river grandma and grandpa lived on was exciting to me. Their house was built on poles, about eight feet high. Grandpa built it himself. There was no electricity and no telephone there. Grandma had a wood burning stove and there was an outhouse close to the house that had to be replaced everytime the river flooded, which was at least once a year. Behind the house were thick woods, with sloughs everywhere and dynamite holes that were always good fishing spots if you knew where they were. I knew. Needless to say, it was a wonderful place to live. I always looked forward to going there.

"What are you doing when you create a thought or a thing?" was what Mudman asked me. Well, he said to 'create' means to bring something into existence. If I create something, then I am bringing it into existence. That sounds too easy to be a good answer. His questions don't have many easy answers. "What was he asking me?" was the question that kept running through my mind. I didn't know what he was asking, but he told me to think about it and that's what I was doing.

Well, that question was on my mind while momma drove to grandma and grandpa's house. Grandma Cora was in the front seat with momma and I was sitting in the back staring out the window, while my brothers were fussin' with each other and making their usual noise.

Grandma Cora saw that I was being still and said, "Johnny, yur being awful quiet back der. Are you sleepn?" Grandma was just teasing me, she knew I wasn't sleeping. Normally, I would have been picking at my brothers, causing them to be even noisier.

I answered, "No, I've just been thinking."

"That's what he told me earlier." said momma. "He's been doin' that a lot here lately."

"You learnin' sump'n new at school, Johnny boy?" Grandma asked.

"Yes ma'am, kinda." I replied, then said, "Grandma can I ask you a question?"

"Shoot." she said.

"If you created something, like a new fangled chair, what would you be doing.?"

Grandma thought a moment and said, "Well, I don't rightly know. I s'pose I'd want it to be a rockin' chair that had a padded seat and a padded back. I'd want dem arms to be low, so they wouldn't interfere with my sewing. An' I'd make dem rockers thick so's the chair'd be solid; cuz skinny rockers make fer a rickety chair an' der ain't nuttin' worse dan a rickety rockin' chair."

Momma interrupted, "For goodness sakes, grandma! You've really thought this through." Then she laughed and said, "You thinkin' about makin' a rocking chair now?"

"Don't ya gon' interrupt me, Ginny." she said, irritated. "I'ma answerin' the boy's question here. Now, where was I?"

(My mother's name was Virginia, but most everyone called her 'Ginny')

"You don't like rickety rocking chairs, grandma." I said.

"Oh yeah," she continued on, "and there's another 'portant thing, dat chair of mine would have a high back. Ain't nuthin' worse than a low back rock'n chair that hurts your neck when you falls asleep in it."

I laughed and said, "Which is worse grandma, a rickety chair or a low back chair?"

That question caused momma to laugh too.

"Don't you go bein' a little smartypants, boy. You knows what I mean. And y'all stop messin' with my train of thought! I'ma creatin' a special rockin' chair right here in the front seat of this car!"

Wow! Grandma was on a roll!

Ricky and Rocky had stopped fussing in the back seat and were listening intently to grandma creating her chair. "Grandma?" piped in Ricky, "can I sit in that chair with you when it's finished?"

"Course you can, child." she said, "that's another thing, I'm makin' my chair wide enough so's my grandchildren can comforbly sit in it wit' me. There ain't nuthin' worse than a narrow rocking chair." and then added, "Johnny, don't you say nuthin'."

Momma laughed again and this time grandma laughed with her.

"What color you gonna paint it, Grandma?" piped up Rocky from the back seat.

"Why child, I'm gon' paint it white," she said, "I ain't ne'er had a white rocking chair afore and I'd lak that."

Grandma was quiet and thoughtful for a while after that. I think creating that chair took a lot out of her. Not long after that, we arrived and momma honked one long and two shorts and grandpa brought the boat over to get us.

I made a mental note to get grandma a rocking chair like that some day. Momma must have been thinking the same thing, 'cause grandma received that rocking chair for her birthday that year. It was handmade, white, and had her name on it. On the back of the chair was engraved, "Created by Grandma Cora". Grandma cried when she sat down in it. I cried too.

You want to know something interesting? I learned a lot that day, listening to grandma create her rocking chair, and began to understand what she was doing as she created. She was making something special, unique to her, that suited her wants and needs. I had an answer for Mudman's question, but had no idea how to apply it to humans getting along with each other. Maybe it didn't apply at all, but I had an answer. Anyway, I figured that he would enjoy hearing how my answer was born.

Chapter 12 - Created That Way

It rained off and on for three days after we got back home and I was interested to know what Mudman meant by "created diversity", so when the weather cleared I finished my chores and walked down to the swamp. The ground was soft and muddy even in the woods. I like the smell of the woods after a good rain. Always have, always will. I think it's the muddy ground that makes the forest smell so good and, of course, the pine trees. I told Mudman about the forest mud after a rain once and he picked up some mud and smeared it on my face. I wore that mud like a badge of honor all that day.

I was eager to talk with Mudman; every time we discussed a subject, my understanding of that subject improved. He wore me down with his questions sometimes, by causing me to think about more than just a word or phrase and grasp their meaning. I like that.

When I arrived at the place where we usually met, he said, "I thought you might be coming out today." I looked, but didn't see him.

"Where are you? I don't see you." I stammered.

"That is the way things are in the swamp, Little Muddy." he said.

"What way?" I asked and looked everywhere around me. I still couldn't find him!

"The way of life my young friend." he said. "You want to know about 'created diversity', do you not?" and he answered his question, "Of course, you do." The voice continued, "There are many diverse creatures and things in the swamp, all different from one another and yet they live in the same swamp."

"Yeah," I replied, "but they don't get along with each other and they mostly keep to their own kind; some kill and eat each other."

Mudman asked, "Why do you think those that consider the swamp home, segregate, kill and eat each other?"

"It is their nature, Mudman. They are creatures who kill and eat each other to live; they do not murder each other like humans do. They do not think things through, they follow their God given nature. Humans hurt and kill each over differences, not for food. Why can't we just get along with each other?

I was getting tired of talking to a voice and wanted to see who I was talking to.

My irritation must have showed because Mudman noticed and asked, "Are you upset with me, Little Muddy?"

"Well," I replied, "I don't like talking with someone who is hiding from me."

"Hiding?" he replied. "I do not hide." He stood up from a tree that he had been sitting against and became instantly visible. "Is this better?" he asked. He had been right there in front of me all the time and I never noticed him until he moved. I was glad to see him.

"How do you blend into the swamp like that? It's like you were invisible," I said.

He replied slowly, "In the swamp, Little Muddy, there are many things. Some can be seen and some cannot; some are seen and some are not. Many come to look, but few see. I was not invisible or blending; I was not seen."

"Next time, I will see you." I promised.

"There is no such thing as 'next time'; there is only now." he reminded. "Now," he said, "what exactly are you doing when you create something? Have you given the question any thought?"

I wondered, "What does creating something have to do with people getting along with each other?" Didn't make sense to me, but Mudman always had a reason for his questions; so, I told him about grandma creating her rocking chair and making it the way she dreamed it.

Then I said to him, "I think that when you create something, you give part of yourself to it and make it like you want it to be."

"Well!, well!, well!," exclaimed Mudman, "Looky here! Little Muddy **has** been thinking about the question. I suppose that you now know the answer to your original question."

He went back, sat down on the ground and leaned back against his tree. I don't care what he claims, he does blend in. He motioned for me to sit down beside him; I sat down and leaned back against the tree too.

"I still don't know why humans can't get along with each other, Mudman." I admitted, "and 'created diversity' is hard for me to think about because, well just because." I didn't know what else to say at the moment.

"Are you religious, Little Muddy?" he asked.

A flag went up in my mind! "Trick question! Trick question!" it was warning. I glanced over at Mudman and said, "You mean like do I go to church? Well, I do. There's a church up on the street where most people in the neighborhood go on Sunday and Wednesday."

"Do you like going to church?"

"It's okay."

"Okay?"

"Well, it's not my favorite thing to do, but I don't mind going and I like singing the church songs."

"You like whistling too, as I remember."

"Yeah, but it's not polite to whistle in church."

"What do you do in church?"

"Mudman, why are you asking me these questions about religion?" I asked. "What does religion have to do with 'created diversity'?"

"It has to do with why diversity was created." he answered.

Suddenly, my attention was focused on Mudman. I felt like a big secret was about to be told me and really wanted to hear it. Hopefully, I will understand what he talks about.

I replied, "We learn about God and Jesus in church."

"I see," he said, "and what have you learned about God and Jesus?"

I knew this was going to be complicated. Why doesn't he just tell me what I want to know instead of asking a bunch of questions? I studied my muddy toes and thought about how good it would be just to take a walk in the shallow water about now.

Mudman saw I was wrestling with an answer. He stood up and said, "Come on, Little Muddy, let's take a walk in the swamp for a bit."

"How does he do that?" I thought. "I was just thinking about doing that myself." I replied.

"Great minds think alike." he commented, and motioned for me to follow him as he slowly glided straight into the swamp.

I followed along, but this was a new adventure. Other than the trip in my barrel boat, I had only been out in the swamp about twenty feet or so before and certainly had never walked out this far. Mudman was leading me into unknown and unexplored territory, at least where I was concerned. I was excited! We went around trees and over water soaked logs. The mud was soft and deep beneath my feet and the water was up to my chest. I had to swim in some places because the mud below was too deep to walk through. But I kept up with him. When we reached a small clearing in the swamp, Mudman stopped, turned and looked at me.

"How is this for a stopping place, Little Muddy?" and before I could answer he asked, "Do you know where you are?" Then he picked me up and set me on a tree limb growing just above the water.

I looked around. I couldn't see the shore line where we started from. There were trees, with moss hanging from them everywhere. And besides that, there were lots of turtles and snakes, some laying on logs or limbs and others were just swimming around. It was a beautiful place!

I answered, "No. Not really. I have never been this far into the swamp."

"You need to learn such things. Many have come this far and stayed, Little Muddy."

"Stayed?" I said. "You mean they moved here?"

"Yes and no. Look at the moss on the trees." Mudman said and motioned to some moss hanging on a limb above me. "Always be aware of the moss when you enter the swamp and you will know your way back." he starkly demanded.

I persisted, "Who would want to stay here, Mudman, and where are they?"

"Staying is never their desire, it is their fate." he said.

"Are you saying that they died here?" I exclaimed.

"The swamp can be dangerous, young friend; look around you." he calmly demanded.

I looked and saw a very large alligator floating behind Mudman and watched the heads of two smaller gators appear a little farther out. I listened and heard sounds that I could not identify. Tree frogs seemed to be competing with birds to see which of them could make the most noise and something under the water was slowly moving close by and causing swirls of mud kicked up by its action. "What is that?" I thought. Then I understood, people would not come here to live; they came for some other reason. If they stayed here, it was because they died here.

"Did the alligators kill the people who came here?" I stammered.

"Among other things." he said, and then asked, "Why do you think the alligators and the people who came here could not get along with each other?"

The small gators were slowly approaching me. I could see the rest of their bodies under the clear water; they were maybe four feet long. I felt safe with Mudman close, but kept my eyes on them while I answered. It was hard to think about an answer to his question with the noise and visible disturbances ongoing, but I gave as honest an answer as I could.

"They are different from each other." I said, "One is an animal and the other is a human. They are not made to get along."

"Who made them?" he asked.

I told him, "God made them. God made everything. He created the world!"

"Why did God make humans and alligators different from each other?"

I answered, "I don't know, probably 'cause He wanted to."

"So, God created them diverse because he wanted them to be diverse." he stated.

"Well, I guess so." I replied weakly. Then I thought about it and firmly said, "Yes! God does not do things that he doesn't want to do."

"Little Muddy, do you remember what you said about your grandma creating her rocking chair?" (*I think that when you create something, you give part of yourself to it and make it like you want it to be.*)

"Yes, I remember." I responded.

The two smaller alligators were floating about six feet away, just looking at us. I can hardly believe that I wasn't afraid of them, but I wasn't. Suddenly I realized something, the swamp was really quiet, no water splashing, no frogs croaking, no birds chirping, no snakes or turtles swimming. It was almost like everything in the swamp was listening to Mudman and me talking with each other and being careful not to interrupt us.

Then Mudman pointed at me, like he always did when he wanted my attention, and asked, "Now tell me, what did you learn in your church about God and Jesus?"

I knew the answer now and told him, "I learned that God created all things: the heavens, the earth, humans, animals, trees, . . . everything and Jesus is his son."

Mudman slid closer to me and softly stated, "So you believe when God created this reality, He gave part of himself to his creation and made everything like He wanted it to be. This means that a part of God is in everything and everything is as it should be because God made it that way."

Mudman's complex statement made sense to me because I believe that God created everything, but something about it seemed wrong, I just couldn't think of why. I needed more time.

Mudman said in a matter of fact way, "That is the explanation of the answer to your question, Little Muddy."

Then he changed the subject, "How do you like this part of the swamp? Does it scare you a little bit? Most people are not comfortable here."

I was feeling a lot of confusion after Mudman's statement because it was not clear to me that my questions had been answered, so I responded to his question about the swamp.

"It's really pretty here, but there are a lot of alligators around. I don't think people are safe here. There is something else here too, I don't know what it is, but it scares me a little. I feel safe with you, though."

"The alligators are the reason people come here." said Mudman. "Humans hunt and kill alligators for their hides. Sometimes, those that hunt do not leave. Be aware of and very careful with things unseen. Let's get you back to shore before your mother comes out looking for you again."

Then he lifted me off the limb and let me down into the water. The tide was out and the water level there was just above my waist. I looked around before leaving. The swamp had come to life again. Birds were chirping and the glassy water was rippling with the activity of creatures, both known and unknown to me. The alligators showed no interest in us. Mudman took my hand and we glided toward shore.

I thought to myself, "I don't know for sure, but I might just come back here someday." Another thought crept into my mind, an answer! "Humans can't get along with each other because God created us that way. God created diversity within his creation, for his own reasons."

'Created diversity' is an accurate answer, but I didn't like it because it gave birth to other questions, even for 12 year old kids like me, and because asking those questions seems a lot like questioning God's reasons for creating everything. Questioning God seemed like a sin to me. I don't know why it should, though. God created me to ask questions. "Didn't He?" I asked myself.

When we got back to where we left, Mudman said, "You're quiet and thinking about something, my young friend. Do you have a question, now?"

"I wonder why my answer that some humans are good and some are bad isn't a better answer to the reason people can't get along together?" I offered.

"Because that answer is a reason that humans **don't** get along together." he said, and added, "They **can't** get along together because they are not created to get along together. Think about that statement, Little Muddy. Saying that humans are **not created** to get along with each other is not the same as saying that humans are **created not** to get along with each other. Do you understand, now?"

"I have to think about that." I said. "It's complicated."

Mudman advised, "Do you remember when we began this conversation, I told you that this subject was difficult to understand and that such understanding would make you unpopular if you ever told anyone else. Well, we are at that point. Let me try to better explain this complicated subject."

"Let's start with a simple math problem. I believe you understand that two plus three is equal to five. The thing is, you were **not** created to understand that $2+3=5$, but you **were** created with the ability to learn that $2+3=5$. Are you with me, so far?" he asked.

That was a little insulting. It seemed that Mudman was treating me like a second grader. I wanted to throw a mudball at him, but controlled myself and said, "Yes."

"Good. Now, you were not created to get along with other humans," explained Mudman in a patient voice, "but you **were** created with the ability to **learn** to get along with other humans."

I was beginning to see some sense in this second grade math lesson and paid more attention to Mudman as he spoke.

He continued, "had you not learned what 2, 3, and 5 were or what 'plus' and 'equal' meant, you would not know how to understand, use, or even write that simple equation." and he added, "if one does not learn how to get along with others, he will have few friends, perhaps many enemies, and even be involved in many fights with others."

"Basically," he explained, "humans can't get along with each other because they have not yet learned how to do so. It is difficult to fault humans for that inability because so many of you are stupid. Normally, I would say 'ignorant', but 'stupid' is more fitting here."

"Are you with me now, Little muddy?" he asked.

"I think so," I said and answered, "You're saying that people can get along together if they want to, because **wanting** to get along with each other will force them to learn **how** to get along with each other. But who is going to teach us how to do that? We don't learn how to get along with others in my school. Also, calling people 'stupid' doesn't help; people don't like being called stupid."

Mudman thought a moment and responded, "The stupid do not realize they are stupid, Little Muddy, but perhaps you are correct. Have you a more fitting word?"

"Well, maybe 'uninformed" is better.

"No," he said, "uninformed implies 'ignorance', which is treatable when ignorance becomes unhappy being uninformed; stupid, on the other hand, is not treatable because those who are stupid do not understand they are stupid and are therefore content with being stupid."

I had no idea what Mudman said and I wish he wouldn't talk like that. No one will ever understand what he means. Well at least I don't, anyway. I just nodded my head and he smiled at me. At that moment, when he smiled at me, I knew he realized that I was lost. That is when I understood what I was and what I wanted. I was uninformed and ignorant, and I wanted to be informed and intelligent. I needed to say something that I was beginning to believe.

So, I said, "Mudman, I believe humans are never going to get along together. There is always going to be arguing, fighting, and killing among people and countries because we humans are a stupid and ignorant race of people. The best we can do is try to be happy with the way things are."

Mudman didn't say anything. I could see that he was thinking about what I said. After what seemed to be a long silence, he made this comment:

"Little Muddy, you surprised me with that declaration. I have been trying to answer your question regarding why humans cannot get along with each other and somewhere in that process you became convinced that humanity is doomed to disorder and chaos. Because of our conversation, you made a leap from an interest in 'now' to 'destiny'. I find that to be interesting.

Then he asked, "So you now understand why humans can't get along with each other?"

"Yes, you have answered my question. Some humans will get along with each other and some won't. Some countries will get along with other countries and some won't. People will hurt or help each other when they feel like it. Countries will do the same thing. God is in charge and knows what he's doing. That is the way things are and we have to learn to accept it or be unhappy. I like being happy."

"Well Little Muddy, you sure have learned how to close a conversation. I enjoyed it. We will talk again in another now." He reached a finger into the wet mud, smeared some on my cheek and glided back into the swamp.

Although it seemed that we had been together all day, only about two hours had passed since my walk down to the swamp. Two hours and it felt like a lot more. I walked away, changed my clothes at the hollow tree, and didn't look back. My brain was tired of thinking. Being with Mudman was tiring. His questions caused me to think about and consider things that never came into my mind away from the swamp. As usual, the things we talked about and the new place he showed me were not secrets, but would not be told. Who would I tell, anyway?

On the way up to the house, my mind was full of all kinds of thoughts and questions. "you became convinced that humanity is doomed to disorder and chaos." is what he said about me.

"I don't want to believe that I believe that because I don't." I said aloud. "Listen to me," I said out loud, "he's even got me talking to myself."

"Well, Mudman warned me that I wasn't intelligent enough for such a discussion." I said to myself. That warning turned out to be true. Truth is, I don't really understand most of what he told me.

When I got back to the house, Rex was waiting and wanted me to go back to the woods with him. I knelt down, hugged him and promised that we would go later in the day.

In the house, momma took one look at me and said, "Go wash that mud off your face, Johnny. I don't see how you can keep your clothes so clean and get your face so dirty."

"The mudman did it, momma." I answered and giggled.

She looked at me and smiled. "Now don't you go telling your brothers any mudman stories. We've been through enough scary tales for one lifetime already. There's a peanut butter and jelly sandwich on the table. Go on out and play with Rex; he's been waiting for you all morning."

"Okay, momma." I grabbed the sandwich and went outside to take Rex for a walk in the woods. My brother Ricky saw me leaving and, uninvited, joined us. Not that I minded his coming along, my little brother loved me and wanted to follow me everywhere, and did whenever he could. I had to share my sandwich with him, though. That mud stayed on my face 'til suppertime.

Chapter 13 - The Big Gator

You have noticed by now that the bulk of this story is about my time with Mudman. I am not sure how else to write his story. I don't write much about my personal life away from the swamp during the time this story takes place because I want to tell you about Mudman and me. We met together, off and on, from the time I was ten until my mother sold the house next to the swamp a little before my sixteenth birthday. As you will see in the coming pages, Mudman seldom answered any questions about himself or where he came from. I never found out how old he was or anything about his life. I mean, he is made of mud! You know, strange looking! And he can disappear in the woods or swamp at a moment's notice. 'Disappear' is the wrong word. I know how ridiculous it sounds, but Mudman blends with or becomes the swamp as he pleases.

His understanding of everything is a mystery. I asked him how he got to know so much about everything and he answered, "If one knows how, information is always available to be absorbed, which you will understand in another now, Little Muddy. It will be interesting to see what you do with such understanding."

Yeah, right! What does one do with "such understanding"? I have tried and failed more than a few times to teach the concept of "such understanding" to others, a testament I suppose to my lack of teaching ability.

Anyway, in over five years, we met together less than a hundred times. This is Mudman's story that I am telling. A small part of the history of what might actually be an immortal or near immortal being, obtained from information gleaned in few meetings. His full story will never be known. Who would tell it? My intent is to capture part of his philosophy and release it for you to consider, except for . . . well, there are always exceptions. As far as I am concerned, his philosophy applies to everything in our reality.

One morning about two weeks later, after a storm, while Rex and I were walking along the edge of the swamp looking for crawfish, I saw something about 30 yards out that really got me excited. It was the nose of a boat sticking up out of the water. I didn't know if it was a complete boat or just a part of one, but in my imagination it was all there in one piece. The problem was, it was about 30 yards out in the swamp and I had never walked that far out before by myself. I didn't even know how deep the water was that far out. Mudman had warned me several times that the swamp was dangerous and to be very aware when there, even on shore. But there was a boat out there and I seriously needed a boat!

Large gators were not a big concern because they usually were not seen that close in during the day where they would be exposed to hunters. There could be a rogue bull gator nearby, but I had not ever heard or seen evidence of one of those. Besides, the swamp was reasonably quiet and I learned from experience that the place erupted with the sound of frogs and birds and other critters when gators were nearby. So I was feeling pretty sure that I could get to the boat without fear of a big alligator.

Most of the snakes in the swamp were not poisonous, the extreme exception being cottonmouths. They were normally not real aggressive unless threatened; however, they could bite underwater. Does it show that I read a lot of books on snakes? I had watched and caught many snakes in the swamp as well, so I was not afraid of snakes, just careful around them.

My boat was out there in the swamp and I was going out there to get it. I went back to my hollow tree and got a rope. I wondered what Mudman would think about my wading out in the swamp. He might be proud of me! I came to play and hunt in the swamp pretty often and only rarely did I encounter Mudman. I often wondered what he did out here all the time. He could get that boat to shore in no time, or 'now' as he would say. But he was not here now. I was. I started slowly wading into the swamp toward the boat. Rex was not happy. He was whining and walking back and forth at the edge of the water. Then he just crouched down and laid there watching me. The water wasn't deep and I was feeling my way as I waded. I left my shoes on because I wasn't sure what might be on the swamp floor and didn't want to step on something that might cut my feet. The shoes actually got in my way as the mud on the bottom was sticky and pulled at my shoes. Bare feet would have been better. I'll remember that.

The water was a little deeper at the boat, above my waist. But when I got there, my excitement level rose because the boat was complete and intact and it was a pirogue! The nose was above the water because it was jammed upon a sunken log, but the rest of the boat was floating below the water. It was a small pirogue, over seven feet long and perfect for me! Even full of water, it was still floating. All I had to do was get it off the log and pull it to shore. I pushed the nose of the boat to the right and it easily slid off the log. The pirogue was full of water and clumsy-heavy, but I had a boat!

I was tying my rope to the ring attached to the nose when I saw the waves rippling the water on the other side of the boat toward the deep swamp about 20 yards away. It was the same thing I had seen two weeks earlier where Mudman had taken me. I couldn't see what it was, but the ripples were there and the thing was moving side to side under the water getting closer with each turn. I pulled on the rope and turned to head back to shore with the boat, but my feet were stuck in the mud above my ankles! The darn shoes! I jerked my leg back hard and one shoe came off. I used the free foot to push the other shoe off and started pulling the boat. All I wanted to do was get it to shallow water where I could easily come back for it another time.

The water thing was close now and then, beyond it I saw the huge gator. He could move very fast in the swamp. I was still at least 20 yards from shore and couldn't outrun him. I let go of the rope and turned to run through the water anyway, but no one runs through waist deep water. My heart was pounding and I didn't want to look back. Then I heard a huge splash and stopped to look. I'll never forget what I saw. The big gator was floating belly up in the water and waves were pushing him farther into the swamp! He was alive, but couldn't get off his back. As I watched, frozen in place, the gator finally flipped over and began swimming toward the deep swamp. I saw the rope floating in the water and walked toward it. My hands were shaking so much that I couldn't pick it up. Looking out to the swamp, I saw the water thing was again swimming back and forth under the water, making waves as it moved deeper into the swamp.

Rex must have been barking during the whole time, but it wasn't until I waded to shore and laid down next to him that I heard the barks. I put my shaking arms around him and cried. He licked my face and the tears. After calming down a little, I waded out to the rope and pulled the boat to the shallows. The small pirogue was easy enough to tip and drain enough water to float it closer in and tie to a limb. That is all I was willing to do; I had enough of the swamp today, and changed my clothes. Then Rex and I headed home. I was going to need another pair of swamp shoes.

"What was an alligator that big doing there?" I wondered. "and what is that water thing, anyway?" I didn't feel so smart anymore.

When we got home, momma was washing clothes and asked, "What was Rex barking at out there, son? I could hear him all the way up here."

"We saw a big alligator turtle crawling out of the water, momma." I lied.

"You stay away from those big water turtles, Johnny." she said. "When they bite you, they don't let go 'til it thunders."

"I know, momma." I replied. "I think I'm gonna lay down and rest for a while."

"Land sakes, boy!" she laughed. "I didn't know turtle hunting was such tiring work."

I slept until suppertime, ate, did my chores, went back to bed and slept all night. Momma came in several times and felt my head for signs of a fever. She thought I might be getting sick. Truth is, that adventure in the swamp took a lot out of me, physically and mentally. I didn't ever remember being that afraid before. That alligator waited, unseen, until no escape was possible and then came for me. I had never see one that big, even at the zoo. . . and he was still out there in the swamp, along with other things. I now had a pirogue, but could I paddle it into the swamp? For the first time in my young life, I now understood that real danger lurked in the swamp and wasn't sure how to fight my new found fear of that danger. Along with that fear came unhappiness. I didn't like being afraid, but I hated being unhappy and didn't know for sure what to do about it.

You remember back when I was ten years old and I was telling Mudman how the swamp was my safe place? Well, I was just a kid back then and didn't know any better. Mudman warned me that the swamp was not a safe place and he was right. I had a boat now and normally would be dying to try it out, but all I could think about was that big gator waiting out there. He was way bigger than my boat.

Getting out of bed that next morning was a job because, in spite of the fear, my new boat was calling me and something had to give. It was an easy choice. I got up, dressed, had breakfast, and walked down to the swamp.

The pirogue was where I tied it and still had water inside. It was an old boat, but new to me. The thing is, the boat was tied about five feet from from shore, in shallow water. Now that don't seem like much, considering how often I wade there all the time, but I didn't go there to get in the water, shallow or not. The purpose of this walk down to the swamp was to face my fear. Everyone says that if you fall off a horse, the best thing to do is get right back on. I don't know who 'everyone' is, but I'd like to see them get chased by a 14 foot gator, get away, and then get back in the water with it. Well, my fear was faced up to a point, which was good enough for the day. I walked back home.

Being afraid was not something with which I was familiar. It is interesting how many reasons there are to avoid facing a fear. Chores, homework, weather, and feeling tired are a few of many and I used them all. Almost a month had passed since I went after that boat and I didn't even know if it was still where I had left it. Momma noticed that my presence at home was happening more often than not and commented about it several times. Even Rex seemed to notice that something was wrong because we were not taking our daily walks anymore. What do you do about fear? I didn't know. I wondered about Mudman; how would he feel about my fear? He didn't seem to fear anything, but why should he? He was like a king in the swamp. My fear was my problem and up to me to solve.

Chapter 14 - The Pirogue

One Saturday morning, a few days later, I woke up determined to go to the swamp every day until that fear left me. Momma and grandma, along with my brothers were going into town shopping for several hours and I chose to stay home. It was raining, but that didn't matter; I had a plan and rain was not going to stop me. I put on my raincoat, walked down to the edge of the swamp where my boat was tied, and sat down there. The rain was coming down pretty hard, but I just sat there and looked through the rain at the swamp searching for any sign of alligators.

I thought to myself, "What would I do if I saw one? Get up and run? No! I would watch."

What was it that Mudman said about looking and not seeing? I was determined to see. So, I watched. There were no gators to see.

After about a half hour, the rain settled to a sprinkle. I sat there for a while longer, then got up and looked at my boat. It was half full of water. I waded over and tipped the boat to drain most of the water, then pulled it to shore and turned it over to drain the rest of the water. I did all that without fear. What happened? Why no fear? Because, I wasn't thinking about being afraid; I was focused on getting the boat to shore. Doing that felt good and I wanted that feeling to last.

I wasn't sure of being ready to take the boat out for a spin, but was feeling comfortable in the swamp again. I looked out toward the deep swamp, noticed the reflection of the trees in the still water and whispered under my breath, "There is so much here to love."

"Things to fear?" I said out loud. "I don't like that word. There are things here of which to be careful, though . . .very careful."

"There are things like that everywhere, Little Muddy." he said and added, "even in your so-called civilized part of the world."

I turned around and there was Mudman, sitting on the bottom of my overturned boat.

"Of course, out here alligators are recognized as predators by all, but in your human world predators look like everyone else, making them even more dangerous."

Excited, I blurted out, "I should have known you were here!"

"Why?" he asked.

"Because for some reason I talk different when you're around. I feel different, too."

"Different? What different?"

"I don't know how to explain it exactly. Smarter, confident, safe and unafraid."

"All of those things are in you, Little Muddy. They do not come from outside."

"Then how come I don't feel them all the time?"

"Because you do not understand Now."

"When will I understand?"

"There is no 'when', my young friend." he said and smiled. "Think about it."

Then Mudman changed the subject. "So, you now have a boat." he stated. "Are you planning to explore the swamp?"

And, there it was, the question! I really didn't want to talk about taking a boat into the swamp, but Mudman **did** want to talk about it. He had to know about my encounter with the alligator because he knows about everything going on here, but he probably doesn't know how I was affected by a brush with death. How do I answer him?

There is only one answer, so I said, "About that, Mudman," and went on to explain my difficulty with fear. "I'm afraid to go out into the swamp now and don't know what to do about it. I can't seem to figure out where this fear came from and am unable to control it."

Mudman sat quietly on the overturned boat and seemed to be in deep thought. He was taking a long time to reply to my confession of fear. I wanted him to say that everything will be alright and the fear will pass. I was tired of being afraid and unhappy, but even at my young age it was clear that my fear was my problem and up to me to solve. I just didn't know how.

Mudman finally moved! He stood up, turned the boat upright and pushed it into the water. I liked that boat. It was a flat bottom pirogue, maybe eight feet long. I had not yet measured it. One day next week, I might take it for a short trip along the shore. It needed a little cleaning before that, though. "I might even paint it." I thought.

Mudman pointed to the pirogue and said gently, "Get in."

"Wha, what?" I stammered.

"Get in the boat, Little Muddy." he ordered, "We need to talk."

I waded out to the pirogue, stepped into it, and sat down on the bottom, feeling tense. Mudman sat down in the shallow water next to the boat and said, "You have a nice boat here. Treat it well and you will see things out here observed by few if any humans."

I weakly replied, "Yeah, I like it. I might oughta clean and paint it before taking it out, though; you know, to check it for leaks and everything."

Mudman knew I was stalling, afraid to take the boat into the swamp. I knew it too, and hated the feeling.

"Little Muddy," he said, staring out into the deep swamp, "the capacity for fear is built into all created species to assure survival. Without fear, extinction results."

"Oh, boy!" I thought, "Mudman is on another roll this morning!"

Remember my saying that being around him makes me feel smarter? Well, sometimes he exposes my ignorance as well. I had no idea what he just said, but I didn't let on and sat there quietly.

"All life experiences fear my young friend. Fear is necessary to survival."

"Except for you, Mudman." I countered, "You're not afraid of anything."

He looked at me and again said, "All life experiences fear, Little Muddy."

That statement made me curious and I asked, "What could scare you, Mudman?"

He simply said, "Sand."

Puzzled, I questioned his answer. "Sand? What's scary about sand?"

"Sand has the ability to change, perhaps even destroy, my essence and its own in the process." he explained. "I both fear and avoid sand."

Once again, Mudman was talking way over my head, so I reminded him by saying, "Did you forget who you are talking to, Mudman? I don't understand anything you just said! What does 'change your essence' mean and what is there to fear about it?"

"to whom you are talking." he corrected me and asked, "Do your instructors teach English in school? I have been meaning to talk to you about your strange way of speaking."

"My strange way of speaking? What about you?" I replied, preparing to make my argument, when suddenly I noticed that our surroundings had changed. We were into the swamp and I couldn't see the shore. Mudman was still by the boat, but in deeper water. He had distracted me with conversation and glided us over a hundred yards away from shore.

I looked at him and nervously said, "What are you doing? I don't think I'm ready to be here, yet."

My heart seemed to be racing in my throat and I quickly looked around, but saw nothing but tall trees and still water. The rain had stopped but the clouds remained and, although it was late morning, it was dark in the swamp. I wondered if the big gator was close by.

"Yet, here you are." Mudman stated in a calm voice. "Many have come out this far and stayed."

"Well, that's wonderful news!" I thought, with sarcasm.

I really didn't want to hear or think about that.

"What do you feel, now?" he asked and seemed interested in a response.

I couldn't concentrate on an answer and said nothing.

Mudman backed away from the boat, pointed at me and said, "Well, Little Muddy?"

"Say the truth, Johnny." I thought to myself. "What **do** I feel now?"

"Tense and afraid." I answered. "and ashamed for feeling that way. I don't like feeling that way and hate that I can't seem to stop feeling that way."

"How do you want to feel?" asked Mudman, as he backed farther from the boat.

"I want to feel confident and brave." I replied. "Being afraid makes me unhappy."

"You said before that you feel safe and unafraid when I am around, Little Muddy. I am here now and yet you feel tense and afraid. Why do you think that is so? What has changed?" Mudman has a way of asking questions that require a lot of thought.

"I don't know." was all I could come up with.

Mudman continued, "Perhaps the confidence and bravery you desire does not come from my presence at all and if that is true, from where does it come? Perhaps from inside you? And if that is true, then it follows that you are the source of that which makes you unhappy or happy."

Like I have said before, Mudman has a way about him. I had already decided that my fear problem likely required a solution from me, but had never seriously considered the problem as coming from within me in the first place. The big alligator scared me for sure, but it is not the source of my fear problem. I am! And I am also the solution.

I looked up to ask what Mudman thought about that, but he was nowhere to be seen. I thought, "Surely he didn't leave me out here by myself. He wouldn't do that, would he?"

There was no answer to my calls. The odd thing is, even though I was sitting in a boat all by myself somewhere in the swamp, it was clear to me that everything was okay. Somehow, I would figure out a way to get back to shore with my boat. Causing me to understand that my loss of confidence in myself was self-created was Mudman's way of getting me back on track.

I said aloud, talking to myself, "I may be lost in the swamp right now, but that part of me that was lost is not lost anymore and I'm thankful for that."

"You can now paddle back alone, Little Muddy. I have things to do." said a voice from somewhere.

"Alone? Paddle?" I exclaimed. "I'm not sure where 'back' is, Mudman and I don't have no paddle!"

"I have no paddle." he corrected. "and have I not taught you the difference between looking and seeing. Look in your boat and see. Remember to notice the moss."

I looked inside my pirogue and what did I see? A paddle was hooked to the inside of the boat and right next to me. In all the time spent sitting there this morning, I never noticed it. I unhooked the paddle and whispered, "Thank you, Mudman, for everything."

The rain started coming down hard again. I looked at the swamp around me, the moss indicated which way was west. I now knew where 'back' was and paddled there, through the rain, without fear. I was still fearful of the big gator out here and was wary of him, but the anxiety of constant fear had left me.

I paddled to shore, secured the paddle, hid my pirogue and walked to the house in the rain. I felt free. I loved the feeling of feeling free. Momma and the rest of the family were not home yet, so I just sat down on the porch in the rain thinking and looking at everything, enjoying my now. It occurred to me that Mudman never completed the story about his fear of sand, other than it could change his essence. I didn't know what that meant, but it must be important in order to be feared by Mudman. I made a mental note to ask him about it at our next meeting, whenever that might be. 'Sand' is to him like the gator is to me. I would never have guessed that. I was thinking about naming that big gator 'Sandy' and wondered if Mudman would see the humor in that. Probably not.

My newly acquired pirogue was life changing for me. During the next year I went to places in that big swamp that very few get to see. Truth be known, few care to see the things I saw anyway. I don't know how many of you reading this are familiar with alligator gars, but there are a lot of them in Texas rivers and swamps and they grow very big. I saw alligator gars that were longer than my pirogue, at least 9 feet long, in the deep swamp. I saw water snakes that were also longer than my boat. I saw more beautiful birds and fish than exist anywhere. There are flowers growing out of dead trees there that I have never seen anywhere else, even in pictures of books about flowers. All of that and more did I see in the swamp during that year. That is the upside view.

The downside to such a beautiful environment must be mentioned. Something else is in the swamp, a life-form that may be the most dangerous thing living there, particularly where humans are concerned. The thing that keeps the human species from the swamp is more insidious than reptiles, quicksand, heat, humidity, poisonous plants and water all lumped together. What is it? Bugs! You simply cannot understand how many different species of bugs exist in the swamp. Much worse than that is the sheer number of bugs. There are billions of them in the swamp, probably much more. I have seen swarms of mosquitoes so thick that animals have choked to death from inhaling them. A horrible thing to watch.

Deer flies are among the worst biting bugs. They live for blood, are very active in the swamp and can drive mammals insane if one cannot get away from their swarms. There are many different types of bugs in the swamp; some bite and some sting. All of them make human living conditions in the swamp next to unbearable.

So how could a young red blooded boy like me survive such a hoard of blood drinking bugs while paddling a boat around in the swamp? I actually don't know. I always smeared myself with mud and wore clothes that covered most of my body, but that wouldn't stop the swarms of mosquitoes and deer flies. I don't know for sure, but it's possible that Mudman had something to do with it. Remember, when I was ten years old he told me that I would be alright in the swamp. Bugs have never been a real big problem for me. Of course mosquitoes and deer flies bite me, but not like they do others. I'm thankful for that too.

Chapter 15 - Biased Compassionate Empathy

I liked baseball and had played in both Little League and Babe Ruth League baseball divisions. I was involved in school events as well, all of which occupied much of my time and limited exploring and playing in the swamp. I seldom saw Mudman, even though I was paddling around in my pirogue at least 2-3 times a week. After he left me in the swamp to get back to shore by myself, I did not see him again until the next summer when I was 13 years old. I had finished playing in a Little League game and after getting home, went down to the swamp to check on my boat, still wearing my baseball shirt and hat. I flipped my boat upright, got in and laid down to think about the game, which we had lost. Losing a baseball game always made me unhappy. I liked playing well but, for me, winning the game was what playing the game was all about. Anyway, my mood was low that day. I must have laid in the boat for fifteen minutes or so, brooding about being a loser, when I heard a loud splash in the swamp. I quickly stood up and looked toward the splash. Mudman was standing about 20 feet out holding a squirming four foot alligator. Now, that was a sight! Okay, a four foot gator is not a big gator in the swamp, but one that size is heavy. Mudman was holding it like I would hold a stuffed toy. The strength of Mudman is something I never before considered. That was something new about him.

Anyway, he began gliding toward me holding the gator out in front of him. I didn't know what he was doing, but he stopped at the edge of the shore and asked me. "What do you think should be done with this big lizard?"

I didn't know what to say. Why would he ask me such a thing? What was he doing carrying an alligator to the shore, anyway?

I answered with the first thoughts that came into my mind, "I don't know. You caught it; he's your lizard now. What do you want to do with it?"

"You might want to think about putting it in your little zoo. A lot of people would pay a nickel to see this baby." he offered. Somehow I felt that Mudman was pulling my leg, but wasn't sure why.

"Come on Mudman, be serious." I said. "What are you doing catching and bringing a gator here?" I replied. "I don't really like alligators."

"It was already here in this part of the swamp, Little Muddy." he said. "All I did was catch him."

It crossed my mind that something was wrong here. Mudman was hinting at a possible problem. In all the times I have gone out in my pirogue this year, no alligators were seen in this part of the swamp. Why was this little one here now and were there more? The more scary question concerned the possible presence of adult alligators.

"Mudman, are there more here in this part of the swamp?" I asked.

"Come down tonight with a light and count the eyes. You know about that, Little Muddy." he answered.

I learned a-while back, when frogging, that the eyes of gators reflect light when it is shined upon them in the dark.

"I don't need to do that," I replied. "your answer is good enough for me." I wasn't about to go to a congress of alligators in the daytime, much less at night. Mudman tossed the little gator out into the water like it was nothing. It hit the water, quickly swam about 20 yards out and stopped. This was not good. Taking my boat out among a group of alligators was not doable for me or hardly anyone else. I was still standing in my boat, now feeling anxious and looking around for gator signs.

Mudman sat down in the shallow water and after a moment advised, "You won't see any of them now, they are farther out among the trees."

"Why are they here now?" I asked. "and why are they all gathering here?" There just had to be a reason for their coming to this part of the swamp and I wanted to know. I stepped out of my boat, walked over to my thinking log and sat down to wait for his answer.

"Fear." said Mudman. "Alligators fear humans and avoid them. Hunters have come in boats to the part of the swamp highly populated by alligators to kill them for their skins. This gathering was herded here for their safety."

"Herded? How can alligators be herded? I asked. And then commented, "They are far too stupid to be herded and way too independent."

"Actually, Little Muddy, alligators are social with their own kind. All but the large ones will try to escape the hunters, but they **are** stupid and, unless forcibly directed, have little chance to survive the slaughter. The large gators have hiding places, which make them difficult to find."

"Forcibly directed?" I questioned. "You mean herded? Alligators have got to be impossible to herd!"

"Not the little ones, they will stay with their mother. The bulls will hide in the swamp, but some will defend their territory because they are stupid. It is their nature. Many die because of that nature."

I had to ask the obvious question, "What can herd alligators, Mudman?"

"Something more feared than humans." he answered.

"Is that something you, Mudman?"

"No. I am dangerous, Little Muddy, but not to be feared."

That answer created more questions than my mind could handle. Right now, I wanted to know how long the gators would be on this side of the swamp.

"How long do you think the gators will stay here?" I asked.

"Until the humans leave or stay." said Mudman. "The hunters should leave now, before dark, but they won't; they prefer hunting at night."

"How many people are hunting there and why should they leave before dark?"

"There are nine and they should leave to live, Little Muddy, but like the gators, they are stupid. The swamp is dangerous and some will stay."

"What is it they should fear, Mudman? The hunters have boats and guns."

"Bugs." was all he said and stared toward the deep swamp.

"Why won't the gators stay here, Mudman?"

"No security for them here. The water is shallow, the food supply is limited, and humans could hunt them from dry ground. The deep swamp is their natural home and they will return there."

Anyway, after telling me about the gators and the hunters, Mudman came over to the log and sat down beside me.

"Stay out of the swamp for awhile until life gets back to normal out there," he warned. "Alligators are more dangerous when they feel threatened and right now the hunters have them on edge."

I didn't know how to feel about the alligator hunters. In the first place, I didn't like gators. They scared me. Second, the hunters were just trying to earn money by selling alligator hides, and killing gators kept the population of those creatures from getting out of control. But although killing gators was legal, in season, and seemed like a good thing to do, I was bothered by the way people went about the killing. Mudman was sitting there with me so I told him how I felt and asked what he thought about it.

"That is another one of those questions you are fond of asking, Little Muddy." he said. "A simple question with a simple answer that begs a complicated discussion." Then he asked, "What is it exactly you wish to understand, my young friend?"

"I want to know why killing alligators for their hides bothers me even though I understand the reason for the killing and go along with it." I said.

"I suppose you feel the same about all animals, including the ones you eat?"

"Well, I haven't thought about them Mudman, but yes, those too."

Mudman continued, "What about bugs, Little Muddy? Are you bothered about the killing of bugs? Of course there are worms about which to be concerned and small creatures like amoeba and paramecium as well. Oh, I left out germs. Do you feel bad about killing germs? Or have you no feelings about them at all?"

"A simple question with a simple answer that begs a complicated discussion." Mudman repeated himself. "Do you understand?" he asked.

I didn't want to get into a complex explanation regarding life; I just wanted a simple answer about why killing gators for their skins bothered me, so I said, "I asked you a simple question

Mudman, which you said had a simple answer. What is the simple answer?"

"Biased compassionate empathy." he answered.

"Well, isn't that just wonderful?" I thought to myself. "This is another simple answer like 'created diversity' that I am too ignorant to understand. Only this one is worse!"

"What does that even mean, Mudman?" I asked. "and don't tell me that I don't have the intelligence to understand! You can teach me and I can learn. I'm almost fourteen now and have learned a lot in the last four years. I feel sorry for the alligators being killed by hunters and don't even like gators much. I don't know why I care or even if I should care, but I care. The truth is, I don't really understand why I care about other animals, and no, I don't really care about bugs or worms or amoebas."

"Well, Little Muddy you are filled with surprises today. I like that about you. You look different, too. What is that shirt you are wearing with the number '6' on the back?"

"It's part my baseball uniform, Mudman. I play on a baseball team. We had a game today and I left my shirt on when I changed clothes to come down here. I wear the number '6' because it is Al Kaline's number and he is my favorite player."

"Did you play well?" he asked.

"Yeah, I got three hits and scored twice. We lost, though." I mumbled.

"Lost?" he said. "What did you lose?"

"We lost the game."

"Where did you lose it?"

"On the baseball field."

"Did you look for it on the field?"

"Mudman, have you ever watched a baseball game?"

"No. Why do you ask?"

"Do you know what baseball is?"

"What is baseball?" he corrected and answered, "You said it is a game and you lost it on the baseball field."

I couldn't believe this. Mudman knows so much about everything that most of the time I feel like I'm talking to a college professor. And now, talking about baseball, he seems like a four year old who knows nothing. It also occurred to me that I didn't realize baseball was so hard to explain.

But I tried anyway, "Baseball is a very popular game played in America, Mudman. We played the game today and lost to another team because they scored more runs during the game than we did."

Mudman said, "Thank you, Little Muddy. I understand baseball more now. It is like many other games your people play where someone wins and someone loses."

"That's right, and winning is way more important than losing. Winning is everything." I said and added, "I love to win and hate to lose."

"What does it mean, 'to win', Little Muddy?"

"It means to be superior or better than someone else." I replied with confidence.

"And being superior to someone is important?" he queried.

"Yes, I guess so." I said, without confidence.

It was starting to feel like I had been ambushed. Mudman was good at that. Like I said before, 'he has a way about him'. I knew what question was coming next.

"Why?" he asked.

There it was! The question that always seems to reveal ignorance of the one asking or the one being asked. But I had been here before and was ready for him.

I answered, again with confidence, "Because I am a living being created by God and designed to be the way that I am. Wanting to win and feeling superior to those I defeat is built into my being during creation and is a good thing because it came from God."

I was feeling pretty good about myself after that answer. Mudman could hardly argue with me there, because much of what I said came from listening to him over the past few years.

I was totally not prepared for Mudman's response. For the second time since I have known him, he laughed, and I mean really laughed! Listening to him laugh, you would think that I had just told him the funniest joke in the world. My response was confusion. What was so darn funny? I had given a serious answer to his question and saw no humor in it. I just sat there on the log, watched him laugh, and waited.

After a few minutes, Mudman got up, walked to the edge of the water and stood there, looking down at his reflection. I was about to ask why he thought my answer was so funny, when he suddenly stepped out into the water and sat down facing me. Then a crazy thing happened. That little four foot gator he tossed back into the swamp earlier appeared from below the water behind him, swam up next to him and settled there. It looked like that little gator was snuggling Mudman. I told you it was crazy! I looked and further out in the swamp and behind Mudman was a gathering of at least 40 or more alligators. Some were large adults, but most were young ones under five feet long. You just cannot believe that scene! It took my breath away. I was frozen to the log under me. They had all come closer to land. I had no thought as to why and wondered about it.

Mudman noticed me watching the gators and said, "They will be leaving soon to return to their place deep in the swamp. You are well known here; they have come this close to see you and say good-by. They don't know why, nor do they question why, Little Muddy. Like you, they are compelled by their design; unlike you, they have no Creator given ability to choose an alternate path. They are slaves to their design and driven by that nature."

"I liked your answer to my question regarding superiority over another being, Little Muddy. It is obvious that you have given thought to creation and a creator. What I found so amusing is the sly way you give God credit for the way you feel and the things you do. It is a 'backdoor' philosophy used by many to credit God for everything that happens, while at the same time absolving themselves of any blame for their actions."

Mudman gave an example, "A bad person might correctly say, 'the Creator created me to be the way that I am!' and less correctly add, 'and since He created me this way, I must be good because God does not create bad things.' That is one's way of absolving himself of any responsibility for his actions, good or bad."

"Do you see the fatal flaw in that philosophy, my young friend?" he asked.

I answered with the truth as I saw it and said, "No, I don't. In a way, it does seem that God **is** responsible for his creation. When He creates a thing to do something, that thing should not be blamed or criticized for doing what it was created by God to do. I understand that we are not always given the reason for God's actions, but when He creates a thing, there is a reason for it."

"You don't often do that. Little Muddy." Mudman commented.

"Do what?"

"Provide an argument to my teachings."

"I wasn't meaning to argue with you, I just don't always understand everything you say. This conversation about God and creation is interesting and confusing at the same time. I never really thought much about God creating everything before."

"Well," said Mudman, "let us see if your confusion can be cleared a little by adding some complexity. Going back to the way you feel about winning and losing, consider what I am about to say and determine if it sounds reasonable."

Then Mudman explained, "If winning makes you better than or superior to someone, then it follows that losing makes you worse than or inferior to someone. It is no wonder that you hate to lose, Little Muddy. Your whole vision of yourself is dependent, not upon playing a game, but upon whether you win or lose the game. Do you not find that interesting?"

Very often, Mudman is not fun to talk with. How did I wind up here, anyway? I became involved in a simple conversation about baseball and wound up entangled in a complex philosophy of life and self worth. Who knew baseball could be so complicated?

I responded by saying, "I don't know, Mudman. I have learned some things about myself in this conversation, though. I don't like the idea of being superior. Heck, I'm not even sure what that really means; I have to think on it for a while. I also learned that my belief in myself should not depend on the result of a game, any game. I intend to remember that because I like playing games."

"What I do find interesting Mudman, is 'Biased Compassionate Empathy'. What is it?"

"It is the answer to your question about killing alligators, my young friend and is defined as: '*only caring about the condition or predicament of another living thing to which you can relate and want to help*'."

"Allow me to explain," he offered, "You feel bad about the killing of alligators for money because you see, or relate to, the gators as victims of the hunters. You do not care about the hundreds of millions of mosquitoes, ants, and flies being poisoned every day for money by humans, because you do not see those bugs as victims, or worth saving, and have no desire to help them. You are biased because your compassion is reserved only for living things to which you relate. Do you have an understanding now?"

I thought about it for a bit, and answered, "Yes." and asked, "Are we just talking about bugs and alligators here, Mudman, or everything?"

"Thank you." was all he said.

I looked out to the swamp and saw that the gators were leaving. Mudman stood up and watched them too. The little one at his feet scurried to get back to the congress.

"It's getting late and they are preparing to go home." he spoke softly. And then said to me, "You should do the same. We have had a long now. Your mother will be expecting you."

Then he turned and glided toward the retreating family of alligators. I went home too, thinking about the alligators that will be killed tonight.

Chapter 16 - Ricky and the Snake

Mudman turned out to be a prophet. According to local reports over the next few days, nine alligator hunters went into the swamp in three boats early that evening and three hunters came back sometime after midnight. The three that returned were suffering from exposure and insect bites. Their claim was that a giant alligator attacked and killed the others in their group, but a more intense investigation revealed that the group got separated in the dark because of a huge swarm of biting insects and two boats were overturned in the panic caused by the bugs. All the survivors could remember was hearing a lot of splashing and screaming as they retreated from the swamp as fast as they could. One of them died a few days later, apparently from infections caused by stings and bites. No bodies were ever recovered. The swamp had just swallowed them up.

The alligators in my part of the swamp were gone the next day, just as Mudman predicted. As I said, no evidence of the missing hunters was ever found. Searchers went out in the swamp looking for a giant alligator and saw no sign of such a monster, but reported that large swarms of deer flies made searching all but impossible to bear. No one stayed out to search after dark. There were too many bugs out at night right now.

Momma didn't know about my pirogue, nor did my brothers, who were getting old enough to be a bother sometimes. Ricky was 3 years younger than me and was developing an interest in going with me to the swamp, but he had a handicap. He wore a brace on one leg because of some sort of problem in his hip that momma claimed he was born with. Momma was afraid that he had polio when he was about 7 or 8, but that was not the case. Anyway, whatever he had, left him with one leg shorter than the other and the brace became necessary. That brace also kept him out of the swamp because it locked at the knee and took walking and wading through mud and water out of the picture. Momma would have none of that.

But Ricky was as sneaky as me. I took him craw-fishing along the bank of the swamp with me occasionally and he loved it. He got pretty good at craw-fishing, too. We made some pretty good hauls for supper more than a few times. Ricky wanted to do more, though. He would follow or come looking for me when I went out. He got to be a bit of a nuisance because I didn't want him to know about my hollow tree or my boat and had to be careful that he didn't find out about them. I knew he would blab about everything. My little brother Ricky loved me, wanted to be like me, and would proudly tell momma and anyone else about the things we did in the swamp. I'll give you a good example.

Once, while we were craw-fishing from the bank, Ricky had to pee and went over to a tree down by the water. It turned out that there was a big snake at the base of that tree. Ricky saw it and quickly ran back to tell me about it. He was excited, breathing hard, and stammering as he spoke and pointed, "Bubba, there's a big water moccasin by that tree over there! I almost peed on it. I think it wanted to bite me!"

Well, that caught my interest because I was interested in snakes and always have been.

"C'mon Ricky, show me." I said.

Sure enough, there was a snake next to the tree. One look told me that it wasn't a cottonmouth, but what I call a fish moccasin and it was a long one too, looked to be over five feet. The reason it had not already slithered into deep water, was because this snake was a pregnant female in the process of having babies! She noticed me and slid into shallow water, with little baby snakes coming out of her.

Ricky hollered, "You gonna kill it, Bubba?"

"No, little brother." I said. "We're in no danger. She's just having babies now. Look at 'em swimming around. Cute little critters ain't they?" I picked one up to show him.

"Babies?" he said, confused; then he looked out in the water and hollered, excited, "Baby snakes! I see 'em! I see 'em!"

Then what do you think happened? My little brother Ricky limped as fast as he could all the way home and told momma about a giant snake having babies in the swamp down by the levy where he and bubba were craw-fishing and bubba was picking them up and playin' with 'em! As soon as I saw Ricky heading home, I knew that I was going to have a devil of a time explaining this.

Sure enough, momma came down to the levy, carrying her gun, and said, "What's going on, Johnny?"

"Me and Ricky saw a snake having babies in the swamp, momma." I said.

"Was it a water moccasin?" She exclaimed, "Ricky said it tried to bite him!"

"No momma, it's just a water snake." I said, "and he wasn't even close to it."

"Live baby snakes?" she exclaimed. "I thought they hatched from eggs."

"Some do, momma. Cottonmouths and copperheads hatch from eggs inside their mother's bodies and they are born alive. Water snakes are born alive and swimming too."

"How is it that you know all that, son?" She asked.

"They teach us stuff like that at school and I read a lot of books, momma." I lied.

Actually, I told the truth about reading books but they hadn't taught us anything about snakes in school yet. I was in the seventh grade at that time and figured school would teach about snakes and animals in later grades. Never happened, though. I had seen water snakes having babies before in the swamp, which explains why I knew what happened that day. Couldn't tell momma about that, though.

"I can certainly testify to your book reading, son." she said. "Your little brother loves being out here with you, so keep an eye on him and make sure y'all stay away from snakes, you hear me?"

"Yes ma'am." I answered, and then added, "I kinda like learning about snakes and things, momma."

Momma pointed at me (kinda like Mudman does) and ordered, "You save that kind of learning for when you get older. Right now, all you need to know about snakes is the only good ones are the dead ones. Now, grab your bag of crawfish and come on back to the house."

You see what I mean? If my little brothers found out about my secrets . . . well, let me put it this way: my little brothers were excellent disseminators of information at their early age and they were even better at enhancing information. Everyone in Texas would know about my hollow tree and boat within two weeks if Ricky and Rocky found out about them. Okay, maybe that's a bit of an exaggeration, but you get my point.

Chapter 17 - Creations of Creations

The next time I met with Mudman was the day after Christmas, 1955. School was out and the day was warm and dry, perfect for going fishing in the swamp. Momma was at work and grandma was watching the brothers, who were enjoying their presents. I had the whole afternoon at my pleasure and intended to make the most of it. This was my first time to go fishing in almost three weeks.

You know, while walking to my boat it occurred to me that my last contact with Mudman was several months ago and wondered if he celebrated holidays. It would appear that he didn't because he was not a human. My family had just celebrated the birth of Jesus Christ, the son of God and the Savior of mankind. I went to church yesterday and sang uplifting songs of joy and salvation. I was happy. Mudman could not experience those things. I wondered if he could even be a Christian if he wanted. It was a sad thought for sure, but was not going to spoil my day. The pirogue was dry, my gear was loaded and the trip to my fishing spot in this beautiful swamp was great. I just sat there and leaned back in my boat, enjoying myself.

"I've been expecting you, Little Muddy." said Mudman. "Would not be like you to pass up a beautiful day like this."

I sat up and didn't see him at first, but then saw his reflection in the water and looked up. He was sitting on a cypress tree limb about ten feet above and behind me. I was really glad to see him and said so.

"What are you doing up there? I asked.

"Just enjoying the view. I can see more of the swamp from here."

"What do you see?"

"Oh, nothing in which you would be interested. Just a lot of trees and water."

"Any animals?"

"Of course, life is abundant here."

"See any human life?"

"Just you, so far, Little Muddy."

"So far? You expecting people to come to the swamp?"

"Well, it is a beautiful day to be out."

"I don't expect you'll see any humans today, Mudman."

"Do you know something I should, Little Muddy?"

"Humans are mostly at home or visiting with their families. It's Christmastime."

"All humans?"

"Well no, mostly Christians."

"Are you a Christian, Little Muddy?"

"No, not really. I think about it, though. Are you a Christian, Mudman?"

"No. Christianity is a religion and religions do not apply to me."

"Why not?

Mudman expertly let himself down from the limb into the water, which came up to his chest, slid over to the edge of my boat, looked at me and said, "Because, Little Muddy, religions are not original creations. They are results of actions by creations of a creator and therefore do not apply to me . . . or you either, for that matter."

Well, that went right over my head! This subject is a whole lot deeper than the water here, for sure. I needed a better explanation.

"actions by creations of a creator?" I repeated his words, "I'm not understanding what you mean by that, Mudman."

"Think of it this way," he began and explained, "many things in this reality of ours are created by a Creator. You will notice that the term 'many things' is used rather than 'all things'. Humanity and this swamp, for example, are original creations. Religion, on the other hand, was founded by humanity and is not an original creation of the Creator. All religion resulted from a human need to explain their existence by the existence of a god. The many religions in existence resulted from the different cultures of humanity, all desiring the same thing and pursuing it in different ways."

"Have I lost you yet, Little Muddy?" he challenged me.

"I think you are saying that original creations themselves are more important than the things they create." I replied.

Mudman slapped his hand on the side of my boat, almost tipping me over, and said, "How is it you can explain my explanation in such a simple way? I was beginning to think you were hearing and not listening and here you are explaining what I mean in one sentence!"

"Well," I said, "you know so much more than me. Besides, I don't understand half the words you use, so I don't use 'em."

Mudman laughed and slapped the side of my pirogue again. "I like that." he said.

Then he continued, "What happened to humanity is they became so enraptured, or caught up, in their religions they forgot who created what and began to worship religion as an original creation of their gods, their invented deity, whom they now believe created them. Mankind has lost it's way in the world because they worship their creations instead of God and no longer realize the uniqueness of their existence."

"Now do you understand why religion does not apply either to me or you?" He asked.

"I think so." I responded. "It's kind of like worshiping wealth instead of God. Wealth is created by us and we are created by the Creator. We should worship God instead of the things we create."

Mudman turned to head off into the deep swamp and said, "Little Muddy, I am going to go now and think about you. At your age, that type of wisdom is seldom observed. You still have time to do some fishing."

I watched him disappear behind the trees and thought about what I learned today, then caught some perch, paddled in to shore and went home. Momma was happy to get the fish for supper. From then on, going to church was not the same as before. It was clear to me now that people worshiped their religion instead of the Creator. My attendance dropped off and eventually stopped. I began reading books about the origin of world religions and paid more attention to the Bible.

Chapter 18 - Diversity

There was so much family stuff going on during the last week of the Christmas holidays that it was about two weeks before I could go fishing again. It was a pleasant Saturday afternoon in January, just cool enough to wear a long-sleeved shirt. Rex was tagging along with me like always. He liked hunting along the shoreline for crawfish and snakes. My dog liked eating crawfish and hated snakes. He was expert at hunting and killing snakes and would go off and hunt them on his own. There were times when he would come home with his neck all swollen from a poisonous snake bite, most likely a copperhead or cottonmouth. He always recovered, though. He would disappear for several days and come home skinny, hungry, and covered with mud. I would go looking for him sometimes, but never found his mud-curing hiding place. I called it mud-curing because swamp mud seems to have curing properties that are under appreciated.

An interesting thing about Rex is that he would not get into my boat for any reason. Several times I picked him up and put him in the boat, but he jumped out as soon as he was released. He didn't like the boat and he didn't like my taking it into the swamp. He would wade out after me until the water got up to his belly and then go back to land, lay down and wait for me to come back. Sometimes when he thought I was gone too long, he would begin barking to let me know it was time to go home.

Rex and Mudman had a strange relationship, or rather a strange non-relationship. They never paid attention to each other. Mudman never said anything to Rex, who in turn never barked at or even acknowledged Mudman. It was sometime later before the reason became apparent. To Rex, Mudman was just an extension of the swamp and he never paid attention to the swamp, just the critters in it. To Mudman, Rex was just another land critter that never affected the swamp one way or another and unworthy of his attention. I sometimes wondered if that was why most people never really noticed, or paid attention to, each other. We only seem to pay attention to those we believe have something to offer, be it something good or bad, or to those who make the most noise. Only then are they worthy of our attention. When you think about it, humans really are strange creatures.

Anyway, Rex and I were wading along in the shallows just off the shore, Rex was hunting and I was thinking. Momma was right, I did that a lot. My thoughts were about the diversity that God had created among all life, especially humanity. I was sort of interested in diversity because of news being reported that colored students were going to be integrated into white schools. I had never met a colored person in my life and really didn't understand what the uproar was about. It was plain that we were supposed to be against the idea of integration, but it just wasn't clear why. There was even talk at school about hating colored people because they wanted to go to our school. I wondered why coloreds would even want to go to our school. They have their own schools. I mean, in town we have our restrooms and water fountains and they have theirs. We have our seats on the bus and they have theirs. What is so wrong about that? We're different from each other and proud of that difference. They're proud and we're proud. What's wrong with that?

There were even some kids at school saying that if colored people start mixing with white people at school, then soon coloreds would be marrying whites and having half breed babies. I laughed at that possibility and told them that no white person would ever marry a colored person. I couldn't even imagine that happening. That's when my interest in created diversity began to grow. Why are populations of people so diverse? I couldn't answer that question and could find no one to explain it. Mudman might be able to have an answer because he is not human.

"Where is he today?" I wondered.

Well, it turned out that Mudman was gliding along behind us as we waded along the edge of the swamp. Gliding through the water is noiseless because there is no splashing and I never noticed him back there. I'm glad I wasn't talking out loud.

"Hello Mudman, I'm really glad to see you." I said.

"You are really glad to see me? I am not sure you have ever greeted me that way before, Little Muddy." he replied. "What has been going on in your world? Do you have something on your mind?"

"What makes you ask that?" I asked.

"Well, you have been in deep thought ever since you got here. Something must be going on in that head of yours."

"I thought you might be reading my mind for a minute there. Yes, I have a question about the diversity of races. The possible integration of coloreds into white schools is big news and I don't know what to make of it."

"Are you in favor of it, Little Muddy, or against it?"

"I don't know, for sure. Why do people want whites and coloreds to mix together, anyway? I don't think that coloreds and whites want to integrate."

We arrived at my thinking log and I sat down; Mudman sat in the water, facing me and Rex continued his search for crawfish.

"Politics, my young friend. The real question that counts for something is, 'do you care and why?' So, do you or not, and why?"

"I don't know if I care. I don't know anything about Negro people, except they are colored and God created them that way."

"That seems to be an accurate observation, Little Muddy. Of course it follows that the same can be said about Caucasians and all other races of humans."

"Do all other races of humans get along with each other, Mudman?"

"I thought we covered that 'get along' thing in another now. I do not know about all the races of people. What I have been able to absorb though, is creatures tend to get along better in environments where diversity is controlled, minimal, or non-existent."

Mudman just can't help himself. That answer probably sounded simple to him.

"What do you mean, 'controlled, minimal, or non-existent', Mudman?"

"Creatures in this reality, generally feel more comfortable with their own kind," Mudman explained, "you know, their own species, their own breed, their own race, and so on. The result of introducing diversity into a mono-cultural society is change, unless diversity is controlled. When diversity is controlled, the diverse minority keeps within reasonable bounds because of majority rules, both legal and societal, creating a type of segregation of cultures where the minority must adopt the majority culture in order to advance, or remain segregated inside their own culture."

"What happens if diversity is not controlled, Mudman? What changes occur?"

"The culture and basic nature of the intrusive diverse population will determine the resulting change, but change there will be."

“Will the change make that society better? Or worse?”

“That depends, Johnny, upon the diversity and its compatibility with the majority.”

“Yeah, Mudman, I understand. Great diversity equals great chaos.”

“I have seen greatly diverse cultures live in harmony, Little Muddy.”

“Tell me how, Mudman. It seems impossible! America needs a solution.”

“America is doomed to failure, my young friend. It has a fatal flaw.”

“How have greatly diverse cultures learned to live in harmony, Mudman?”

“Mutual respect for each other under a system of order.”

“Why can’t America’s diversity produce harmony? What fatal flaw?”

“Freedom. The obstacle of freedom, Little Muddy.”

“That can’t be so! Freedom is what made America great, Mudman.”

“Freedom also creates a sense of inequality and unrest among cultures. Unrest prevents unity.”

“How can freedom create inequality? Freedom promotes equality.”

“Humans are not equal, my young friend; some are smarter, faster, stronger, better.”

“So what, Mudman? Everyone in America has equal opportunity.”

"That is a fallacy, my friend. Opportunity? Yes, of course. Equal opportunity? No."

"But Mudman, freedom allows everyone to be the best that they can be."

"Little Muddy, one person's best may not be equal to another's best. Guess who wins?"

"But that's the way it's supposed to be, Mudman, the best is supposed to win."

"Only in a free society, my friend, is the best supposed to win. To your credit, you understand, but those who are physically or intellectually less talented than another, for whatever reason, resent losing. Many of them are not capable of respecting the greater ability of another; rather, they want their betters to be penalized for being better at something. The less talented do not like a free society where the best prevail; they will demand a rule change, where the inferior have as good a chance of winning the prize as the superior. Not only is this true of individuals, but of cultures as well. Weakness and destruction results when a society bends to the will of the less talented, leading to leadership by the less qualified, meaning that people get exactly that for which they ask. Interestingly, they will lay the blame for failure, elsewhere."

Mudman continued, "Since you are a student of your bible, Little Muddy, you will be familiar with a revelation of Jesus concerning equality. He is reported as saying, '*For him who has, more will be given, and he will have abundance; but from him who has not, even that which he has will be taken from him.*' That alone is enough to get Him crucified again, should He return today. His statement defines how things work in a free society, like that in which you exist. Defying that truth leads only to destruction, the path upon which your American leaders are presently leading and will continue to lead America."

"What do you mean, 'cultures, as well', Mudman?"

"I was talking about equality there, Little Muddy, explaining that, like individuals, cultures are not equal to each other. The culture of every created race of humans differs, one from another. One culture will depress human conditions while another will improve human conditions. Some of the differences are minimal and tolerable among some; some are major differences and are intolerable among most. When the culture of a diverse minority imposes its beliefs upon a society it occupies, that society is changed, but seldom, if ever, strengthened. The various races of humans were not created to co-exist, as evidenced by their conflicting cultures; however, they were created with the ability to do so, if willing, a willingness seldom displayed."

"Little Muddy, the idealogical conflict between Negroes and Caucasians will unlikely be resolved. There is too much hatred there between factions within the two races for reason to prevail. Like many such differences, opponents will derive no less satisfaction than the blood of those who do not share their passion. Humans are interesting creatures."

"Mudman, are you saying that the integration of whites and coloreds will result in conflict?"

"What I am saying, Little Muddy, is that 'forced integration' of Caucasians and Negroes will result in division, not unity, and conflict will result; perhaps lifetimes of conflict. The freedom so cherished by America will disappear under a slowly rising tide of big government control, exercising its power, 'for the good of the people' by creating laws to assure the equality of everyone. I have observed it. Foolish people, you humans. Your saving grace is the created ability to make choices, but you always choose leaders who follow that which is in their own best interests because that is what you are led by your teachers to do."

"Mudman, sometimes I think you forget to whom you are talking. I don't understand what you just said and kinda believe that a lot of older and smarter people than me wouldn't understand either."

"You know something, my young friend, you are absolutely correct. There are times my observations of the human condition find their way into our conversations and I get carried away talking about them. What was it you were asking"

"We were talking about the integration of white and colored people resulting in conflict." I replied.

"Yes, Little Muddy, forced integration of Caucasians and Negroes in America will result in conflict, and more."

"Why do you say 'Caucasians and Negroes' instead of 'whites and coloreds', Mudman?" I asked, interested in his reply.

Mudman replied, "Because Caucasian and Negro are racial designations. White and colored are skin color designations. The two races differ in more ways than skin color."

"Mudman, it seems to me that the two races could live peaceably without conflict if they would just tolerate each others differences."

"Yes, that does seem like a simple and logical solution. Why do you think such a thing will never be accomplished?" he asked.

"Why would I even think that Mudman?" I replied.

"Because you already know why those two races will never get along with each other." he answered. "They differ from each other in important ways."

Mudman's words, "never get along" made realize that he was getting at, "created diversity". They will never 'get along' because they were created not to get along by the Creator.

I looked at Mudman and saw that he was watching me. "You understand now?" he said.

"Yes, but I have heard that some Negroes and Caucasians do appear to get along with each other. How does that happen, Mudman?" I asked.

He responded, "Very often, in this reality, appearances are deceiving, but all humans have the created ability to choose good over their basically evil nature. Those individuals you heard about made the good choice of friendship over conflict. Individuals can make such choices; collectives cannot."

I was confused and asked, "What do you mean by 'their basically evil nature', Mudman?"

Mudman revealed this, "There is a little known truth about life, Little Muddy. All life follows its created design, but mankind alone is allowed to learn and choose to do otherwise. Evil and goodness were created by the Creator specifically for humans, who were designed with an inherently evil nature. Also designed into humans by the Creator is an ability to learn and choose. Other life forms have no such designs."

"Mudman, I was always taught that humans were created basically good and went through life choosing good or evil in the course of living. You just said that humans are created with an evil nature but go through life with an ability to choose goodness over that evil nature. I'm not sure how that works."

"You must follow the logic in the Creator's design, Little Muddy." he explained and continued, "If humans are created basically good, they do not have to try to be good because they **are** good. In such a format, humans have to try to be evil."

"On the other hand, if humans are created basically evil, they don't have to try to be evil because they **are** evil. In this format humans have to try to be good."

"Which of the two formats do you suppose applies to our reality? In the first format, there is no need for morals, ethics, or kindness because everyone is basically good. In the second format, there is great need for morals, ethics, and kindness because everyone is basically evil."

Mudman concluded, "Obviously the second format applies to our reality, where humans have to make an effort to be good; otherwise, they remain evil and will reap evil."

"Are you still confused, Little Muddy?" he asked.

"No Mudman, I see the logic behind our creation as you described it. There is divine value in goodness because it must be strived for and earned; conversely, in evil there is no value because it is free and doesn't have to be earned. We humans are free to determine the value of our lives by striving for goodness and resisting evil."

"Young Johnny," he smiled and said, "you have an interesting way of explaining a complex teaching in few words. Now let us return to racial diversity."

Mudman continued, "Diverse racial culture is what separates the races and fuels racial conflict, Little Muddy, not color. Color is an indicator of a particular culture, but diverse culture is the culprit. Contrasting cultures will always invite conflict, which can be avoided by mutual segregation of the cultures or by one race adopting the culture of the other."

"What about mixing the different cultures into one blended culture?" I offered. "Would that not avoid conflict?"

"That is a surprising question from you, my young friend." he stated. "I did not mention it myself because your suggestion has often been, and is, being attempted. In America, the primary racial problem to be solved is the Negro / Caucasian jigsaw puzzle. You know what a jigsaw puzzle is, do you not, Little Muddy?"

"Of course, Mudman," I answered, "grandma and momma are always working at putting one together. It's a kind of game that has a bunch of different pieces that will only fit together one way. You solve the puzzle by connecting all the pieces correctly. Once a jigsaw puzzle is completed, it usually turns out to be a pretty picture of something. I like working on them. They are real popular."

Mudman replied, "That is an accurate description, my young friend. I shall try to show you how a jigsaw puzzle applies to racial conflict and why it is such a difficult problem to solve."

"Imagine that you have two boxes of jigsaw puzzles," he began, "one has a picture of a Caucasian to assemble and the other has a picture of a Negro to assemble. Then you combine the two puzzles into one pile, mix them up (integrate them) and begin assembling. When you finish the mixed puzzle, what will you have? You will have a picture of a Caucasian and a picture of a Negro. When you integrated the two puzzles together, all you did was create a more difficult puzzle to solve. In the end, the integrated puzzle pieces segregated themselves from each other because they were created to be different from each other."

Mudman continued, "Now imagine that you mix half the pieces from one box with half from the other box and begin assembling them. What will be your result? Chaos! Some pieces will fit together in various individual groups and the rest will fit nowhere. You might be stubborn and force some pieces to integrate in order to get a completed puzzle, but your result will be a conflicted mess."

"Little Muddy, until humanity understands and accepts its diversity as being part of their Creator's plan for this reality and works within that plan, there will be no end to conflict and chaos. What that means is, there will be no end to conflict and chaos between and among Negroes and Caucasians. There are just too many stupid humans for such a resolution to be successful."

"I'm beginning to understand, Mudman." I replied. "If either integration or segregation of the two races is forced, conflict will result. In order for diverse races to live in peace with each other, integration or segregation has to be mutually agreed upon by the races involved. A good resolution is for one race to adapt to the other's culture."

"So is there a solution to racial discord in America that avoids conflict, Mudman?"

"No."

"Is there a solution to racial discord in America as a result of conflict?"

"No."

"C'mon, Mudman. Every problem has a solution."

"Why does racial discord in America need to be solved, Little Muddy?"

"Because Mudman, a unified America is better than a divided America."

"America won two world wars and became powerful in spite of racial discord, Johnny."

"Yeah, but being racially unified seems better than not getting along with each other."

"Caucasians and Negroes must discover their own way in America, Little Muddy."

"Why can't they be taught how to just accept their differences, Mudman?"

"People have to discover those things themselves; there is magic in discovery."

"What can be done to keep diversity from destroying America, Mudman?"

"Make everyone equal under the law and enforce that law; then, leave them alone."

"Yeah, right. Leave us alone. That's never gonna happen. America is doomed."

"What a depressing thought, young friend! Doomed? Unlikely. Changed? Big time!"

"You don't care, do you Mudman? You just watch."

"Human affairs do not apply to me, Little Muddy; but yes, I watch humans; they are interesting."

"What will change, Mudman?"

"America's government. That change will cost many lives, much freedom, and perhaps most of both."

He explained further, "It is only a deduction based upon the basic design and nature of humans and their created racial imperatives, my friend. If anything, humans are consistent."

"Mudman, what is a racist?"

"A person who believes his race is superior to another race." he replied.

"What is wrong with being a racist?"

"Nothing, unless discrimination is involved, Little Muddy, and everything when it is."

"Why do you say that, Mudman?"

"Discrimination is the ultimate enemy of unity, Johnny."

Mudman paused, thought a moment and explained, "If discrimination is not involved in racism, Little Muddy, no one seriously cares about differences in races. Racism, in that environment is just an opinion, similar to believing that one make of car is better than another. However, when people driving Ford cars begin discriminating by treating the people who drive Chevrolet cars as inferior and questioning their humanity, conflict will occur and people will die because of it. All over a differing opinion of cars!"

Mudman advised, "Be proud of your race, Little Muddy, without denying the humanity of others."

"What about prejudice, Mudman? What is wrong with being prejudiced?

"All humans have their prejudices, my young friend; none are without."

"Is being prejudiced a bad quality?"

"It is deceptive, with the potential of being incorrect or correct, because it is a belief."

"Mudman, what does prejudice mean? How do I avoid being prejudiced?"

He replied, "Prejudice is a belief about someone or something based upon your perception of their identity. You cannot avoid being prejudiced; however, you can practice objectivity."

"Why do people fear being called a racist, Mudman?"

"Cowardice." he answered.

I took issue with that answer and stated, "That's pretty extreme, Mudman, and not a nice word to describe someone who does not want to be referred to as a racist."

Mudman hesitated, as if considering my comment, then asked, "What word would you use refer to someone who fears being called a racist?"

He caught me off guard and I could only reply, "I don't know. I never thought about it before now, but maybe 'careful' is a better word."

"Hmm," he mumbled, "I thought for sure that you would answer, 'stupid', but on to your word 'careful'. Careful of what? Being revealed as a racist? Someone afraid of being called something of which he is not? Is that not cowardice, Little Muddy?"

In thinking about it, 'stupid' was a much better answer, but I was stuck with 'careful' and wanted to see where Mudman would take the conversation.

"But Mudman," I responded, "being thought of as a racist is shameful and will hurt a person's reputation."

"Is that how you think as well, Little Muddy?" he asked, quietly.

"Well, it depends on the kind of racist a person is accusing me of being, Mudman."

"So, Little Muddy, you consider racism to be relative?"

"Relative? What do you mean?"

"You know, on a variable scale, like one to ten, where two is a little racist and ten a lot."

"You mean, a scale to define good and bad racists, Mudman?"

"That depends upon whether the scale is a 'good' scale or a 'bad' scale, young friend."

"So Mudman, on the 'good' scale, all racists are good, but some are better than others?"

"And vice-versa, Little Muddy."

"I don't like it, Mudman."

"What is it you do not like?"

"I don't like the idea of believing all racists to be either good or bad."

"Why not, Little Muddy, most things are."

"Mudman, you told me there was nothing wrong with being a racist."

"Yes, I did."

"You also defined a racist as someone who believes a particular race of humans is superior to another or all races of humans." I reminded him.

"That is not exactly what I said, Little Muddy, but your definition is accurate."

"I do not consider being a racist a bad thing, Mudman."

"That is interesting, Little Muddy; what is your reason for taking that position?"

"It seems that many people in the world believe their race is superior to another."

"You are saying that much of the world is racist?"

"That is my conclusion, Mudman." I stated. "It makes sense to me."

"So," Mudman began, "by that definition, there are racists everywhere on earth, most of whom do not realize they are racists. Also, being a racist is not a bad thing unless people begin thinking they are superior to people of other races and develop a prejudice against those people and begin discriminating against those people. Where have we heard that before, Little Muddy?"

I answered, "Stupidity leads to stupidity leads to stupidity leads to stupidity leads to destruction. Does that have to happen?"

"No," he replied, "but in order to change, 'stupidity' must be removed from somewhere in that equation and 'smart' inserted."

"How is that made to happen, Mudman?" I asked, "Can it be made to happen?"

"No, it cannot be made to happen, Little Muddy," he instructed. "People have the built-in ability to choose their life's path and, in the process, the path of their civilization. But there are obstacles."

"Obstacles? What obstacles?" I inquired. "That does not seem promising for civilization."

"Diversity, for one. You know about diversity." he stated.

"Yeah, I still don't completely understand the necessity for creating diversity." I complained. "Seems like mankind would be more unified without diversity splitting everyone up into different races and languages."

"The Creator has a reason for everything in this reality.", young Johnny.

"I know, Mudman." I said. I felt guilty for complaining. "But this racial stuff does not promote unity. Differing cultures of the various races will never compromise with each other. I hate the idea of forced integration." Then I asked,

"Am I a racist, Mudman?"

"What is your race, Little Muddy?"

"Caucasian."

"Do you like being Caucasian?"

"I like it a lot."

"Would you like to be another race?"

"No." I said.

"Why?" he asked.

"I am happy with what I am."

"Yes." Mudman stated.

"Yes?" I asked, not understanding.

"Yes, you are a racist." he affirmed.

I thought about his statement for a moment and asked, "Mudman, are you a racist?"

He looked at me and said, "I have no race."

"I don't understand that." I responded. "What are you, Mudman?"

"Now?" he asked.

I looked at him and said. "Always."

"The swamp." was his reply.

That was going to have to be enough for now, but I had questions . . . for another now.

Chapter 19 - Stupid or Smart

It was late afternoon and I had chores to do. Rex and I walked home. The things I learned today were on my mind and would always be in my mind. I thought it was sad that races were not designed to get along together, but the Creator gave them a path to do so if they were willing to work at it, which they would not do because segregation was a path of least resistance. It was interesting to see where their individual cultures led them. Culture was a compelling design.

I saw Mudman several times during the next five weeks and I turned fourteen years old in March. You know something? The realization that I live in a created reality designed by a Creator changed my outlook on everything. Any question on anything can be explained by virtue of a created reality. The reason for anything and everything became clear to me through the understanding of creation. At the age of fourteen, I understood something that was unknown to everyone I knew, including momma and grandma. Because of that understanding, my way of looking at the world changed. I know why the world exists and how it came into exist in the first place. I see people and animals in a new light and understand why they do what they do. There was a downside, though; there is not a person I can talk to or tell about my discovery. How do you tell someone the moon is not real? The answer is, you don't try.

I had Mudman, though and he was a legitimate mystery, something I did not know or understand. I loved talking with him because he kept me grounded by making me realize my knowledge is not really a big deal compared to all there is to know.

It was a nice Spring day in late March, the likes of which make the swamp one of the best and most pleasant places in the world and I am here with my dog, Rex. Life is good.

"I am where I am supposed to be." I said to myself. I was happy.

To be where you want to be is a special feeling. I hoped that most in the world were also feeling it. I was cleaning out my boat and whistling while I worked when a movement in the swamp attracted my attention. Looking farther out, I saw Mudman playing with something in the water, something I have seen before. Actually I have never seen it, only evidence of it. I still couldn't see it because it was beneath the water, making waves. This was the creature that herded the alligators, stopped that big gator from getting me, and helped me escape the poachers. Once, several years ago, Mudman told me about certain things not seen in the swamp. This was one of those things and he was playing with it like I do with Rex. I watched from a distance and realized that Mudman was also exactly where he was supposed to be.

My conversations with Mudman had become important. He was like a wise grandfather who seemed to understand things I didn't know could even be understood. I mean, where else could I go to learn about creators and creations? That was not taught in Sunday school or any of the other schools that I attend and no one in my family knew any of the stuff that Mudman talked about. As a matter of fact, no one in my family even wanted to talk about religion, creators, and their creations. They went out of their way to avoid them. I, on the other hand, loved those subjects. Mudman appeared at a time in my life when I needed someone to explain the questions about life of which my mind was constantly bombarded. How does something like that happen, anyway? Grandma always said that everything happens for a reason and is supposed to happen. She called it fate. I thought about that and wondered how Mudman explained fate. Probably had something to do with creation, which seemed to explain so many things.

We had been studying about the rise and fall of nations in history class at school and I was wondering how nations rose to power and what caused their fall from power. From the things we were taught, it seemed that great leadership was responsible for a nation's rise to power and poor leadership caused its fall. The question my teachers never could seem to answer was how poor leaders are able to assume leadership of a country. I didn't understand how that could happen and brought up the question with Mudman when next we met.

"Stupidity." he replied.

That was it! All he said was 'stupidity'. I protested, "That is not enough of an answer, Mudman."

"Well," he said, "you want to know how bad leaders assume leadership of a country. Stupidity is an answer. There is another, perhaps more accurate answer, but stupidity will suffice."

"That might be true," I argued, "but there has to be more to it. Who is being stupid?"

Mudman answered, "Those who choose or enable the leaders."

"This is frustrating." I thought. "Every question I ask seems to result with stupidity being the answer, almost appearing as if stupidity is the alpha and omega of all questions concerning stupidity."

"Mudman, what does stupid mean?"

"Possessing little or no common sense."

"Are people born stupid?"

"No. For the most part, stupidity is taught."

"Taught? Stupidity can be taught?"

"Of course. Why do you think there are so many stupid people?"

"But I thought stupid people were created." I argued, "and couldn't learn."

"Some humans are born without an ability to reason well and will be stupid throughout their lives because of an inability to learn well." he explained and continued, "Those humans have a reason for being born, but that reason is seldom examined or considered."

"Little Muddy, all life is designed with a potential to make choices." he instructed. This inherent ability to choose is peculiar to all species, more so for humans because of their innate ability to reason. It is important to understand that humans are not born either smart or stupid; rather, they are born with the **potential** of becoming smart or stupid, because of an ability to learn. What humans learn is a direct result of what they are taught! If humans are taught 'stupid', they will be stupid and if they are taught 'smart', they will be smart."

I thought about what he said and asked, "What is 'teaching stupid', Mudman? I don't know for sure and don't think anyone else does either."

"There are different methods of 'teaching stupid' young Johnny." He replied. All of them seem to revolve around false teachings or lies."

1. 1, When people are taught that their problems are the fault of others, that is teaching stupid.

2. When people are taught what to think, that is teaching stupid.

3. When people are taught what to believe, that is teaching stupid.

4. When morals and ethics are not taught, that is teaching stupid by omission.

5. When people are taught government is their friend, that is teaching stupid.

6. When people are taught superiority over others, that is teaching stupid.

"Those are 6 examples of teaching stupid, Little Muddy. There are more. Add your own."

"Something important to realize is, very many intelligent people are stupid. They became intelligent through education and experience, but were taught stupid; therefore, they are stupid. Intelligent-stupid."

"Now, the methods of 'teaching smart' revolve around teaching basic truths that magnify freedom of the individual and respect for others."

1. When people are taught to accept responsibility for their actions, that is teaching smart.

2. When people are taught to think for themselves, that is teaching smart.

3. When people are taught how to form their own beliefs, that is teaching smart.

4. When people are taught morals and ethics, that is teaching smart.

5. When people are taught to be watchful of government, that is teaching smart.

6. When people are taught to respect the humanity in others, that is teaching smart.

7. When people are taught the value of kindness, that is teaching smart."

"Those are examples of teaching smart. There are more, young friend."

Mudman continued, "So, why do some intelligent people support bad leaders? Because they are stupid. You must understand, Little Muddy, that all people increase their intelligence through education and experience. An intelligent-stupid person's intelligence is derived from stupid sources or teachers who themselves had stupid teachers. When you do the math, you begin to understand why there are so many of them, stupid people, I mean. Intelligent-stupid people do not realize they are stupid, which makes it difficult to criticize them for their stupidity because, like all intelligent people, their actions are determined by what they were taught. The problem that arises for humanity when intelligent-stupid people become leaders is: the stupid intelligence of those leaders causes them to make stupid decisions and do stupid things, like violating ethical and moral codes that bring about destruction. Are you with me, Little Muddy?"

"So that's how stupidity causes the downfall of a nation,?" I exclaimed.

"The downfall of civilizations." he corrected. "Intelligent, stupid leaders making stupid decisions, and doing stupid things has caused the downfall of civilizations."

"How do stupid people get to be the leaders of a nation?" I asked. "Aren't most people smart enough to identify good, smart leaders and support them?"

"No," said Mudman, "but it would make no difference if they were. People do not care if their leaders are smart, they care about themselves. Selfishness is designed into the human being as a necessary part of the first law of life."

"The first law of life?" I questioned. "You haven't said anything about a first law before, Mudman! What is it?"

"Survival." he said. "There are certain laws designed into the creation of life as necessary to give its existence a chance to succeed. The first law of life is survival. The primary imperative of that first law is selfishness. That means life will always do that which it perceives to be in its own self-interest."

He continued, "All any potential leader must do is:

1. convince people that he has their best interests at heart, or

2. convince people that it will not be in their interests to oppose him, or

3. convince people that his opponent will threaten their best interests."

"Convince people of any one of those three and you own them."

"Successfully achieving just of one of those will give that potential leader the power he desires. That is how people achieve power, Little Muddy. Intelligent, stupid people are good at such things because they are not often encumbered by ethics or morals."

"Okay," I said, "just for the record let me see if I have this straight:

Some life is stupid and some life is smart.

Some life is ignorant and some life is intelligent.

Stupid does not mean the same thing as ignorant.

Smart does not mean the same thing as intelligent."

"How am I doing, Mudman?" I asked.

"Well, life is more complicated than four simple sentences, Little Muddy." he said. "And there are degrees of those four words, meaning that they are variable, which in turn means that life is variable within the imperatives of creation law. Your reasoning is well formed, though."

"That's nice Mudman," I said, laughing. "as if I understood anything you just said."

"You never asked the single, most important question, Little Muddy." He reminded.

"The single, most important question?" I wondered aloud. "This has got to be good. What is that 'single, most important question', Mudman?" I asked.

"He patiently answered, "How does one recognize 'stupid', my young friend?"

I thought to myself, "Wow! Mudman is right. How did I miss that? I wish I **had** asked it because I do not know the answer. He might have been hinting at the answer though, in his list of teaching stupid. I'm going to ask now."

"Mudman." I said, "You are right. That is the single most important question regarding our conversation. I wish it had occurred to me to ask it, because I have no idea how to identify an intelligent stupid person and would really like to know."

"I am surprised that it did not occur to you as well, normally you would have been all over that question." he said, "What is going on in that mind of yours, Little Muddy?"

"To tell the truth, Mudman, I never realized that almost every question that comes to my mind can be answered by referring to creation and the Creator. It almost seems too easy to explain the actions of all life with an understanding of creation. I wonder about the people who reject the truth of a Creator. How do they explain questions regarding life without creation? Are they the 'intelligent stupid' people that you referred to earlier?"

"You know Little Muddy," he replied, "you have an interesting habit of answering your own questions in the way that you ask them. Yes, those who come to an understanding of creation are able to comprehend the way things work in this reality. Something you must understand though, is this: A majority of humans reject the idea of this reality being created, much less created by a Creator."

Mudman began, "Many people explain the origin of this planet and the life here with the biblical story of creation in the book of Genesis, which began with the creation of a great number of regular humans and later, two very special humans. There are large majorities of humans that have faith in a deity, whom they credit with their creation. Of course, there are those who reject the very idea of God or any divinity. They are the atheists, who seldom think about the origin of life, but explain existence with an interesting idea of chance when pressed for an answer. Your beliefs make you part of a small minority, Little Muddy; so if it ever comes to a vote, you will be among those burnt at stake. It will be a small consolation for you to realize that the humans killing you are only following their primary imperative, but that understanding will allow you to forgive them."

"Okay my inquisitive young friend, back to your first question about how to recognize stupid. I regret to inform you that once again you have asked a question with a simple answer and a complex explanation. The simple answer is, you will know stupid by its fruits, which is a reference to an answer by Jesus, in your bible's Gospel of Matthew, to a question concerning how to recognize false prophets: 'You will know them by their fruits.' You are a reader, Little Muddy. Read Matthew, chapter 7. You will find it there."

"Anyway, you will know the stupid by their fruits, meaning by what they say, do, or produce. A basic truth is, stupid cannot say, do, or produce smart. There is a problem with that truth, though. Unless you are an intelligent-smart person, the fruit of the intelligent-stupid is difficult to immediately recognize from what it says or does. You then must wait to see what it produces before you will recognize that it is stupid. Often by that time, stupid is in power and 'ruling the roost', so to speak. Happens often."

Mudman continued, "So how does one go about quickly identifying an intelligent-stupid person? First, one must be well educated about morals and ethics. Intelligent-stupid people seldom have either, much less all. Look for and notice continuous violations of one or more ethical or moral principles and oppose those who exhibit them. The stupid and ignorant are unable to make such decisions and will support those whose voices are strong, convincing, and promise them safety and prosperity. It is unfortunate, Little Muddy, that the populace of your civilization is mainly composed of the stupid and ignorant. They will follow the voices of false prophets (the intelligent-stupid), ultimately causing the end of their civilization. Such has happened before and for the same reason, "Stupidity.""

"Wait a minute, Mudman!" I demanded. "Are you saying that America is going to fall? We just won the World War against evil in the world and now America is the strongest country in the world! We stand for God and freedom for all. We have good, smart leaders and with the Creator on our side, who can stand against us?"

"Your nation will enjoy the power and privileges of victory for a period, Little Muddy, but intelligent-stupidity is already weaving its web of dissension around the very fabric of your leadership. Too many will get entrapped by false prophecy to save your fragile freedom or your nation, as you know it. You should also realize something else important, young Johnny, 'sides' is something the Creator does not recognize."

"Why not? I mean, why did you say that the Creator doesn't pick sides?" I asked.

Mudman replied, "I said he does not recognize 'sides'. The Creator gave this reality everything it requires for existence, which means humanity has all it requires to make its own way. The Creator will not be involved in bringing about the fall of America, the populace of the country gets all the credit for its country's fate."

I couldn't believe what I was hearing. Mudman was predicting the fall of America! I have great respect for him and his simple understanding of everything, but the fall of America? That's just crazy! We have a great country, a powerful and important country. Then I thought of something, Mudman said nothing about time! Maybe it's going to take a thousand years or more. I mean, who knows for sure? Right?

So I said, "Mudman, can America keep from falling? I mean it doesn't have to happen, does it? How long will it take? There has to be a way for our country to save itself from destruction! The Creator's designs always include a way for humanity to save itself, why not a way for humanity to save a nation?"

"Little Muddy," he replied, "your last sentence is a great example of faith in the Creator's wisdom. You are correct my young friend, there is a way for America to save itself. The populace of America is the hope of America. People must come together to support leaders who display personal ethics, high morals, and good sense in their lives.

The stupid do not possess those qualities and will do everything in their power to defeat those who live moral and ethical lives. Stupid will support stupid, because stupid does not understand that it is stupid. The sad truth is, very much of America is populated by stupid people. America's real hope is education. Her young must be taught morals and ethics and shown the value of an ethical and moral life. Teachers are, and will remain, the single most influential people in the lives of a populace. Never allow the stupid to become teachers. Intelligent-stupid teachers will teach stupid ideas to children, resulting in a stupid populace that will, in turn, select stupid leaders who will bring about the fall of America. You will recognize the stupid by their fruit: immoral and unethical behavior, along with foolish decision making."

"Well young Johnny," he asked, "are you still awake? This subject is interesting only to a few."

"I'm awake, Mudman." I replied and asked, "How long before the fall of America?"

"Babies born today will see it." he replied. "What do you think about the future of America, young Johnny?" he asked. "Will America save itself?"

"I don't know," I said, "I want to believe America's leaders are smart and intelligent, but it's just too easy to be stupid. I think most people are stupid. Heck, I often wonder about myself; sometimes I do stupid things."

"That self awareness you just displayed," he pointed out, "is an indicator of smart. The stupid cannot do that."

"Anyway," I said, "I'm not sure why, but it seems to me that stupidity will prevail in America, causing the fall of our country. We may never be a country of morals, ethics, and good sense. The truth is Mudman, I'm not even sure what those things are."

"Volumes have been written on those subjects Little Muddy," he said and added, "let me see if I can come up with a brief explanation. Morals and ethics are learned qualities. Morals tend to refer to the right or wrong of a human action or thought, whereas ethics tend to refer to the good or bad of a human action. Ethics is the code of conduct of a society that teaches mankind how to honorably navigate that society. Morals are a divine code that teaches mankind how to honorably and rightly navigate their lives."

Mudman continued, "The why stupidity will prevail in America is easy to answer, young Johnny. One does not have to work at being stupid and/or ignorant and can become or remain stupid by doing little or nothing. Being smart and/or intelligent requires effort, meaning that work, often hard work, is required. Very many people follow the path of least resistance and find ignorance. As a consequence, they will support leaders who advocate ignorance among the populace and strive to make their herd obedient and happy."

"Why would leaders want their people to be ignorant, Mudman?"

"Because, Little Muddy, a blissfully ignorant populace is the boon of the powerful. In other words, when one's cattle and sheep are fat and happy, his purse and stomach are secure."

"Mudman, you have mastered a confusing language; I hope one day to understand it."

"You will young Johnny," he chuckled, "one day you will."

Chapter 20 - Mating

You know, Mudman had a great impact on my life and I had little understanding of who he was, what he was, or where he came from. Apparently that was not important. Because of my relationship with him, I was different from the rest of the kids I knew at school and members of my family, as well. For example, my vocabulary was much wider than that of my peers. Heck, I used words that momma and grandma never used or even heard about. They were the first to notice and bring it to my attention. Both were convinced that my appetite for consuming books was the reason but, while reading contributed to my use of words, it was Mudman who explained what the words meant.

Another example was evident in the social aspect of my young life. I was not one of the popular kids, mainly because I did not socialize a lot. I liked the other kids and had some friends at school, but really did not have a lot of time for them. Because of Mudman, I understood why they did the things that kids do. They were all products of their creation, driven by a biological imperative to do and say things meant to make them feel good about themselves. Later on, I came to realize that applied to all humans. That is the human design. Mudman taught me that choice and learning were also in that design and by learning morals and ethics and applying them to the biological imperative, we choose to do and say good and right things. Too many people never learn and those around my age were not being taught, because their parents never learned and schools did not include morals and ethics in their teaching. Probably the two important tenets of human life. Yes, Mudman is a guiding influence in my life.

At ten years old, when I first met Mudman, I did not know what to make of him. He scared me at first because he was big and came out of the swamp. I realized he was made of mud, a mudman, and glided through the swamp like it was normal, but I didn't think too much about it after a while. I just liked him and liked talking with him. But that was almost five years ago and now that I'm older, questions are beginning to surface. I am curious about his age, what he eats, if there are more like him in the swamp, and how he got here in the first place. He once told me that he absorbs knowledge. I want to know how that works. I have a lot of things to ask him. I mean, a mudman? Who wouldn't have questions?

I was noticing things at school that I had just accepted before now and never really thought about them. It had to do with how students treated each other. Everyone seems caught up in how they look, not like that is something new or anything, just not noticed. Some of the kids at school are more attractive than the others and get more attention because of it. Some of them are not attractive and that works against them, socially, in school. What is more confusing is that smart unattractive students are less popular than stupid attractive students! This results in a great deal of time being devoted to looking good for the purpose of attracting attention. Mudman and I have talked several times about stupid and smart, but never about beautiful and ugly. I have read about those two descriptive words and still do not understand why I am influenced by how someone looks. It probably has something to do with a creative imperative and I'm hoping Mudman can explain it better than the books I've read. I'm headed to the swamp now to go fishing and hope to see him out there. He always seems to know when I'm around.

This is one of those days in the swamp when bird calls and singing were all around, not noisy, but intermittent like the birds were talking to each other. Mudman was there, sitting by my boat watching the birds flit around in the trees. They would fly to a limb of the tree, bob their heads up and down, then fly off the limb, return to the limb and bob their heads again. It was a ritual of sorts.

I sat down next to Mudman and watched the birds with him. "What's going on with the birds?" I asked.

"They are courting, young Johnny."

"Courting?"

"Yes, it is time for them to choose a mate."

"So, that is what all the chirping and flitting around is all about?"

"Every male bird is demonstrating his physical and singing abilities."

"Why, Mudman?"

"To convince the females that he is a good quality breeder, young Johnny."

"The females choose which male they will mate with?"

"Yes, she will mate with the male that impresses her the most."

"Mudman, what if an ugly female chooses a handsome male?" I asked, "Will he reject her offer to mate? Or do the males only court pretty females?"

"Are we still talking about mating birds here, Little Muddy?" he questioned. "Sounds to me like you have something else on your mind. What is going on in that young mind of yours? Something I can help you with?"

I told him about the students at school and my recent questioning of attraction and said,

"I understand a little about the biological imperative being a part of the human condition, but I want to understand why I am attracted to the prettier girls when some of the other girls are smarter and easier to talk with. It doesn't make any sense, Mudman."

Mudman continued watching the birds, seeming to be in deep thought. After a few minutes, I said to him, "What are you attracted to, Mudman?"

"Attraction does not apply to me, Little Muddy," he replied, "and I am still considering your first question, without any more interruptions." Then he went back to thinking.

Finally he was ready and stood up only to sit back down across from me.

"Little Muddy," he began, "your question about being attracted to pretty girls is a good one and has a simple answer. The fact that you asked it in the way you did says much about you. It is doubtful that young male humans ask that question often, if at all. As I said, the answer is simple but you are not going to be satisfied with such an answer."

"Why not, Mudman?" I asked.

"Because it is a simple answer and you often want complex explanations."

"That is because your simple answers create more questions in my mind."

"Little Muddy, you are an interesting young human."

"You have said that before, Mudman."

"So I have, my young friend. So I have." he admitted.

"Okay Little Muddy", he offered, "here is the answer: your feelings about being attracted to pretty girls are partly the result of a biological imperative built into the human design at creation and partly the result of learning from intelligent-stupid teachings."

"Oh wow!" I thought, "Mudman has done it again! He suckered me into asking for more by giving me an answer that begs for more. He left me the choice of accepting an answer beyond my understanding or asking for an explanation that will not be simple.”

“Alright Mudman,” I replied, “you are right, I want an explanation. And I was right too, because your simple answer created more questions in my mind. Please explain the intelligent-stupid teaching I received from who knows where.”

“We have covered all this before, young Johnny.” he said. “Intelligent-stupid people teach stupidity. They cannot help doing that because they teach what they were taught. It is important to realize such people neither realize or believe they are stupid, nor did those who taught them. . . and so spreads the disease.”

“Is this disease curable?” I asked.

“Yes. However, as in all illnesses, the sick person must recognize that he is sick; otherwise, he will neither seek treatment nor tolerate advice. As I mentioned before, intelligent-stupid people do not believe or realize they are stupid.”

“Sounds like an incurable, terminal disease to me.” I commented.

“Well, not for the patient,” Mudman replied, “but it will eventually kill his country.”

“Yeah,” I said with sarcasm, “I remember. ‘Stupidity’ is the cause of the fall of empires! That is awfully dark, Mudman. I mean, why does everything having to do with stupidity seem to lead to destruction?”

Mudman thought a moment and answered, “Where else is there for stupidity to go?”

Then he returned to my question regarding attraction.

"Little Muddy," he began, "there is little, if anything, one can do about the biological imperative to preserve their species. All life is driven by their created nature to reproduce offspring that are best qualified to preserve their kind. Just as birds are driven to choose mates that exhibit high quality bird traits, so are humans driven to choose mates that exhibit perceived high quality human traits. Birds and other creatures instinctively sense those traits and are attracted to mate with those of their kind who exhibit them."

Mudman continued, "Humans have the same instincts which, when followed, produce the most qualified offspring for the survival of their species; however, humans have choice designed into their nature and mostly choose their mates based upon perceived value and self interest, a perception imposed by their society or culture. Very often, such imposition overlooks qualities that produce lasting, loving relationships. These imposed values create an attraction based upon the external rather than the internal qualifications of a potential mate. What does this mean? It means that it is stupid to choose a mate mainly based upon attraction to external appearance. And where does stupidity lead, Little Muddy?"

"Stupidity ultimately leads to destruction." I replied. "Marriages mainly based upon external attraction will likely end in divorce and broken families. That is destruction."

Mudman replied, "In regard to human mating, there is a battle going on between the biological imperative to preserve the human species and the stupid human tendency to make appearance the determining factor in choosing a mate. The fact that you, young Johnny, questioned that tendency is a glimmer of hope for mankind. Perhaps there are more smart young humans in the world who will reject the intelligent-stupid teaching of judging a mate mainly by their external appearance and pay more attention to character and uprightness. Could happen, probably will not. Humans are interesting creatures."

I went home that day with a way of looking at something I knew nothing about, that being the human mating ritual. What did I learn? I learned that a potential relationship should be determined by the internal qualities of a person rather the external, a lesson that should be taught to everyone. Could be the hope of the world. I also went home with a nagging sense of doubt that humans would ever kick their habit of 'judging a book by its cover'.

Chapter 21 - The Moon

"What is on your mind this fine day, Little Muddy?"

"Mudman, I've been thinking about the moon. What is the moon?"

"A creation, a satellite, an anomaly, a mystery. A symbol of light."

"Come on Mudman, I just asked a simple question."

"A simple question brimming with complexities."

"Complexities?"

"Little Muddy, how do you even know the moon exists? You cannot smell, taste, hear, touch, or see it."

"Because I **can** see it, Mudman."

"How is it that you see it?"

"Because light from the sun makes it visible, except when the earth blocks the light."

"Tell me, Little Muddy, when you look at this thing you call 'moon', what do you see?"

"I see light, reflected light of the sun." (I was proud of that answer.)

"So, you do not actually see the moon, you see sunlight, reflected sunlight, but sunlight all the same."

"Well, yes. But Mudman, the sunlight is being reflected off the moon!" I exclaimed.

"Still, my young friend, all you have ever observed is light, and you call the light, 'moon'.

"But Mudman, light reflected from something." I argued.

"Yes Little Muddy, from something you have never seen."

"But reflected light is evidence of a moon."

"No Johnny, it is evidence of something."

"Something?"

"A thing which is unspecified or unknown, Little Muddy."

"I have a question, Mudman."

"I would have expected nothing less. What would you like to know?"

"I would like to know if the moon is an original creation."

"Yes. No. Take your pick. One answer is, maybe; A better answer is, maybe not. The best answer is, probably not."

"The Bible says it is an original creation, Mudman. Created on the 4th day."

"Do you believe the bible, Johnny?"

"I don't know, Mudman; I do believe, but I have doubts about how Genesis was written. Some things don't make sense."

"Little Muddy, the Creator of this reality does not have to make sense; like your grandma and her chair, the Creator created what he desired, in the way he wanted it to be."

"But Mudman, He created light on the first day and the sun and moon on the fourth day; that seems backwards to me! The bible says He called the dark, night and the light, 'day' and that was the first day, but the sun and moon did not yet exist! That makes no sense. It seems that the writer of Genesis made a mistake in the order of creation."

"Yes Johnny, so it would seem to your young mind, but your view of the order of things is from a creation's perspective. Your viewpoint is that light is the result of an emitter of light, like the sun, and cannot exist until after the emitter is created; however, from a creator's point of view, light must be created first, otherwise, creating an emitter has no purpose, since light would not yet have been created. That being the case, it was necessary that light be created first. There was no mistake made in the bible's order of creation."

"Wow Mudman, that is simple! How come I didn't think of that?

"You have not yet begun to see from the viewpoint of a creator. Your grandmother did, at your request, while creating her chair from the front seat of the car. What questions have you about the moon that cannot be answered by saying, 'because the Creator desired it.' Little Muddy?"

"My question was if the moon was an original creation, Mudman."

"There is no such evidence, Johnny."

"But Mudman, the bible says the sun and moon were created on the 4th day!"

"No Johnny, the bible says no such thing. It says God created two great 'lights' on the 4th day. There are various modern versions of your bible where humans have applied their own version of what the Creator meant to say, but He actually made no mention of the sun or moon; rather he created two 'great lights'; the greater light to rule the day, and the lesser light to rule the night. Bible 'experts' inserted 'sun' and 'moon' in their revised versions of the great book, explaining what the Creator 'meant to say'. It takes great ego to do such, does it not?"

"I don't know, Mudman. You have taught me that humans tend to follow their created imperatives and have selfish reasons for their actions. I guess 'revised versions' are just an example of humans being human. Understanding that makes them easier to forgive."

"Did I say that, Little Muddy? It is nows like this that make me realize how great a teacher I am! Did you find your answer regarding the moon?"

"Well, it seems pretty clear that you don't think the moon is an original creation and I'm not sure why."

"Johnny, this is one of those things that cannot be explained now."

"So you know, don't you, Mudman?"

"Knowledge does not exist here Johnny, but for your understanding, yes. No, the moon is not an original creation is the answer to your question."

Mudman, will additional questions get satisfying answers?"

"No Little Muddy, not now. Your ignorance at this point in your now does not permit the understanding of such a truth. 'Waves of light' is the secret that hides it and which you will understand in another now. Be careful with such understanding as it will attract predators."

Chapter 22 - Integration

At our next meeting, Mudman caught me taking a nap in my boat. I had leaned back against the bow, watching mosquito hawks flitting around in the air and the next thing I knew the boat was rocking, waking me up to see Mudman laughing while shaking my boat back and forth. I thought I was dreaming! This big man of mud was standing above me laughing, with mosquito hawks sailing all around him. Did I ever mention that Mudman has a way about him? Well, he certainly has a way about him.

"Little Muddy," he chuckled as I sat up rubbing my eyes and yawning, "have you been staying up late at night doing your homework again? You have been sleeping out here a long time now."

I glanced at my watch and was surprised to see that my nap lasted almost two hours. The truth is, my late night studying and thinking was not due to homework activity; my time was being spent thinking about racial diversity in America and the talk about integrating all the white schools with colored students. As far as my school is concerned, allowing colored students to attend was not only hard to imagine, but also hard for me to understand. Why do Negro students want to attend my school? I don't want to attend their school. My reasoning is that colored students don't want to go to my school either, but I don't know any Negroes. Maybe they do want to go to school with Caucasians. Are their schools so bad that they want to go to our schools? I don't believe that to be true. If Negro schools are good schools, why are our leaders pushing so hard for integration? I don't know, but maybe Negro schools are terrible schools. I don't know that either.

I wish that I knew more about Negroes; I know nothing about Negroes or Japanese or Chinese, or pretty much any other races. I do, however, have a good friend who is Mexican and is on my Babe Ruth baseball team and goes to my school. We practice baseball together and have a lot in common. We both have guitars and play and sing together, making up songs and having fun. He is brown skinned and I am white skinned and we never think to talk about that difference. An interesting thing about Billy Joe is, he is against integration too. Unlike me, he knows and associates with colored people; but, he is very much against their attending our school. I asked him why he feels that way and his answer was that Negroes didn't like him much and made fun of him and his brother. That didn't make sense and bothered me because all of us on the ball team liked Billy Joe. Something was wrong about this racial thing that was outside of my understanding. Why would the coloreds make fun of my friend when the color of his skin was close to theirs?

I was beginning to believe that different races were created for the purpose of keeping humans from getting along with each other. Mudman once told me that forced integration would not work because each race would eventually segregate into their own groups because of a created racial imperative to do so. I was far too ignorant to understand the diversity thing and wanted to understand more about it. I was determined to ask Mudman about it.

Mudman was looking at me, waiting for me to finish waking up and answer him. You have to understand that talking to him was often not easy. Right now is a good example of what I mean. Even though my eagerness to talk with him and ask questions was pushing me to say something, the image of him standing there in front of me with mosquito hawks darting around and landing on him dominated my attention. Why were they doing that? It looked so strange that all of my attention was focused on them. I just had to ask why. So, I did.

"Mudman, why are all those mosquito hawks flying around and landing on you?" I asked. "You have know that is strange, don't you? I mean, mosquito hawks don't do that; they chase and eat mosquitoes and land on bushes, trees, and clotheslines. They also don't seem to gather together in groups, but they are all over you! What's going on?"

"Little Muddy," he said, "you sometimes ask the strangest questions in response to a question asked of you. Technically these are dragon flies, but the term "mosquito hawk" is perhaps more appropriate since the majority of their diet consists of mosquitoes. They are swarming around me because mosquitoes are gathering for mating purposes and are easy prey. Most of these mosquitoes are males and are gathering to attract females. Dragon flies do swarm together when they migrate in Spring and Fall, so there is much to learn about them. Do you want to engage in a long conversation about dragon flies, or mosquito hawks? They are very interesting creations."

Well, that is a subject that I was not about to get sucked into when there were other things on my mind. Mudman was expert at steering conversations toward the things he was interested in talking about. The huge amount of knowledge and understanding he demonstrates is impressive and he claims to have never read a book! How does one "absorb" information anyway? Talk about strange? That is strange. Anyway, I had some steering of my own to do.

"No Mudman," I replied, "I like mosquito hawks, but don't want to talk about them now. Maybe another time. What I . . .

Mudman interrupted, "There is no other time, Little Muddy; there is only now. The mosquito hawks are here now and we are here now; another time does not exist, nor will it ever. But you already understand about 'now'. I sense that you have another subject on your mind. So let us see if we can indulge in a conversation infinitely more important and interesting than mosquito hawks." He then sat down at the side of my boat and looked at me expectantly.

It was pretty obvious that Mudman was being sarcastic. Why would he want to discuss mosquito hawks anyway? Then something really strange began to happen. There I am, sitting in the front of my pirogue facing the swamp, when the mosquito hawks leave Mudman and start settling all around me on the sides and inside of my boat. Some were even alighting on me! I knew about mosquito hawks and had caught many of them to put in jars to add to my private zoo. I knew there were different types; they all had four independent wings, allowing them to fly backwards, kinda like hummingbirds. Those in and on my boat were different colors. Some of their colors were blue, yellow, green, brown and even a pink one. Some had striped brown wings or just tan wings. I had never seen so many mosquito hawks in one place in my life. I was sitting in a boat covered with mosquito hawks! No one would ever believe this. Heck, even I thought this might be a dream!

Mudman was just sitting there beside my boat looking at me as if everything was normal, but it wasn't normal to me and wouldn't be normal to anyone else, either. I lifted my arm to gesture to Mudman and the mosquito hawks on my arm flew up and landed on my shoulder.

I stammered, "Mudman, what is going on here? Why are they doing this?"

He looked around and replied, "Well, it looks like I am not the only one wondering what interests you more than mosquito hawks."

"Come on, Mudman," I argued, "these little creatures can't think or reason about things like our conversations."

"How is it that you know such a thing with so much certainty, young Johnny?"

"Mudman, they're insects and do not think or reason or even understand what we say."

"How is it that you know such a thing with so much certainty, young Johnny?"

"Because they are insects, Mudman, not humans."

"So, young Johnny, insects are not human and as such, have no understanding of our conversations or feelings? Is that what you are saying?"

"I can't believe we are having this discussion, Mudman. I know, and I know you know that is true. Of course insects have no such understanding."

About ten mosquito hawks flitted up and alighted in my lap and stayed there.

"How is it that you know such a thing with so much certainty, young Johnny?"

I thought, "This is getting a little crazy! Why does he keep asking me that? I know that bugs can't think, but these mosquito hawks seem to be paying attention to our conversation!"

Then a new thought occurred to me. "How do I know for sure these bugs cannot understand us? I absolutely believe that bugs cannot think or reason, but I do not **know** that they can't. That must be why he keeps asking me how I know. He's right, I don't know!"

I answered quietly, "I do not actually know such a thing with certainty, Mudman."

Mudman stood up and at that moment, the mosquito hawks began flying away into the swamp and all other directions. I have to say again that I have never seen anything like that, before or since. Mudman watched them fly away, then turned to me, picked me up, lifted me into the air above his head, held me there for a moment looking at me, and put me back in the boat. He never said a word and I didn't know what to think, much less say anything.

He glided out into the swamp a little way, then turned, came back and sat down again by my boat. Then pointed at me and said, "What is it that you want to talk about, Little Muddy?"

I wasn't sure how to begin. There are so many questions to ask and they were not yet organized in my mind. But as Mudman reminded me earlier, there is only now; so I just started talking.

"Mudman," I began, "of all the things you and I have discussed over the past years and all I have learned from you, the most puzzling is diversity. When my mind wanders with random thoughts and finally settles on one, that one is always diversity. Should America fall within the next 100 years as you seem to think, diversity will be a main cause unless mankind adapts to racial differences like those between Negroes and Caucasians. I don't know anything about Negroes or any other race and have never met any in person. I don't understand why Negroes want to integrate our schools. No one at my school wants to integrate theirs. You said Negroes and Caucasians differ in important ways, but never mentioned what those differences are. I understand all humans were made by the same creator for a reason and made different from each other for a reason as well. I just don't get it. Are humans some kind of experiment or something? You know, like I do with bugs in jars and snakes in cages."

Mudman listened, without interrupting, and appeared to be interested in my statement. He nodded as if understanding when diversity was being questioned and shook his head at references to integration. It was the question about humans being an experiment that caused him to stand. It seemed that he was deciding what to talk about first.

He made up his mind and began explaining, "First and foremost, Little Muddy, you should understand that America will fall within the next hundred years because of the stupidity of the people of this country. It is likely they will choose godless leaders who will, in turn, make stupid decisions that will result in the end of the nation."

"I believe that result can be avoided if we just knew how." I argued.

"You already know how, Little Muddy, he replied, "but it will not be done. Knowing how to do something and doing it are very different concepts."

"Why will it not be done?" I asked.

Mudman continued, "Because of the selfishness of the people who choose the leaders of the nation. The people are interested in that which profits them, or rather that which they believe to be in their best interests. Usually those best interests are money, pleasure, safety, and comfort. Any potential leader that convinces people he can provide those things or frightens them into believing his opposition will take those things from them, will own their allegiance.

"But what if the potential leader is a good human being, an intelligent-smart person?" I countered.

"Not possible." said Mudman. "Intelligent-smart people have morals and ethics; they will not make such promises. The kind that do make those promises plant destruction in a nation, the harvest of which, is destruction."

"So, Little Muddy, can America's imminent destruction be avoided?" he asked and answered his own question, "Yes! Will America do what is necessary to avoid its downfall? No! Its people will submit to their basic evil nature of selfishness and support those who promise to take care of them."

I protested, "But Mudman, after winning the World War, America is united, strong, and great. We should get even greater over the next hundred years."

"Your positive outlook is encouraging, young Johnny." he replied. "I like it and admit your logic is appealing. Your prophecy will be fulfilled if Americans maintain their trust in God, love their country, and teach ethics, morals, and kindness to their young. There is a test coming for America though, that will determine its future and the success of your prophecy. Should be interesting to watch."

Mudman has a way of baiting a hook that makes it almost impossible to avoid biting it; his last two comments hooked me.

"What test?" I asked, "and why do you find humans so interesting to watch?"

He answered, "Humans are interesting because they have free will to choose their way through life and very often choose wrong, which makes all of you difficult to predict. I suppose the mystery of humans is their appeal."

"What test is coming, Mudman?" I inquired.

He simply said, "Forced Integration. It is a flawed concept with the ability to destroy."

That was a great hand-off to the subject I was wanting to discuss and took me by surprise. I wondered if Mudman already knew what had been dominating my thoughts recently and chose a path to that destination. He believes that humans are a mystery? That may be so, but Mudman is a real mystery.

"I have been wanting to talk to you about that subject. How did you know? I asked.

"Well, as I recall, you mentioned it in your opening talk, young Johnny." he replied and asked, "What is on your mind?"

"Mudman, I wonder if you can tell me why Negro students want to go to my school? I mean, why are Negroes so interested in integrating Caucasian schools?"

"Why do you care if your school is integrated, Little Muddy?"

"Because I am a white person and they are colored people. I would not like to go to a school for colored students and believe they won't like going to my school. We are different races. What is wrong with leaving things as they are? Maybe integration is not a good thing. Will their presence in our schools make us smarter and better students?"

"You ask some good and important questions, young Johnny. I can see you have given this mystery significant thought. Allow me to ask you this, what would be wrong with permitting all students to go to the school of their choice?"

"That wouldn't work, Mudman. One school would be more popular than another and would be over-run with students while the other school wouldn't have enough students. Unless all the white students wanted to go to school together and all the colored students wanted to go to another school. They might segregate or integrate themselves."

"Would you go to a school with some Negro students, young Johnny?

"Of course."

"What if that school had a majority of Negro students?

"No, Mudman, I would not want to go there?"

"Why not?" he questioned.

"I don't know anything about Negroes and would be uncomfortable there. I don't know for sure, but my thought is, coloreds and whites would not get along well in that school. The reason being that we are different from each other."

"Other than color, how are you different, young Johnny?"

"I told you, Mudman, I have never met a Negro before and know nothing about them."

"Even though you do not know any Negroes, you believe the two races cannot coexist?"

"Well, you taught me that the races were created to oppose each other but were also created with the ability to learn, meaning different races can learn to get along with each other. I take that to mean that a Negro and I can learn to become friends, but our races will always oppose each other because of imperatives created into our basic human nature."

"Wow, Little Muddy! I never realized that I was such a good teacher." exclaimed Mudman. "You answered your question with that long comment."

"No, Mudman. I asked if you could tell me why colored students want to go to white schools. You have not answered me yet. Do you know the reason?"

"It is unlikely Negroes want to attend your schools anymore than you want to attend theirs, young Johnny." he stated.

"Why?" I asked, surprised. "At our school, we feel like they want to invade us and we are being forced to accept them, which is causing a lot of resentment."

"Why do you care?" Mudman asked gently and continued, "If all schools are integrated or if they continue to segregate, why do you care? One should always have a reason for allowing anything over which they have no control to seriously affect their emotions. In the case of race relations, prejudice, politics, religion, opinion, and money are a few culprits. What is your reason?"

"I like the way things are right now and don't want them to change." I replied. "Also, I don't like the idea of being forced to integrate with Negroes. Something about forcing people to associate together against their will does not sound right to to me. If the coloreds oppose integration too, who is doing the forcing?"

Mudman sighed, "Little Muddy, you often ask the most difficult of questions. Your question is actually not about 'who', but rather, 'what'. More specifically, the primary force driving integration is, 'linear time'. Of course, the ridiculous idea of freedom is involved as well. It is time for America to begin eliminating racial segregation from her list of historical carryovers and forced integration is the method your leaders have chosen. Perhaps it is not the best choice, but a logical choice once one understands how those leaders think."

"What do you mean, Mudman? How do our leaders think?" I persisted.

"It is not something you will hear government leaders say, young Johnny, but they are convinced Negro students are not as intelligent as Caucasian students because Negro schools are inferior to Caucasian schools. Your leaders also believe that Negroes will never reach equality in American society unless they are forcibly integrated into Caucasian society, something they believe will not occur naturally. They are wrong."

"What do you think, Mudman?" I asked. "Will forced integration be successful? Will our nation become happier, smarter, and more unified?"

"Not even hardly." he replied. "Of course, there are individual exceptions, but the created imperative of racial opposition will prevail in the American collective because people will not choose to do the things required to achieve unity."

"Why not, Mudman?"

"You will object to this answer; nevertheless, it is true: Because they are stupid."

"Stupid? What does being stupid have to do with racial unity? Stupid people can unify."

"Only under special circumstances, Little Muddy. In this instance, they will not unify."

"Are you saying that nothing can be done to keep America unified, Mudman?"

"Well, I did say there are exceptions, longshot possibilities at best, Little Muddy."

"Tell me Mudman! I want to know! What could keep America unified?"

"In the first place, Little Muddy, America is not now unified. How to unify America is the question. One solution might be a common enemy, which would cause unity for a period of time. A second solution might be a group or thing perceived to be so fearful that Americans are forced to unify for their personal safety and the preservation of the nation. That type of unity will last as long as the fear of the common enemy exists or the nation is destroyed."

"I don't like that, Mudman. I like the idea of unity, but living in fear and at constant war with a dangerous enemy seems like an unhappy existence. Anything else we can do?" I asked.

Mudman pointed to me and firmly stated, "A collective choice to live a moral and ethical life, have deep faith in God, and teach your children to do the same."

Then he softly added. "And that, Little Muddy, is the longest of longshots."

"Why, Mudman?" I replied, "That seems easy enough to do. We are doing that now in my family. What makes unity unlikely to exist in America?"

Mudman explained, "In this discussion, young Johnny, our subject is racial unity and the lack thereof in America. The answer to your question is, *a false idea of 'equality'*. Racial unity has not yet been achieved in America and will likely never be achieved because the Caucasian and Negro races **are not now and will never be, equal to each other**.

That is true for all races and until each race recognizes inequality does not necessarily mean 'inferior' or 'superior', unity is a hopeless dream. Basically what that means is, unity has no chance to prevail. The idea of human equality divides people instead of unifying them. Although the terms 'equal under the law' and 'equal opportunity' sound nice, there is no such thing in this reality."

Chapter 23 - Freedom and Unity

"Another concept that will divide, not only the races, but the nation itself is the abstract idea of national freedom, or a free country. The statement, "America is a free country" is a misnomer; it should read, "America is a limited free country". Depending upon how freedom is defined, America is not now, nor will it ever be a free country. In America, one is free to breathe, if able, to enjoy sunshine, if able, and to feel, hear, taste, and smell different things, if able. If those freedoms are the criteria that define a free country, then America is indeed a free country; of course, so is every other country on earth."

"Think about it, Little Muddy, from a creation point of view. Humans were created with an evil nature, the ability to reason, and freedom without boundaries. Freedom, on the surface, is a wonderful concept, but dangerous beyond description; hence, the ability to reason. Through experience and the ability to reason, humans learned that freedom of individuals was destructive and had to be restricted, or limited, for the good of the collective of mankind. This restriction took the form of laws, with penalties for violations, and enforcers of the law. What resulted is a variable Freedom Scale from zero to ten, with zero freedom on one end and complete freedom, a ten, on the other end. Where a society of humans rate on that scale reveals much about them."

"**Every** society of humans is forced to limit freedom for the good of the that society. Some have more restrictions than others and penalties for violations are more severe in some than in others, but **all** limit freedom because unlimited freedom is chaos."

"The concept of limited freedom is now making America great, rich, and powerful. How did freedom do that? With the idea that anyone can advance in America through hard work, talent, and desire. That idea has resulted in many great accomplishments in the America of today; however, because not everyone is equal, some do not enjoy the same benefits of freedom as the more capable. A logical reason for the success of America is, freedom is prejudiced. That prejudice favors those who are achievers, meaning those who exhibit good work ethics, reliability and persistence. When leaders apply equality to freedom's prejudice with the forced distribution of profits for the purpose of assisting the less capable population, great division occurs and rebellion ultimately results."

Mudman has always amazed me with his ability to explain how things work and I often wonder how he acquired his understanding of those things, so I asked.

"Mudman, your prophecy of the approaching fall of America and the reasons it will occur are not taught in school. The adults that I am around never talk about such things, even my teachers. The books I read do not say the things about equality and freedom that you taught just now. Your way of explaining a question is different than anyone I know. You have told me that you absorb information and I am not sure what that means or how it happens. I don't remember if I ever told you this, but being your friend means a lot to me, and all that you have taught has allowed me look at life in a way that would never have been considered without you."

Mudman smiled and said, "Much of what I have told you is not taught in your schools because your teachers only know to teach what they were taught. Anyway, even if they had an understanding of what I talk about, they would not be allowed to teach it as a truth. It is an intelligent-stupid thing." he explained, and continued, "The same goes for all the adults with whom you associate. Books do exist that deal with the subjects you and I talk about; you will eventually read them. I also have the advantage of having seen this unfold in another now. How do you learn, Little Muddy?"

"Well," I answered, "I learn through my five senses. I observe, hear, taste, smell, and touch things." I was feeling rather proud of that answer until Mudman asked a followup question.

"I wonder, Little Muddy, how does the information you obtain from those senses get into your brain or mind? They are not solid or liquid or gas. What are they and how do they get into you?"

I was stunned by his question because, not only had I never even thought about it, but had no idea of how information gets into me or anyone else. Mudman could see that I was wrestling with his question and proceeded to ask another question.

"Could it be, my young friend, that you absorbed that which you think you know?" he asked quietly.

"How does he do that?" I thought, surprised by the way he allowed me to answer my own question by asking questions.

All I could say was, "Yes, Mudman. That is how I learn, I absorb information. Thank you."

Then he said, "I have great affection for you, Little Muddy."

"Mudman," I said, "some time ago you commented that there are important created differences between the Caucasian and Negro races, but you did not explain them. Why?"

I could see that Mudman did not want to talk about this because of the time he took to answer and, after a few minutes of silence, I pushed for an answer by hinting that he did not have an answer to the question.

"Is this something which you have not absorbed?" I asked.

He looked at me, cocked his head, smiled and stated, "You know, young Johnny, for asking that last question, you almost deserve the dark consequences of understanding."

"The dark consequences of understanding? What does that mean?" I questioned.

"It means there are some truths of which one should not be aware, now." he replied, "particularly those like you who, because of youth and inexperience, may not keep them secret."

"Why not now?" I persisted.

"Now you have asked a question that I cannot answer because I do not know the answer." he replied, "but I can see that you are not going to let this go away. I am opposed to revealing a truth which you are unprepared to process, as it is something that should be discovered on your own; however, your serious interest in race relations deserves information that will inspire continued investigation into the subject."

Then he told me this, "Young Johnny, hear a simple truth:

The created imperative of the Negro race is to destroy, anything and everything, knowingly and unknowingly. They are, by their very nature, excellent at destruction. They do not build, nor do they labor at building, of their own will.

The created imperative of the Caucasian race is to build, anything and everything, knowingly and unknowingly. They are, by their very nature, excellent at construction. They build, they labor at building, and they also destroy, in the name of progress.

Understanding that should be kept to yourself; it should remain untold for now. The current civilization will object to such a truth and attack you for revealing it.

"Why?" I asked.

"Generally," Mudman explained, "humans do not understand the concept of a created reality, much less that of a Creator. The idea of a created imperative that governs their thoughts and actions is offensive to them. They want to believe they are in charge of their lives and oppose the idea that their 'want to' or 'desire' is part of a design, or imperative, placed there during creation."

"I don't understand." I complained. "How can the Negroes destroy everything?"

Mudman replied, "You should listen better, young Johnny. Just because the Negro race has a created imperative to destroy does not mean they will destroy everything. They, like all humans, are created with the ability to choose. Their race, due to its imperative, has little chance to choose rightly, as the path of least resistance is very compelling, but some learn morals and ethics and apply them to their lives, thereby becoming intelligent-smart humans. In any event, it is not the Negro race to fear of destroying everything; that, Johnny, is reserved for the ultimate destroyers, the Caucasians."

"But Mudman, you teach that Caucasians are builders!" I protested.

"Yes they are builders, young Johnny, of many different types of structures, all of which destroy something in the name of progress, for profit and power. Caucasians build war machines and armies in the name of national security and use those structures to wage war in the name of God, which they firmly believe justifies their actions. There are many things in the world that were built by Caucasians, for they are a multi-versatile race of humans. Think about it, Negroes may very well be the hope of the human race; they do have a destructive nature, but since they are not builders, they do not build things that threaten creation. Caucasians do build such things, very often unknowingly, which makes them the ultimate destroyers in this reality and very possibly, of this reality."

Mudman continued, "Much can be learned about the various races of humans, Little Muddy. Each race has its own culture and segregates itself in it's own unique way according to created imperatives, which heavily influence their beliefs, customs, and actions."

I was thinking as Mudman was talking and commented when he finished, "I don't like the idea of my race being destructive, Mudman. We should be saviors, not destroyers. What can Caucasians do to change such destruction from the things they build?"

"It is unlikely Caucasians will do it do it, Little Muddy."

"Why not? I questioned.

"Because of a created imperative." he replied.

"To build?" I responded.

"Yes, Little Muddy! Along with a belief that building is progress and progress is good."

I considered what he claimed in that statement and admitted, "You're right, Mudman; Caucasians will not stop building."

He replied, "Well, that is something as yet undetermined." and pointed at me, emphasizing a point.

I thought a moment about our conversation and realized what had happened. His last comment told me the answer to what had been bothering me. "Mudman certainly has a way about him." I said to myself.

I looked at him and said, "You have answered my question, haven't you, Mudman?"

"I think so, young Johnny." he answered softly, then added, "You can do what you wish with your discovery, but it is best that you keep it to yourself for now. You are in this reality for a reason, Little Muddy, and you may have just discovered it, but cannot know for sure. You must think about it, now. There is more to learn and moments to talk in another now."

I thanked Mudman and walked slowly home, not knowing what to think about today's discussion. More had been absorbed than expected and I felt a need to talk to someone. But whom?

Chapter 24 - A Talk With Grandma

My new discovery was a revelation of sorts, but was really more a confirmation of suspicions that have been nagging me recently. I mean, how can one believe that everything here in this existence is created by a Creator and not have questions and suspicions? Unless, of course, one believes there is no creator and everything in this existence came about on its own by some sort of natural selection by evolving through generations into something better. Truth is, the natural selection explanation is easier to believe than creation. What bothers me about something being easy, is the teaching of Mudman that 'easy' is a crowded path of least resistance.

He would say, "It is crowded because it is easy to travel, because there is little or no resistance for one to overcome, and the company you keep on such a journey is stupid." Mudman has a way with words.

Anyway, the idea of creation appeals to me, but that of being an experiment does not; however, it does make sense. The driving force for creating a reality is curiosity, a desire to understand something not understood. According to Mudman, our Creator designed us with an evil nature, imperatives, free will, and the ability to learn, all of which are a map of the path of least resistance, leading to destruction.

What a great experiment! A creation game with sentient pieces! Will mankind exercise their free will and choose goodness over evil, learn to live moral and ethical lives on the difficult path to virtue or will they take the easy way? I certainly don't know and the Creator must be interested in knowing as well, since this reality is his creation. The heavy bets are probably on destruction. No wonder Mudman says humans are interesting to watch.

I wanted to hear a different point of view on creation and thought that grandma might be a good place to start. She is a Christian, familiar with bible quotes, and I have heard her discussing the bible with momma. One afternoon, while she was sitting in her chair on the porch, I kissed her on the cheek and sat down on the steps.

"Whatcha been up to today, child?" she asked. "Bin out fishin' agin? I seen 'ya in dat boat. Ya can't keep sump'n like dat seecurt 'ya know."

"No, I've been reading a lot and thinking about things, grandma." I replied.

"Whatcha bin read'n, boy?" she inquired. "Ya still turnin' dem pages in dat 'White Fang" book."

"I finished that book last week, grandma. Today, I am reading the bible about the creation of the world."

"Land sakes alive, Johnny!" she exclaimed, "you thinkin' 'bout bein' a preacher now?" then she laughed and slapped the arm of her chair. "Now dat der would serve yur daddy right, him bein' cathlik and all. Watcha findin' out 'bout creatn' the world, son?"

"Well, I'm interested in how people were created and why they were created, grandma. I mean, did God create people to be good or bad? What was their race? Did God create white people first or colored people first?

"Lawdy, lawdy, child!" Grandma replied and leaned forward in her chair, "You got a bunch o' questyuns there. Ya might wanna slow down sum on dat read'n a bit. I'ma gon' tell you sump'n nobody else will, Johnny. Ain't nobody knows nuthin' 'bout dem things yer askin'. Dat God feller wurks in 'serous ways and don't nobody know how 'r why He duz 'em. You jus s'pose to bleeve He made everthin' and ya jus got to reelize that ya ain't ne'er gon' kno how or why."

"Grandma," I said, "That is hard for me to do. My mind is full of questions that need answering and I believe that God wouldn't have let me have those questions if he wasn't going to let me discover the answers."

"Well now, son," she responded, "it jus mite be He sees sump'n special in ya'. Lord knows I do. Now c'mon up here and give me a kiss. You back off dat read'n awhile an' go fishin'. I got a yen fer some perch at supper. Rite now, I'ma gon' lay down 'n rest a bit. Talkin' wichya tires me out at times."

I stood up, kissed her cheek, and helped her into the house. Then I went out and caught some perch for supper. Darned if I didn't have something else nagging my mind after my talk with grandma, but what it was just wouldn't come to me. I made a mental note to talk to her more often about some of my thoughts. Besides, I liked listening to her talk. I wonder what she would think about Mudman?

It seemed to me that as I grew older, my conversations with Mudman became more complex, a logical reason being that as my intelligence increased, my ability to process more complex information increased as well. It is easy to see that Mudman inspires me to think about new ways of looking at everything by pushing me to see the things at which I look. I wish the teachers at my school were inclined and able to teach that way; however, in their defense, my teachers have 20 or more students in a classroom and Mudman has only me. I wonder about that, too. I have no idea how long Mudman has lived or if he actually lives, in my sense of what living means. He says that age does not apply to him, which is confusing. Mudman teaches me; I wonder if he teaches anyone else or has taught anyone else. There seem to be many things to learn about Mudman, but the real truth is this: I do not care about knowing any of those things! What is important to me is, I am his friend and he is mine.

While I'm thinking about Mudman, a thought has occurred to me. The last time we met, when we were talking about equality and freedom, he said something about having an advantage over my teachers in that he had seen the results of the same stupid decisions in "another now" that are being made now. I didn't follow up on that comment then, but it caused me to wonder, when was that other now? I have more questions to ask when next we meet.

Chapter 25 - Be Careful Who You Talk With

The month of June in Beaumont is wonderful for some people and miserable for others. Most of the time, the windows in our house are open and being in front of our two electric fans is the most popular place to be. Where we live, surrounded on three sides by forest and swamp, there is seldom any movement of air experienced. With the exception of a storm, when it rains, which is often, the rain comes straight down and it might rain for five minutes, five hours or five days. Summer in Beaumont seems to be either hot and humid or hot and raining. I love it here.

The next time I met with Mudman was one of those on and off rainy days in the high seventies, in other words, a great day. For some reason, fish seemed to bite better on these type of days. Whether it is the temperature or the rain, or both, what makes them active is a mystery. Anyway, my expectations for a stringer of fish were high.

The best fishing spot for me is less than a hundred yards from where my boat was tied. The great thing about my place is that no one can see me from shore; the solitude is comforting. Last year I discovered an underwater hole there, where the water is pretty deep. The depth of the swamp where I usually take my boat is three to four feet, but my fishing spot is very deep and almost always yields good results. It is my spot because I am the only one who knows about it; well, except for Mudman; he knows everything about the swamp. Anyway, I had already caught three perch and a catfish when Mudman came gliding up to my boat. It was raining steadily when he arrived. He took a long look at me sitting in the boat in the rain with a fishing pole in my hands and shook his head, laughing. I saw the humor in the way my fishing in the rain looked and laughed with him.

"Little Muddy, why do you like fishing so much?" he asked.

"Well," I said, "We eat a lot of fish at home, but the main reason is, I do some of my best thinking when I'm fishing. I don't know why that is, it just is."

It was raining pretty hard now and the water in my boat required me to begin bailing out some of it.

Mudman commented, "What can you possibly be thinking about in this downpour? Most people would be a bit depressed about the rain ruining their fishing trip and here you are acting like it is perfectly normal to fish in the rain."

"The truth is, Mudman, fish often bite better in the rain." I answered. "On top of that," I continued, "rain like this is really pleasant. It isn't cold and there's no wind out here. Besides, when that cloud passes, the rain will stop until the next one gets over us. I'm glad to see you though, because there are some things I want to talk about that we have never before discussed."

The rain eased up to a sprinkle and I had bailed most of the water out of my boat. To my surprise, Mudman untied my boat and guided it back to shore.

"Young Johnny," he ordered, "take off those wet clothes, put on your regulars, then take your stringer of fish and go home. Whether you admit it or not, you are cold and shivering. Also, the subject on your mind will get us into areas of thought that I know little to nothing about and you should talk to others before we begin our conversation. Few, if any, will want to talk with you about such things, but the experience will be enlightening. We will talk in another now."

"Mudman, what makes you think you know what I want to discuss?" I asked.

"In our last conversation, you came to an understanding of reality and the purpose for its creation. You left with that revelation on your mind. Having questions about such an experience is to be expected. You have been wondering about the Creator, who is among the most interesting and important subjects about which to have a discussion."

I went home thinking about Mudman's comments. Also, I came down with a fever and a cold and had to stay in the house for several days. It goes without saying that I had to suffer a scolding from momma about fishing in the rain. She was not happy with me, but got over it when she saw that I was sick and then worried over me like I was a little kid.

Having to stay at home because of sickness sounds boring, but for me that confinement was a benefit. Having the time to think without interruption was needed and refreshing. Mudman's suggestion to talk to others about the created reality in which we exist dominated most of my thinking. For example, who do I know to talk with about creation? Heck, there is probably no one in my circle of society who ever thinks about creation, much less the idea that this reality is an illusion! I can only imagine the response to my idea that this reality might be a type of experiment or game created for the amusement of its creator. I can hear their the response now, "Break out the strait jacket! Johnny's done gone and lost his mind." I don't know, maybe I'll just talk to momma. If I'm going to do this, she's as good a starting point as any.

I got the chance to talk with momma later that day when she came in to check on me. Even though my fever was down to normal, she checked my temperature and made me take two aspirin. While she was fussing about with my pillow and bed covers, I asked her if she had time to talk with me.

"Why Johnny boy," she declared, "I always have time for you and it's important you know that! Nothing is more important to me than my boys. You'll be sixteen next year and have a lot of things going on in your life that might be hard to talk with your mother about, but I am always here for you when you need me."

"I know all that momma, it's just that I've been reading the bible a lot the last few days and am wondering how the world was created. There are a bunch of things in the Bible's version of creation that are hard to understand and I'm pretty sure that you know more about it than me."

Momma stared at me intently for a few moments, finally smiled and said, "Son, have I ever told you how difficult you are to read? You're just chock full of surprises and I love that about you, but you sure do come up with some interesting questions. I don't know which subject is more difficult, the one I was expecting or the one I got. No matter, what is it you want to know about creation? Before we begin, you should know that I'm not an expert on the bible and believe that there are some things we are not supposed to understand about God."

"That's what grandma said, too. I think most people think that way, but I don't. It seems to me that God created a world full of questions that have answers, but you have to work for those answers and most people don't want to work that hard."

Momma thought about my comment and said, "Maybe God created those questions to test the faith of people. When you believe in God, you just trust that He had a reason for creating the world and the people in it. Our knowing why He does what He does is not important, but trusting that God knows **is** important. That is faith."

"But momma, that kind of faith keeps people from asking questions and looking for answers by making them believe that asking a lot of questions about creation is the same as questioning God, which is a sin. I believe God wants me to ask questions and try to find answers."

"Well, think of it this way son," she suggested, "maybe God does want people to ask questions about His creation of the world, even though answers cannot be obtained. It is possible that the journey to obtain answers is the way faith in God is obtained. In other words, the journey is important and in some cases necessary, but the answers aren't. At some point in your search for answers, you are going to have to make a decision and that decision is going to be based upon faith because you can never absolutely know there is or is not a God. No one can. You will either believe in God and have faith that He created everything and all that happens is according to His will, even though you don't understand why, or you will believe that everything happens by some sort of universal accident and people are on their own. No matter how long and hard you search, it will eventually come down to faith because no one can know for sure what this life is all about."

"Wow!" I thought to myself. "My momma is smart! She has already given me some things to think about that had not occurred to me. I should have started talking to her long before now." But I couldn't help thinking that there was something wrong, or at least incomplete, with momma's explanation.

When I think about it, the idea of faith and a belief in something is the end of a discussion about anything and everything, because it always comes down to what someone believes, or does not believe, to be true. It seems that everything in this reality is based upon faith and it makes no difference how wrong or stupid that belief seems to be. For example. If someone truly believes that 3 + 5 equals 9, then it **is** 9 for them and you are wrong for saying the answer is 8; so, one of you, in the interest of peace and harmony, eventually says, "We will just have to agree to disagree" and both of you let it go at that because each of you believe the other is wrong. It is interesting to me that there is no truth, in this reality, that everyone believes to be true, which means there is no absolute truth because this reality itself is an illusion and not real. How do I tell momma something like that?

Momma saw that I was thinking about her answer to my statement about God and inquired, "Whatcha thinking about, Johnny? Did you understand what I was trying to say? Most of the time conversations about God get complicated and challenge another person's way of believing. Discussions about religion are uncomfortable for most, and often embarrassing, which is why they avoid talking about it in the first place. I am glad that you are open to talking about God, but you should be careful who you talk with. God is a subject that can and will make you unpopular with many people."

"I understand what you said momma, it's just that no one has ever explained God and faith to me that way before. The truth is, I'm not real sure about anything. I think that believing in God is a good thing, but I'm not sure why. The preacher at church talks about how God is good and the devil is evil, but I'm not sure how anyone knows which one they're praying to when they pray. I mean, how am I supposed to tell the difference between them if the devil is as smart and good a deceiver as the preacher claims he is? Don't you want to be sure who you're praying to when you pray, momma?"

"Land sakes, boy!" she exclaimed. "Where do you come up with those questions? Now you've done gone making me wonder about those things! I don't know the answer to what you're asking, but it's a good question. I'm gonna have to talk to the preacher about that; he knows a lot about such things. All this talking we've been doing has made me forget about fixing supper and I best be getting at it. I'll be thinking about your questions while I'm cooking, though. You've got me to wondering."

Have you noticed, in your own life, the strange way that small things you do turn into big things that were not your intention? Something seems to be going on that you really don't have time to analyze and think through and is definitely beyond your ability to control because others are involved. That is basically what evolved from my discussion with momma. She followed through on her intent to talk with the preacher at our church. I didn't attend church often anymore as explained in a previous section of this book and was surprised when the preacher showed up on Wednesday of the next week and announced that he was there to talk with me. I was over my spell of that cold and was practicing some chords on my brother Ricky's guitar that he received last Christmas. He didn't much care for guitar playing at that time, so I adopted that guitar and used it.

Anyway, the preacher was there to see me and I figured it had to do with my discussion with momma regarding God. Momma showed him in and gave us some privacy in the back room of our house. The preacher was Brother Yoes; I was friends with his son, Louis. Back when both of us were twelve, Louis and I had an unfortunate adventure in the swamp which led to his being banned from playing with me for almost a year; however, everything was good now, or so I thought. Brother Yoes was very cordial and asked me to join him in prayer before beginning our meeting, to which I agreed. I was impressed that the preacher of the local church would take time off from his busy schedule to talk with me. After the prayer, he asked me if I was happy at home and got along with my family. He expressed his concern that I was no longer regularly attending church and invited me to come this next Sunday. I answered that I was very happy at home, other than the fact my brothers were a nuisance sometimes. Then he got down to the reason for his visit.

"Johnny," he began, "your mother tells me that you have questions about Christianity and God that she cannot answer and asked that I talk with you about them. What do you think?

Are you up to a conversation about religion? Perhaps I can be of help to you in understanding the way of God in our lives."

Now, you have to understand this from my point of view. This was the first time in my life that the opportunity to talk with a man of God, one on one, had ever been given to me. I was fifteen years old and the church preacher, Brother Yoes, wanted to talk with me about God. I had so much to tell and ask him, but momma's warning to be careful who I talked with about God kicked my defenses into gear. I needed to know a little more about him and his understanding of God.

"Brother Yoes," I asked, "I've been reading the Bible about creation and wondering why God created humans and why He created them to look like Him and His people. You probably have read a lot more about that than me and can explain it too."

"Well now Johnny," he responded, "you seem to have given some thought to this subject and I have to admit that it is refreshing to see a young man like you reading the bible. In regard to your question, God created mankind out of love for the purpose of spreading love throughout the world. You believe that God loves you, don't you Johnny?"

"But Brother Yoes, the bible says that mankind was created to rule over all the creatures of the earth. Nothing is said about humans being created to spread love. Where is that love you talked about throughout the world? We humans cannot get along with each other throughout the world. We humans are killing each other out of hatred of each other. There seems to be more hatred than love in the world. Shoot, even the Negro and Caucasian races don't seem to get along. I'm not seeing the love you talked about. As far as believing God loves me, I'm not real sure who God loves, but his human creations sure don't love each other."

Brother Yoes opened his bible to the first few pages, read a moment, then closed it. "Johnny, are you happy?" he asked.

I was surprised that he asked that again, but thought a moment and answered, "Yes."

"You seem to be unhappy with the world right now. Why is that?" he asked.

"Brother Yoes, I am not unhappy with the world, I am fascinated by it. I love the world and am grateful for the opportunity to live in it. The problem humans have getting along with each other is interesting, though. Where do you think all the hatred between races comes from? You think maybe God created them that way? I often wonder why He created different races of humans, anyway. Do you have any ideas about that?"

"Johnny, do you understand the meaning of faith?" he asked.

I replied, "Faith is a word that is used to end religious discussions in harmony. For instance, after continuing a religious discussion without resolution, one can say he has faith that God is in control and everything is going according to His plan. The discussion is then over."

"Do you believe God has a plan for humanity, Johnny?"

"Gosh preacher, I honestly don't know what to believe about that." I answered.

"Johnny, a major part of my calling is to counsel teenagers with personal problems, as well as problems of faith. I want you to know that you can call on me anytime you have questions or just want to talk. I enjoyed meeting with you today."

"Thank you Brother Yoes," I answered. "I enjoyed talking with you too, but you never did answer any of my questions."

While walking away, he glanced back at me and replied, "That is because I did not know how to answer them, Johnny."

I asked momma after supper, while we were washing dishes, if the preacher said anything to her about our meeting today. She told me, "The only thing he said was that he was unprepared for a meeting with a teenager like you."

Momma then asked, "What did you think of Brother Yoes, son?"

"I don't know, momma," I replied, "he didn't really say much and never answered my questions."

"Well son," she replied, "in his defense, many of the questions you ask are difficult to answer. How do you come up with them anyway?"

"I pretty much only ask questions of some people when I know the answer, momma. You know, 'what is gravity?' and 'who were the people in the land of Nod?' If I had not asked those questions of myself and searched them out, I would never have found the answers, because no one I ever meet can answer them."

Momma stopped washing dishes and looked at me. "You found the answers to those questions, Johnny? Are you telling me that you know the answers to those questions?"

Sometimes I let my guard down and say too much. How do I get out of this? I couldn't tell momma about Mudman because if I did, the next meeting I attended would be with a child psychiatrist. I don't like lying to momma, but sometimes you just can't tell the whole truth; so, I decided on part of the truth.

"Yes, ma'am," I replied, "I found those answers a month ago. It's not like it was real hard or anything, anyone can do it if they are willing to read."

"But son, no one knows how gravity works or even what it is, not even Albert Einstein!"

"Oh, he knew, momma." I said, "He just wouldn't tell anyone. I don't blame him, I wouldn't tell either."

"What are you talking about, Johnny? You told me!" she exclaimed.

"Not really, Momma," I replied, "I only said that I found answers to some questions and that it was easy to do."

Momma went back to washing dishes without saying anything. I was drying the dishes and could see that she had something on her mind. Finally she couldn't take it anymore and turned off the water and dried her hands on her apron.

"Come with me, son." she ordered. "I want to talk with you."

When momma used that voice, it usually meant trouble. What for? Only she knew, because it was a mystery to me. I followed her outside, where we settled into a couple of lawn chairs. It was getting dark and I was wondering how she was going to handle the mosquitoes that get worse as the sun goes down.

Momma got right to what was on her mind. "Johnny, have you talked to anyone else about these questions of yours and discussed their answers?" she asked.

"Well, I ask a lot of questions about things that are hard to understand," I said, "but I never tell anyone the answers."

"Why is it you never tell anyone the answers, son?"

"Because the questions I ask don't have easy answers for people, momma."

"Johnny, if the answers are not easy for people to find, how do you find them?"

"You're not going to understand, Momma."

"Try me, son."

"I have an understanding about some truths that almost everyone else doesn't."

"How did you learn to understand these truths?"

"I read and think about what I read, momma."

"Are you telling me that you learned to understand gravity by reading books?"

"Pretty much." I replied.

"Son, if you already know the answers to the questions you ask, why do you ask them?"

"I want to see who else understands what I understand."

"Who have you found, so far?" she asked.

"No one yet, but I don't often get a chance to talk to a lot of people and actually don't want to."

"Why not? There may be many who would enjoy talking with you, Johnny."

"I don't think so, momma, and anyway that's a bad idea."

"Why do you think talking with people is a bad idea?" she questioned.

"Because it is hard sometimes to tell the bad people from the good ones."

"Yeah son, I have found that to be true myself, but you should talk with someone."

"I am, momma; I'm talking with you."

"I mean someone smarter than me, Johnny."

"That all depends upon how you define 'smart', momma. You are smart."

"You know, son, I don't know what to do with you. You're not like your brothers."

"Sure I am." I replied, "I just understand more than they do. They don't like reading."

"I don't agree," she said, "I think your brothers like to read; they just don't interpret what they read in the same way as you. You seem to have a different way of looking at things than the rest of us."

"There's a big difference between looking and seeing," I responded. "We all look at the same things, but not everyone sees things in the same way."

"Did you get that from reading a book, Johnny?"

"No, mostly from watching my teachers and the kids at school." I answered.

I wanted to tell momma something, but our discussion wasn't going in that direction so, I just blurted it out.

"Momma, I know you thought it was a good idea for the preacher to talk with me, but the kind of counseling he does is for unhappy people. I'm happy, momma. Just because I want to understand things and have questions about God and Jesus doesn't mean I need to talk with a preacher. Brother Yoes didn't understand a thing I asked him, anyway. You told me to be careful who I talk with and I am, but don't you think you should be careful who you arrange to talk with me? Besides, I like talking with you and grandma. You may not think you're smart, but you are. I don't want other people bothering me about the way I see things. Maybe some day I will, but not now. I just want to play baseball, go fishing, and go to school. Heck, I'm not all that special anyway; there's a lot of kids smarter than me at school."

Momma laughed and said, "Lord goodness, child! I don't know who's talking to whom right now, but I think you're right. We'll just leave things the way they are; no good comes from trying to make a mountain out of a molehill."

Then she continued, "You're mistaken, Johnny. You are "all that special", at least to me, and I seriously doubt there are any kids like you at school. Now, lets get back in the house before the mosquitoes get out and about and carry us off."

"They're already "out and about" now, Momma." I quietly responded, but she was already going in the door and didn't hear me.

That talk with momma turned out better than I expected. There were no more meetings with "do gooders" intending to help me and interestingly, I never saw Brother Yoes again. I heard that he up and moved his family to a small town, just outside of Beaumont and took to preaching at a small church there.

Momma and I were more open in our conversations after our talk, allowing me to learn more about how she felt about life and what she wanted to achieve. I never thought before about what momma wanted to do with her life. She was thirty-one years old when we had that conversation and had dreams of going places and doing things that I didn't know she even thought about.

I regret failing to help momma realize the importance of now. It is not an easy concept to absorb though, when your "now" is far less pleasant than what your non-existent "when" seems to promise.

"A common malady among humans." as Mudman would say.

Chapter 26 - The Poachers

I went fishing a few times to my fishing hole in June, but never saw Mudman. Funny thing about that is, whenever I'm in the swamp by myself, fishing or just looking around, I have the sensation that Mudman is also there. I'm not claiming that he is or isn't, it's just a feeling. I guess it sounds crazy, but sometimes I talk to him like he is there. Of course I talk to Rex, too. Either way, it is always a one-sided conversation, except that Rex barks sometimes; kinda makes me think he is answering, in his way.

It was a few days after Independence Day when Mudman and I had an opportunity to talk again. So far, July has been a rainy and foggy month. If spooky places are not to your liking, stay away from the swamp when the fog is laying on the water. I learned a few years earlier that the swamp on a clear day and the swamp on a foggy day are two different places. It's probably just a mental thing, but fog has a way of messing with with a person's mind and has cost more than a few people their lives out here.

Now, you have to understand that my swamp is a scary looking and scary feeling place on a clear day, with moss hanging from trees, strange bird calls (if they are birds), and splashing in the water that you can hear but not see what's causing it. However, when the fog is on the water, sight is limited and the animal noises are muffled and sound like they are closer than they actually are. Everything is different. It is really easy to get lost out here when you're only twenty feet from shore. I know that from personal experience.

Sometimes it seems that the swamp changes itself in the fog by messing with directions when you're in there, making your way back a best guess situation. Now, that's spooky. Mudman warned me about the fog when I was just a kid about nine years old; said to keep my wits about me and never panic in the fog. "Panic kills with fear." He told me. That advice stuck in my memory; it was not only about fog.

One day last year, I took a friend from school out fishing on a foggy day and in an hour or so, after we had a stringer of fish, we decided to paddle back and call it a day. Well, darned if I didn't get turned around in that fog and lost my sense of where we were. My friend Jack was sure that we paddled in next to a nearby cypress tree, so we went in that direction. After about ten minutes of paddling, the trees were getting farther apart. I recognized my mark on one of the trees and realized we had navigated to the edge of what I refer to as the deep swamp, where I rarely go for various reasons; so, I stopped the pirogue to get my sense of direction under control. We were next to a big clearing in the swamp that always seemed like a lake to me because it had no trees in it. Jack was obviously nervous about where we were and was probably wishing he had not insisted on going fishing with me.

Jack was popular at school, used to getting his way and began demanding that we go back home. I felt bad for him because this was his first time in the swamp and, like I mentioned, this place is spooky enough on a clear day when you can see, much less a blind foggy day. Besides, the deep swamp is where the big gators hang out and my little pirogue tipped easy. I didn't tell Jack about that though, as it was obvious he was beginning to panic and the thought of gators being around might tip him over the edge. People who panic have no concern for anyone or anything other than themselves; that makes them dangerous to others, in this case, me.

Jack motioned to me and excitedly pointed, saying "What's that?

I looked through the fog to where he was pointing, and saw what seemed to be two boats, each with three people in them, and motioned for Jack to be quiet. They were close, but had not noticed us, mainly because of the fog and the fact the pirogue was hidden behind a large bush next to the tree where I stopped to get my bearings. There was less fog in the middle of the clearing, where they were and we could see them better than they could see us.

Jack was afraid now and whispered "Johnny, who are they and what are they talking about?"

I shook my head and put a finger to my lips, indicating silence, and wondered, "Why in the world does he think I know and understand them?"

Then I realized it was reasonable for him to have that thought, since I spend a lot of time in the swamp and they probably do the same; but, they were strangers to me. What was important, though was for him to sit still and not talk.

Their boats were side by side in the water and the men were talking in a backwoods slang that my grandma used sometimes. They were alligator hunters and already had killed two gators. I guessed they were poachers or they wouldn't be out hunting on a foggy day. Most gator hunters I heard about, preferred clear nights. These guys here might not appreciate two teenage kids witnessing their illegal activities and I sure didn't want them to know we were here. I whispered those thoughts to Jack, which didn't make him feel any better and it was becoming obvious that he was getting antsy. I wanted to be quiet and wait until the hunters moved on, but Jack kept motioning that he wanted to get away from here and I kept motioning back for him to sit still in silence.

Well, that's when fate stepped in and made our decision for us. Our stringer full of fish was still in the water and, unknown to us, had attracted an alligator or two. I couldn't see the gators well because they were below the water, but there were at least two pulling on the stringer and rocking the boat. I quickly pulled my knife and cut the rope holding the stringer, but it was too late. Jack had seen the tail of one of the gators and leapt to his own conclusion as to what was happening and totally went berserk! He stood up and screamed, "Alligator! Alligator!" If I hadn't been holding on to a limb of the tree, the pirogue would have turned over.

There was nothing to do now but run, or rather paddle. Jack had broken down, crying, and was standing up in the boat holding his paddle and mumbling about alligators. I reached, took his paddle and told him to sit down and be still. I was scared now, too and doing everything possible to keep the pirogue afloat as it was our only hope of getting away from there.

It was obvious the poachers had not yet seen us, but because of Jack's screams, they knew our general direction. Both of their boats were metal, with motors, and were heading our way. I began paddling directly away from them, heading for the heavily wooded swamp area. When I earlier saw my mark on that tree, the way back home was clear. I was confident that if I made it to the woods, their bigger boats could not navigate through the thick trees and would have no chance of catching my smaller pirogue, especially in this fog, because those trees were my area of the swamp and I now knew my location.

I made a mistake though, about the distance to the thickly wooded area. It was further than it looked and although I was steadily paddling my pirogue, they located us and one of their motor boats rushed ahead, cut off my escape route, and stopped ahead of us. I stopped paddling, trying to be calm. Jack was frozen in the front of my boat, gripping the sides like his life depended on it. The man standing in the front of the boat blocking us had a rifle. He held his hand out, motioning us to stop, but my boat was still slowly coasting forward. He hollered something at me, fired his gun into the air, and then pointed it at us. Poor Jack snapped and threw up in the front of the boat when the man fired his gun into the sky. Then he laid down in the boat and stayed there. We were trapped. One boat in front and the other behind us. I just sat there with the paddle in my lap, wondering whether our situation was life threatening or not. I smiled, trying to look harmless, which was easy to do because we certainly were no threat to them. But we had seen something we were not supposed to see and no one would know where to look if we mysteriously disappeared in the swamp; truth is, no one even knew we were in the swamp. I was trying to be brave, but yeah, these guys really scared me. They also had guns and I had a hunting knife, two paddles, and a peanut butter and jelly sandwich. Jack had eaten his food earlier.

The man standing with the gun pointed at us was gesturing and hollering something that I didn't understand and, as a consequence, he didn't see it coming; but, I did. A ripple appeared on the surface of the water to his left about 20 yards away from his boat and quickly became a wave, which was approaching from the open water and got higher as it neared. I couldn't see what was causing the wave because the thing was under the water, but I knew what it was; I had seen it before and witnessed what it could do. It was headed straight at his boat and in seconds, slammed into its side, crushing the aluminum inwards and knocking the boat upwards and upside down! The two men in the back of the boat were thrown out towards the trees and the man standing in front with the gun was heaved up in the air and landed in the water on the left side and went under. I didn't see him come up. It was over in a moment! The sound of the crash and the screaming of the men in the boat behind shocked me into action. Those few seconds of chaos took all attention away from us and provided the time I needed; I grabbed the paddle and maneuvered my pirogue into the swamp forest faster than I thought possible, then disappeared into the fog.

Jack didn't move from the floor of my boat the whole trip back. It took me longer than it should have, partly because of the fog and partly because of stopping and listening for any sign of our being followed. I never heard a thing indicating unwanted company. We were approaching land and when I told Jack that we had made it back, he sat up and jumped from the boat before it reached shore. It was about knee deep there and he waded to shore, kept going, never said a word, and never looked back. He just went home.

I wanted to tell him to keep quiet about our encounter in the swamp because those men would be wanting to know who we are and where we lived, but he was gone before I could say anything. He had ridden his bicycle to my house, so he had a way to get home and get home is what he did. I kind of expected Jack to wash himself in the swamp before going home because he smelled really bad, probably because of the vomit all over him. But I figured he needed to get away from here as fast as possible. I kind of understood how he felt, since fear like that had once gripped me as well.

I sat there in the boat for a moment thinking what to do now, when a bad smell in the front got my attention. It didn't take long to see the cause. Jack had made a bigger mess than vomit and left me to clean it up. This experience actually scared the crap out of him. In his defense, today's adventure was incredibly dangerous and should not have occurred. We could have been hurt or even murdered that day. It was my fault, too. It happened the way it did because I got turned around in the fog, causing us to paddle into the deep swamp area. Jack panicked because he was taken too far outside his comfort zone and was unprepared to mentally deal with the consequences of the experience.

My relationship with Jack became non-existent after that day and I understand why. Jack is a four sport athlete at school and popular among the student body. When I walked up to talk with him the week after our outing, Jack was dismissive and verbally abusive, calling me a liar and warning me to never talk to him again or say anything about him. He was embarrassed by his response to to a tense situation and desired to "sweep it under the carpet" and pretend it never happened. I never said a thing about him before or after our encounter at school. I didn't have to, Jack later exposed his true nature on his own without any help from me.

Chapter 27 - The Creator

I warned you at the beginning of this book about my tendency to go off course sometimes when an old memory comes to mind that needs to be told before it gets forgotten. Anyway, as I was saying, I met Mudman again a few days after Independence Day on a drizzling, foggy day in the swamp. As I mentioned before, a foggy swamp is a spooky place. I much prefer going into the swamp on a clear day because there is so much more to see. Mudman probably loved the foggy days because, for all practical purposes, he is invisible in the fog.

I was barefoot, wearing an old hat to fend off the occasional shower, and enjoying walking in the mud at the edge of the water, one of my favorite things to do. Mudman was on my mind because there were many things to ask him about creation and the Creator. The last time we met, he claimed I was about to ask him questions about something unknown to him. I wonder what that something is and am planning to ask him about it.

"What are you thinking about on this wonderful morning, Little Muddy? You seem to be in deep thought, walking back and forth in the mud there." Mudman seemed amused.

I looked down and saw a mud puddle created by my pacing around in the same spot over and over. Being so caught up in my thoughts, I never considered my actions. As a result, there was a nice, shallow mud hole about six feet across at the edge of the swamp with me in it. If it looked as silly as I felt, then it must have looked ridiculous. I stepped out and waded into some clear water to wash off the mud.

"Yeah," I admitted, "sometimes when I get to thinking about something in particular, there's no room for paying attention to anything else."

It was difficult to determine where his voice was coming from, but a quick survey of my surroundings revealed that he wasn't close by me. Knowing him, he could be up to his neck in the water or watching me from a tree. It's no wonder that he is seldom seen; he blends in perfectly with the swamp.

"You know," he responded, "the human mind was not created for thinking about more than one thing at a time, Little Muddy. Those that try to do so are seldom rewarded with great achievements. Still, it is possible to think and be aware at the same time."

Mudman's voice was clear and sounded close, but sounds are deceptive in the fog. Once again I looked around, determined to look further out, and saw him about twenty feet away in the swamp, sitting on an old overturned tree where I sometimes go to fish for perch. Although the water is not deep, the sun perch go there to feed on bugs and they really like my homemade flys. I waved and he motioned for me to come on over, so I waded out and climbed up beside him.

"You were hard for me to locate for awhile there, Mudman. I heard your voice, clear as a bell, but couldn't pinpoint where it was coming from and was surprised to see you out here. Why are you out here, anyway?" I asked.

"couldn't pinpoint from where it was coming" he corrected.

"What?" I questioned.

"Just a small lesson in the use of your language, Little Muddy." he chuckled. "It's a tough job, but someone has got to do it."

I realized what he was talking about, laughed and said, "I know and I'm working on it. Getting rid of old habits and forming new ones takes thinking practice."

"Thinking practice?" he queried.

"Yeah, you know, thinking about doing something a certain way and then practicing doing it that way." I explained.

"Did you read that somewhere, Little Muddy?"

"No, I just now came up with it as a way of explaining how I learn or re-learn things."

"Do you often come up with different ways of doing things, young Johnny?"

"Sure Mudman, everybody has their own way of explaining what they do or think."

"So, young Johnny, you believe that everyone is free to think what they want to think?"

"Why not, Mudman? No human knows what another human is thinking, anyway."

"So, someone is free to think about hurting someone else and planning to do so?"

"Yes. That probably happens all the time; anyone can have bad thoughts, Mudman."

"Should a person be punished for having bad or harmful thoughts, Little Muddy?"

"No. You can't do anything about something you know nothing about."

"What if you knew someone's thoughts, young Johnny? Would you act on them?"

"I don't know. Probably." I replied. "It would depend upon what they were thinking, though." I felt like Mudman was up to something, but I didn't know what.

"So," said Mudman, "everyone is free to think what they want to think only if no one knows what they are thinking, which indicates that everyone is free to do what they want to do if no one knows what they are doing. Once someone knows what you are doing or thinking, you are no longer free to do either, without redress of some measure, unless that someone approves of them which, in itself, is a restriction of freedom."

"Come on, Mudman," I complained, "no one understands what you just said, least of all, me. Where are you going with this conversation? I'm lost."

He answered with a question, "What do you think I am getting at here, young Johnny?"

I didn't really know what to think about Mudman's comment and, being a little frustrated, spoke without thinking, "The only thing I can figure out about the point you're making is that no one is free from God because He knows what we think and do, which doesn't make any sense if you believe He created us to be free."

"Young Johnny, what do you mean by saying that no one is free from God?" he asked.

"If God knows everything that we do and think, we have no privacy. I believe that people are not free when their now is constantly under observation, whether they know about the observation or not. You teach that humans are created with unbound freedom and have to learn to set boundaries on that freedom for the benefit of the mankind collective; however, if our actions and thoughts are constantly being watched by the Creator, does that not interfere with our so called free will?"

"Young Johnny, it is obvious why you paced a hole in the ground this morning. You have been giving a great deal of time to thinking about this created reality. You are probably the only human on earth doing that right now. Why are you so passionate about your discovery of this created reality? Having that understanding should be comforting."

Mudman continued, "What is it, anyway, that causes you to believe that the Creator knows your thoughts and sees everything you do?"

"Well," I began, "the Creator created this reality and everything in it, including you and me. Then He installed the rules that determine how everything works here and gave humans the freedom to learn morals and ethics, which helps them to resist their basically evil nature and follow His will along the path to heaven. God is aware of everything that happens in this reality because He is the architect of it."

Mudman was silent for so long that I felt maybe he expected me to say more, but he raised his hand at my attempt to continue. After a few more minutes, he pointed at me and exclaimed, "Little Muddy, I'm having difficulty responding to your answer. You have a knack for condensing long, complex conversations into a brief explanation. This particular explanation is unique, in that it reflects some of what you have learned about our created reality and at the same time exhibits your arrival at a false conclusion, which resulted from your interpretation of incomplete and erroneous information. Where you are now is where most of mankind is to be found, lost in ignorance and bound there by content."

"Mudman, your way of talking is often confusing to me. Sometimes it seems that you overlook the fact that I am not as intelligent as you. My mind needs explanations of things you take for granted that I understand, when the truth is, I don't understand. For instance, what 'false conclusion' and what 'incomplete information' caused that conclusion? And what do you mean by 'lost in ignorance and bound by content'? I'm interested in understanding that about which you are talking."

Then I added, "How did you like the way I spoke that last sentence, Mudman? Because of you, I'm learning a new way of expressing that which I say."

"Little Muddy," he said, laughing, "have I mentioned how much I like you? Well, allow me to say it again in a different way, I have grown very fond of you, my young friend."

Then he got right down to answering my questions.

"Alright Johnny, it is time now for you to learn some truths. Many of those who represent religion teach religious truths and consider such truths to be divine, meaning revealed by God. They cannot possibly know their truths are divine because their beliefs are flawed, similar to your current belief, Little Muddy."

"Listen closely," he warned, "you should realize that such a statement should not be verbalized in your society, as condemnation will most surely result, some of which carries with it an element of danger."

Mudman then continued, "People are not rational when their long held beliefs, especially religious beliefs, are challenged. Imagine how they will react when told that their beliefs are flawed. It is understandable when one considers the fact those beliefs of theirs have continued for millenniums, representing wealth and power for many, as well as peace of mind for others. A belief in the Creator is considered by many to be the mortar that bonds humanity together in a strong wall resisting evil. That sounds wonderful! But that belief is flawed."

"I wouldn't dare tell that to anyone, Mudman." I said.

"Really? Why not, Little Muddy?" he asked. "You live in a free country, with free speech."

"Yeah," I retorted, "but not **that** free!"

Mudman smiled and advised, "Remember that statement in another now."

I was impatient and had to ask, "What is that flaw you keep talking about, Mudman?"

"I'm getting there," he stated, "but there are some questions of yours still outstanding and begging to be answered, one of which regards my statement that mankind is lost in ignorance and bound by content. What I basically mean is this: out of ignorance, early mankind made a stupid decision regarding their god, which benefited them and gave them direction and contentment in their lives. Simply put, they chose the wrong path and lost their way, but the benefits of that choice resulted in contentment. As a result, mankind has since remained lost in ignorance, because they do not know better and are content to be where they are. Mankind has been content with their ignorance for millenniums, a contentment unlikely to change."

"Will we ever leave and take the right path?" I wondered aloud.

"You have heard me quote the poet Gray before, saying that 'ignorance is bliss'. Who would want to leave bliss? Mudman questioned.

"Mudman, I am not sure this result is bliss. A lot of people are unhappy, but do not realize it is their ignorance causing the unhappiness. They blame it on other things, like poor health or lack of money."

"How does one go about changing millenniums of ignorance, Johnny?"

I thought about his question for a moment and asked, "Mudman, have you ever thought that mankind's way back to the right path is to correct the original stupid decision made because of ignorance in regard to God?"

"Few ever ask that question, Johnny." he said, surprised. "How is it you thought to ask?"

"Your question about 'millenniums of ignorance' caused me to wonder about the original stupid decision that made a mess of everything." I replied. "Mudman, why was it stupid, anyway?"

"Johnny, earlier I told you that your belief was based upon a false conclusion you reached from having incomplete and erroneous information. You made a stupid decision based upon ignorance, just as did early mankind. It is interesting that both stupid decisions were caused by the exact same flawed information, resulting in the exact same false conclusion! How is that for coincidence?"

"Well now," I said sarcastically, "that is wonderful, Mudman. It's good to see you so self-satisfied, but are you ever going to explain the flaw in our beliefs that resulted in mankind and me making the same stupid decision? I cannot even imagine what that might be and believe me, I have spent a great deal of time thinking about it. This is a huge moment! I'm expecting fireworks and wouldn't be surprised to see thunder and lightning and feel the earth quiver under my feet!"

Mudman was quietly looking at me, without saying anything. I felt a little embarrassed by my outburst and meekly said, "Okay. Okay. Maybe that is a bit of an exaggeration, but I feel like I'm about to learn something from you that not only do I not know, but neither does anyone else. That gets me excited."

Mudman exclaimed, "No kidding! Thunder and lightning and earthquakes! I am thinking about putting this off until another now; that is more excitement than I can take."

Then he got serious and said, "I think you may be disappointed in what you are about to learn Johnny, because it is a simple revelation. You are correct though, it is a truth very few have considered. Understanding it gives you great insight into the Creator and this reality."

Then Mudman simply stated, "The Creator is not God, Little Muddy."

He did not make a big display about it or make any pretense about stating a great revelation. Just an ordinary, everyday piece of information spoken in a 'matter of fact' manner as if it were common knowledge. But it wasn't. "The Creator is not God!" No one knows this, least of all me!

"That can't be right!" I objected, "I don't understand how that can be true, Mudman. All my life, I have read and been told that God and our Creator are the same and now you're saying that the Creator is not God. I'm very interested to hear your reasoning for that conclusion."

Mudman patiently listened to my response to his announcement and waited afterwards, a few minutes, to hear if I had anything more to say. When he saw that I was waiting for an answer, he said softly,

"Tell me Johnny, what was it you discovered about this reality in another now?"

"That this reality is an experiment created by the Creator." I replied.

"So," Mudman stated, "this reality is the result of the curiosity of the Creator?"

"Yes." I agreed.

"Do you believe that God is all powerful, able to do anything, and is everything?"

"Yes, I do."

"Tell me Little Muddy," Mudman pointed at me and demanded, "how is it that a curious creator can be God?"

I was stunned by his question, because I knew the answer. A curious creator is not all knowing and able to do everything. The creator of our reality is not God! I looked at Mudman and saw that he already knew my answer. He stood up and easily lifted me off the downed tree and into the water.

"Go home, Little muddy," he ordered. "You have much about which to think now and I have things that require attending. Remember my young friend, there is only one absolute. We shall meet in another now."

I waded to shore and turned to watch him fade into the fog. It was drizzling rain again, but I walked home slowly, thinking: "Who and what is the creator? And what the heck does, 'there is only one absolute mean', anyway?"

On days like this, there is little to do outside, which was alright with me; I needed time to come to terms with this different idea of God and creator. That was a lot for my young mind to sort out.

Chapter 28 - OOO

Something that became clear to me later on, as I learned more about existence, is that God always does whatever it is that He does and we have nothing to do with it. Think about it, God is thought to be Omnipotent (all powerful), Omniscient (all knowing), and Omnipresent (present everywhere at the same time). Whatever that is, it is certainly beyond definition and giving it a name, like God, Allah, Jehovah, or anything else is pointless. At least that is the way I thought at that time.

The thing is, I never thought of God in that way before, being omnipotent an all. He was always someone we prayed to for help and wanted us to be good so that when we died, we could go to heaven and be with Him. But I never actually thought about God until after I met and began talking with Mudman. That is when I began to understand that God is more than most people know. . . way more! He is described by the three O's I mentioned before, OOO. An interesting way to describe Him, "OOO!" That sounds great, but is not quite applicable.

You know, looking back on that particular now, something happened to my attitude ever since I began learning more about the creator, creation, and the different ways people think about God. Now, I understand. God is not relative to anything, period. It is not accurate to make the claim that God is infinite because He **is** infinity, itself. God does not just love, He **is** love. God is Everything, and Everything is incomparable. God is not just omnipotent, rather He **is** Omnipotence. He is not just omniscient, He **is** Omniscience, itself. He is not just omnipresent, He **is** Omnipresence. All that was discovered by me much later, after much thought and more than a few discussions with Mudman. There is more that will be discovered as the Mudman story unfolds.

That discovery is similar to a cave that you've heard about all your life and been told of its greatness; so, you go to see it. Upon going inside, you are fascinated by the wonder and beauty there and notice there are many other cave entrances inside. You are curious and enter one of those caves, find even more wonderful things and discover even more caves. You enter one of those, and so on and on and on. At some point you will realize the cave cannot be fully explored, its origin cannot be learned, and its reason for being will not be understood in this now; you just accept its existence. You are forever changed by the experience and get on with your life in the realization that life is also a limitless cave, being constantly explored by limited minds.

Here again, I have stepped outside my story timeline. Let's get back there. What was I thinking back then about Mudman's revelation? For a day or two, I didn't know what to think. Actually, I tried not to think. I listened to the radio, played my guitar for hours, and read comic books; I had a large collection of comics. Those activities worked for a while, but quickly wore off. The fact is, more important and interesting questions were begging for my attention and getting it; questions regarding God, Creator, and Created Reality.

I had no idea what to think about God. It is obvious He, or It, is far outside my ability to understand. I cannot even imagine God anymore. Who can imagine something that can do anything and everything? Mudman said that the Creator is not God, leaving the possibility open that God is the Creator, since He can do anything. I don't like the idea of questioning an ultimate thing like God, but why would It create? What would be the point? It already knows everything. Like I said, It is outside my ability to understand. Heck, I don't even know how to talk about God anymore. She? He? It? What is God? I really need to hear what Mudman has to say about it. Who is the creator? Is there a creator? From where did it come? Is it human? What is it? I have no idea anymore. The idea of a creator made sense to me when I saw him as God. Now, everything is a mystery that needs solving. I'm not sure why, but life was better explained and more comfortable from a simple creation point of view.

I believe that we live in a created reality, in fact I am sure of it; but what do I know? Who created it and why? I don't know. The bible says God created everything. Maybe I should just let go, accept the bible's version on faith like everyone else, and get going with my 14 year old life. Not likely. Why not? That is a difficult question. I don't know why I care, but I care.

Chapter 29 - The Mistake

I didn't see Mudman again until the last part of July, mainly because of baseball practice and games. I was also picked for the All Star Team as a pitcher-outfielder, which required extra practice and social plans, like the league dance. It was a hot and humid Sunday when I had a chance to go out in the pirogue. I had my fishing stuff with me, but was more interested in just paddling around in the swamp and doing nothing but thinking. It had been storming all month and to have a sunny day for exploring was great. I could feel that Mudman was around, but then, I always felt that way in the swamp. Over the last week, I had come to terms with the thought that our creator is not God and was close to just accepting things I could not change. Hearing Mudman's thoughts on a few questions that are bothering me is important.

I was less than 200 feet from shore when I spotted Mudman standing next to my hollow tree. He seemed to be waiting for me. I paddled there and pulled my boat onto land. He was glad to see me.

"I have been waiting here young Johnny, watching you paddle around out there; you have learned to handle a pirogue well."

"Thanks Mudman," I replied, "I am really glad to see you."

"Good!" he said, "I pulled a couple of big logs here for us to sit on. I suspect you have done some thinking since last we met."

"It's been hard for me to think much about anything else," I admitted, "and the truth is, I'm confused and unsure how to sort this new information regarding God and the creator of this reality."

"Well now," he replied, "lets see if we can help with that sorting process. I want to warn you though, this is the most difficult subject we have ever discussed and there are many things in regard to God of which I know little to nothing. Where would you like to start?"

"What can you tell me about God, Mudman? You have already made it plain that God is all powerful and capable of doing anything. That being true, God could be the creator if he wanted. I just can't think why He would to do that. I mean, if He is all powerful and can do anything, what would creating a reality do for him?"

Mudman answered, "I actually said God was 'able to do everything', but your question indicates you have really given this subject much thought. God is not the creator of this reality, Little Muddy. The Creator is an individual entity, with his own reasons for doing what he does. Notice that I always refer to the Creator as a male or 'He', but in truth the Creator may be a 'She', an 'It', or a 'Them'. In some ways, the creator is a more fitting example of what most humans believe to be God, which is why they worship him. Pretty much all religions arose from faith in a creator, not faith in God. This is where things get a little complicated, so pay attention and listen closely without interrupting."

"What can I tell you about God?" he repeated my question, and began, "There is a problem with that question, in that it cannot be answered as it does not apply to anything or everything. You might as well ask me to tell you about the square root of your pirogue or about the color of color. Those seem to be non-sensible questions without sensible answers. When attempting a serious discussion about God, one has to realize the futility of discussing something about which no one knows anything. That is a complicated way of saying that I cannot tell you anything about God, nor can anyone else, because no one knows anything about God. I can talk to you about appearances or 'what seems', though."

"God seems to be indefinable." he began. "It appears that God is everything, meaning, **Everything!** It also appears that God is the source of everything and anything, making it incorrect to claim that God does or does not exist because, being everything, God **is** existence itself.

"God appears to be non-intrusive, meaning He does not intrude in your life in any way. God does not punish you, reward you, protect you, heal or harm you; however, He does provide all of those things, and more. It is entirely up to you as to what you receive, good or bad. In other words, whatever good or bad happens to you in this reality, or the next, is of your own doing . . . basically, to your credit and your own fault."

Mudman added, "Another interesting thing for you to consider Little Muddy, is this: All I just told you is something of which the Creator may or may not understand. After all, like everything else, he is a creation, too."

"And that is a great lead-in to the next subject." Mudman continued. "I can hear you now, asking what can I tell you about the Creator. Unlike God, the Creator can be defined and explained. Something you will find nearly impossible to tell anyone is this: *the Creator is not a divine being.* Divine has been defined as, something (or someone) that has the qualities of a god or deity."

Mudman pointed at me and said, "First, you should understand this: There is no such thing as 'a god'; there is only God, and 'having the qualities of God' is mankind's stupid attempt to assign qualities to God. I want to emphasize this Little Muddy: God has no qualities, He **is** qualities! He is everything. Qualities are what creations have. For instance, the Creator has qualities."

Mudman looked at me and paused. "How are you doing, Little Muddy," he asked, "are you absorbing my lecture? I am aware that much of what is being revealed here opposes conventional religious beliefs, some of which you were taught as being truth."

"Yeah Mudman," I answered, "what you are revealing today is opening my mind and closing my mouth. There is no one to tell what I am learning here today. For example, the reason you said ancient mankind turned in the wrong direction and got lost so many millenniums ago has become clear. They began to believe that the creator is God and lived their lives 'lost in ignorance and bound by content', a condition that continues today. A condition that may have become incurable."

"Mudman, before you continue, I have a question. Since the Creator is not divine, can he make mistakes?

Mudman looked at me, then pointed at me and said, "Somehow, I just knew you were going to ask that question! The answer is, I do not know. Is the Creator infallible? I do not know, but a logical conclusion is that since the Creator is a creation, he is fallible. By the way, I like your interpretation of mankind's mistake, but your deduction is wrong because you left something out, something important."

"Something important? What do you mean? What am I missing? Mankind's mistake was to follow the Creator instead of God."

"No, Johnny. Mankind's mistake was much more serious."

"Wha . . .What?" I stammered!

"Think about it a moment. Who was Mankind's God? Who did they worship? Who parted the sea? Who led them into the wilderness? Who fed, protected, and watched over them?"

"Jehovah! That's who it was, Mudman!, wasn't it? Jehovah is the Creator!"

"and therein lies mankind's greatest mistake." murmured Mudman and without saying anything else, glided off into the swamp.

"What happened?" I thought. "Where did he go? What did I say?" I had no idea what was going on. Mudman left and my mind was chock full of questions about Jehovah God being the Creator.

Chapter 30 - Jehovah

Mudman is fascinating; what he actually is or how he came to be is not known, at least to me. Heck, **when** he came to be is a mystery, but it must have been thousands of years ago. Why would I think that? Because he told me about events in history from the viewpoint of someone who was there at that time.

"Written history is not truth; it is interesting fiction loosely based upon the results of events as reported by witnesses and recorded by those who have a dog in the hunt."

Mudman told that to me when I was about thirteen years old. I ran home and wrote it in my notebook because it sounded impressive, but had no idea about that to which he was referring and thought it must have something to do with the bible. We were talking about the bible, Moses, and Jehovah when he looked into the deep swamp for several minutes, then turned and made that statement above about written history.

Several times have I said during the writing of this book that Mudman often gave me more credit for understanding than I deserved. You see, at thirteen, the bible was my moral compass, the word of God and, as such, absolute truth . . . even though I had never read more than two or three excerpts from the New Testament. All that I believed was absorbed from preachers and Sunday school teachers at the churches I attended. I knew about Jehovah God, Adam and Eve, Noah and Moses, but little else. In my mind, Moses looked like Charlton Heston in the Ten Commandments movie. It was at that age that the bible was added to my library of books read.

That was last year. I have learned much more since then. Our conversation began today with me asking Mudman about God and the creator and evolved into my deduction that mankind's creator is Jehovah, to which Mudman said something about that being mankind's greatest mistake and abruptly left. I sat there on the thinking log for about 15 minutes, wondering if he was coming back today. Suddenly he appeared from the swamp, glided over and sat down beside me.

"Little Muddy," he said, "sometimes when we are discussing certain subjects, I tend to overlook the fact you are a very young human."

"Come on, Mudman, I'm not all that young!" I interrupted. "I'm almost fifteen. Anyhow, the way you explain things makes the subjects we talk about easy to understand."

"Well Johnny, our subject today has found its way into a sensitive subject that could have an effect on your life, something for which you may be unprepared at your age. I know you want to talk about why mankind's belief that Jehovah is their creator was such a great mistake. There is much for you to learn about the great Jehovah, God of Moses, David, Solomon and the Jews. Much to learn.

"What is it about Jehovah you would like to discuss, Little Muddy? Jehovah is a big subject."

"I have been reading the bible a lot, here lately, and coming up with more questions than answers."

"Well, let us begin with one question. What is on your mind, my young friend?"

"Who is Jehovah, Mudman? The only person to see him is Moses, but I haven't read the whole bible."

"According to your bible, what did Moses see?"

"Well, actually God told Moses that no man could safely see His face, but let Moses see His backside."

"So, God's backside is less holy than his face. Makes you wonder, doesn't it?"

"A whole lot of things about Jehovah make me wonder, Mudman."

"Well, Jehovah is a wondrous subject. His presence shaped several great religions in this world."

"Mudman, why did God allow Moses to see his backside and not his face?"

"Have you any ideas about that, Little Muddy? I see that you have been thinking again."

"Well, maybe Jehovah thought his appearance might frighten Moses to death."

"Why would Jehovah worry about how he looks, young Johnny? Afterall, He is considered by very many people to be God and God can do everything, even change his appearance."

"Then why was Jehovah concerned about letting Moses see his face, Mudman?"

"Well, maybe he thought his appearance made him look ungodly, young friend."

"But Mudman, that would mean Jehovah is not God! He must have been something else."

"So, there are you, Little Muddy. What else about Jehovah would you like to discuss?"

That was it! Jehovah is not God!

A very surprising conclusion, which Mudman treated as if it were just common knowledge. I was only fourteen, but everyone in my life believed that Jehovah **is** God; I had been taught all of my young life that Jehovah and God were the same being. No one had ever suggested otherwise, until now. Good grief, I even said my prayers to Jehovah God! This was a huge surprise to me; more surprising was that it made sense to me and answered many of my questions concerning the limitations of Jehovah. So, the Old Testament Jehovah was not God. He was someone or something else. So, was Jehovah the Creator or not? Did Mudman know? I had to ask.

"Mudman, was Jehovah the Creator of our reality?"

"No, Johnny. That belief is the great mistake of humanity."

"Why was it a mistake?"

"The deification of Jehovah as the 'One True God' set certain civilizations on a destructive path."

"A destructive path?"

"Yes. A path from which they have yet to turn."

"I don't understand, Mudman; why would Jehovah do that?"

"He just followed his created imperative, Little Muddy; humans deified him, that was their mistake."

"Who is Jehovah? Who was Jehovah? Who is the Creator, Mudman?"

"Who? Who? Who? Sounds like a familiar sound in the swamp. That is not the question you want to ask, my inquisitive friend."

"Huh? What is the question I want to ask, Mudman?"

"That is correct, Little Muddy, 'What?' is the question."

"Uhh, Mudman . . ."

"I am just messing with you, my young friend. You want to know, 'What' is Jehovah?"

"You know what Mudman? That is a better question! That is my question. What is Jehovah?"

"It is a dangerous question; one that is seldom asked and may not be answered without consequences."

"Consequences? What are consequences?"

"Consequences are a lot like results or outcomes of an action, Little Muddy."

"What outcome results from answering questions about Jehovah?"

"Remember, I said that his presence shaped the beliefs of many who worship him."

"So what? Can people's beliefs keep me from asking questions and getting answers?"

"Yes, Little Muddy, when your questions are in regard to Jehovah. For many, he is God."

"What is he, Mudman? Is he a god?"

"There are no gods, young friend; there is only God."

"What is Jehovah, Mudman?"

"Jehovah is an effective legend; one that is taught, written, and believed. He was a great owner of people."

"Owner of people? You mean like a slave owner?"

"Not all owned people are slaves, Little Muddy, most are subjects who trade themselves away."

"Trade themselves? You mean their freedom? For what?

"Security. Power. Food. Humans always seem to trade themselves for some one or some thing in which to believe. Jehovah became something to worship, fear, and give their lives meaning."

"Why is Jehovah great, Mudman? What made him great?"

"His skills in controlling people were extraordinary. He gave them what they wanted in return for their devotion."

"What skills, Mudman? Why was devotion from people so important to Jehovah?"

"He caused the Jews to rely upon him, in return for his protection and provision. Jehovah demanded obedience and severely punished detractors."

"Why Mudman? What did Jehovah get in return?

"Money and power, Little Muddy. Precious metals, earthly goods, and the devotion of his human subjects; he became God to them. Being treated as God is both seductive and addictive. Jehovah came to believe he was the One God of humans and acted accordingly."

"But Jehovah did a lot of good; he freed the Jews from captivity in Egypt and protected them."

"Jehovah slaughtered many Egyptians (men, women and children) and severely damaged Egypt's economy and security in order to own the Jews."

"But the Egyptians were bad people, Mudman. They made slaves of the Jews."

"The Hebrews simply traded one type of master for a different type of master, Little Muddy."

"You make Jehovah look like a bad person, Mudman. He protected the Jews in the wilderness."

"All the while creating their dependence upon him. He made himself their God. He remains such, whether he still exists or not."

"Was Jehovah a bad person, Mudman?"

"When it came to humans, He followed the path of least resistance and acted according to his created nature, Johnny. Other choices were more difficult. You will see in another now."

"But was he a bad person, Mudman?"

"What is a bad person, young friend? Besides, Jehovah was not a person; he was not of this world."

"What? He was not created by the Creator? How can that be?"

"Jehovah was created by the Creator, just not created of this world. He came from elsewhere."

"Elsewhere? He was an alien?"

"He was not of this earth, Little Muddy and was in possession of great power that made him superior to men of earth."

"The Creator put him here. Why, Mudman?"

"No one knows the mind of the Creator, my young friend. Perhaps He was curious to see how humans would react to something they could not explain."

"There is something wrong with that idea, Mudman; I just can't think what it is right now."

"Have you additional questions, Little Muddy?"

"I don't know; my mind is full and needs time to think."

"Until another now, then."

Mudman sat there and watched me leave for home. I looked back to watch him glide into the swamp, but he wasn't there. He left me with a lot about which to think, though. . . as always.

Chapter 31 - Ricky and Rocky

Mudman was sitting by my boat the next day when I walked down to the swamp; I was hoping to see him as a few questions were floating around in my mind, begging to be answered.

"Good morning, Mudman; I was hoping you would be here"

"Very happy to see you as well, Johnny. I am always here."

"I have been thinking about what I learned from you yesterday and have a question."

"There is no 'yesterday', Little Muddy, only now. Do you want to talk about 'now'? You are obviously having difficulty absorbing the concept."

"No. Well yes, I do, just not at this moment. Mudman, I have a different question."

"Why am I not surprised?"

"Well, Mudman, your talks create questions."

"I know what you are going to ask, Little Muddy."

"So Mudman, you're a mind reader afterall?"

"No, but I can often read you, my young friend."

"You don't have any idea what I am going to ask, Mudman!"

"You want to know who created the Creator."

"How do you do that? How did you know?

"It was the logical next question, Little Muddy."

"What is the answer, Mudman?"

"I do not know the answer, young friend;" he confessed, "however, it does seem likely this reality of ours is not the first of its kind, nor is our Creator the first or only creator of realities."

"C'mon Mudman, no one is going to believe that!" I objected. "Multiple creators and realities sounds like something I read in my 'Out of this World' comic books."

Mudman advised, "That is an excellent reason keep our conversation to yourself until such time the world begins to understand the sense of it. It is not logical to believe that only one reality has ever been created. It is more logical to believe that our reality is one of very many creations."

I argued, "Our world has difficulty understanding the sense of one creation, Mudman, and the idea of multiple creators will make human's heads explode! To be honest, the idea of many created realities is difficult for me to accept."

Mudman exclaimed, "Exploding human heads! That is a great display of imagination. Did you read that in one of your comics, Little Muddy? They sound exciting! I'm going to have to absorb some of those books."

He continued, "Seriously though, the concept of multiple created realities is interesting, do you not think? Particularly since we exist in one. We should talk about it."

"Sounds like it will take an awful long 'now' to cover that subject, Mudman."

"What are your thoughts about creation, Johnny?"

"My first thought is the bible reveals that God created everything."

"Is that your belief, Johnny?"

"No, the explanation that God **is** everything makes sense to me."

"That alone puts you in rare company. What else is on your mind, young friend?"

"My second thought is that our creator might be a human. A very smart human."

"How did you come to that way of thinking?"

"It makes sense that the creator would create mankind in his image, Mudman."

"Do you have thoughts about why the creator wanted to create this reality, Johnny?"

"Yes, but I don't know what his reality is like. Maybe for pay, or power, or curiosity."

"A key question here, Johnny. Which do you believe humans worship, God or Creator?"

"Creator. In their defense, humans believe their creator is God."

"Johnny, do you see anything wrong with worshiping the creator as God?"

"You know what, Mudman? Worshiping the creator seems to work for humans. So, no."

"Whom do you worship, Johnny?" Mudman asked gently.

"I'm not really sure, Mudman." I replied. "My whole life, as much as I can remember, has been spent believing the creator to be Jesus or God, but that belief never felt right; there are just too many unanswered questions with that way of thinking and now that I have come to believe the creator may be an intelligent human, the thought of worshiping him is not an option. I do talk with someone I believe to be a type of guardian angel, but I have no way of knowing if it exists, or not"

"Mudman declared, "So, you believe in God and angels."

"Mudman, this is a hard subject about which to talk. I believe God is everything, but I'm not sure that I believe **in** God. There is something though, that listens to me. I talk with it. It never talks back, but it is always with me. That's why I say it's a type of guardian angel, kind of like you are when I'm in the swamp."

Mudman looked at me sitting there on a log, then stood up, walked to the shallows and glided out into the swamp. I watched him, not understanding why he was leaving. He stopped just short of the trees and stood there. If I had not been watching him, he would be invisible out there.

"Whatcha lookin' at Johnny?" Rocky hollered.

I looked away from Mudman and saw my two brothers running to me, laughing. They were holding string and raw bacon. Ricky promptly informed me, "Momma said we could go crawfishing as long as you went along, so we got our stuff and found you. Come on, let's go!"

"Wait a minute, you two," I warned, "does momma know you're with me? You're not supposed to be near the swamp by yourselves."

"Well, uh, no," Rocky admitted, "momma told us to wait until you got home, but we couldn't wait any longer and went lookin' 'til we found you."

"Yeah," said Ricky, "I don't need no babysitter noways, Johnny! I know how to catch crawfish all by myself 'cause I've been fishing with you before."

My brothers talked like a couple of country hicks. Grandma was rubbing off on them. I made a mental note to talk to momma about that. I really loved my grandma and enjoyed our conversations, but her country way of talking was infectious.

Whatcha doing anyway, Johnny?" interrupted Rocky, "I ain't never been down here before. Is that your boat? Can we ride in it? I ain't never been out in the swamp, Johnny. Can we go now? Please?"

How Rocky was able to get all that out in one breath is a mystery, but I know what he's feeling. The swamp is fascinating. My talk with Mudman would have to be postponed; my brothers wanted a boat ride.

I pushed the pirogue into the water and told them to get in. Ricky in the front and Rocky in the middle, then me. They were excited to go in the swamp. I paddled them just outside the shallows, in and out of trees, through limbs with hanging moss, and showed them birds, turtles and fish they had never before seen. My young brothers enjoyed a 30 minute ride through my version of paradise. That was the upside; the downside being their total inability to keep their adventure a secret. The moment the pirogue nosed to shore, they were off and running.

Yeah, they told momma that I took them for a ride in my boat, but it didn't turn out anything like expected. She asked if they had fun and told them to thank their brother for the boat ride. Momma didn't make a big deal out of it and my brothers, seeing her mild reaction, didn't either.

Momma had the mandatory talk with me and again reminded me to look after my brothers. Turns out she knew about my ventures into the swamp and was okay with my fishing there. Strange, isn't it? Sometimes things just work out in your favor, but just maybe there are other forces at work, as well. I was happy with this result, though.

Chapter 32 - Created Equal

The next day, when I went down to check on my boat, Mudman was already there, out sitting on the old tree in the swamp. I was really glad to see him. We never did finish our conversation yesterday because he left without saying anything; however, the questions I asked him were mostly answered anyway. The subjects of God, Creator and creations are almost too sensitive to talk about. That is probably the reason most people avoid talking about them.

Imagine telling anyone that the Creator mankind has worshiped for millenniums is not God or that the God of the Old Testament is not God. No! Forget that! Don't imagine that! Keep that a secret and don't talk about it. That's what I'm going to do. I will think about it often, though and talk with Mudman.

"Anyway," I said under my breath, "what difference does it make who people worship as long a their faith produces good results?"

"Would you like to think that statement through a bit before casting it into cement, Little Muddy?" I turned and saw Mudman standing behind me; he sure glides quietly through the water, with no waves.

"Oh, hi Mudman." I stammered. "You caught me talking out loud to myself. Sorry about that, but the idea of mankind worshiping our creator as God for thousands of years is crowding my mind."

"Crowding your mind, Little Muddy?" exclaimed Mudman. "I have not heard that reference before; I like it! From where did it come?"

"Heck Mudman," I admitted, "I don't know; you caught me off guard and I just blurted it out."

Mudman laughed, "You are adding new terms and words to the language, Little Muddy; 'off guard' and 'blurted' are new to me! Did you make them up? You are good at doing that, you know."

"No Mudman," I replied, "I didn't invent anything; lots of people use those words when talking." Then I changed the subject back to my earlier comment. "Why did you suggest that my comment about faith should be thought through a little more."

Mudman, after a brief hesitation, answered, "Little Muddy, your assumption that it makes no difference who one worships is troublesome. How you arrived at that thought is interesting to me. What caused you to come to that conclusion?"

"Frustration." I confessed.

"Little Muddy, are you frustrated by an inability to understand that about which we have been talking in regard to God and the creator? In these discussions, beliefs you have held all your life have been challenged. Such information would frustrate and even anger many people in your society. We can talk about those feelings if you like."

Mudman seemed concerned about me, but he had the reason for my frustration all wrong. I was getting tired of standing and went over to my boat, got in, and sat down. How do I explain my feelings to him? How do I admit surrendering to wrong, because it appears impossible to make right?

"On the contrary, Mudman," I began, "my frustration is a result of concluding that your explanation of God and creator is sensible. Understanding that the creator is not God means that all who have worshiped the creator since ancient times have been, and are, worshiping a false god. It frustrates me that this wrong cannot be righted, but then I ask myself why worshiping a false god is wrong, anyway. All the religions that grew from worshiping the creator seem to be good for the world; so, maybe who you worship is less important than faith. You know, it is written that Jesus said faith moves mountains; however, I sometimes wonder how Jesus is explained, too."

"Talk about frustrating, Little Muddy, your way of reasoning your way through complex philosophical questions is more than interesting; it also is frustrating."

I could sense that Mudman was getting into his teaching mode, so I leaned back in my boat and got comfortable. That is my listening mode.

"Little Muddy," he began, "everything 'crowding' that mind of yours right now is a result of realizing that the creator is not God. That understanding has weakened your entire belief structure and caused you to think less of our Creator. You have not given the creation of this reality and its Creator the reverence due."

"But Mudman," I objected, "the creator is himself a creation, making him no different than us! How does he deserve reverence?"

Mudman pointed at me and softly stated, "Remember, Little Muddy, He created you and is the reason you exist."

Wow! Mudman just threw a bucket of ice water on my mind! I stood up in the boat, my mind racing. Why did that not occur to me? I knew it all the time but, for some reason it did not register.

I looked at Mudman, pointed at him and said, "Thank you, I needed that."

He laughed and commented, "Little Muddy, you remind me of me." and laughed again. Then he walked to the side of the pirogue and sat down facing me. "What is on your mind, Johnny?"

"Mudman, is our Creator divine?"

"No."

"Is he a great Creator?"

"He is that and more, Little Muddy."

"Does he know that I don't worship him?"

"No. He is just a creator, not all knowing."

"Does he know that we think about him?"

"I suppose he wonders the same thing about us."

"Does he answer prayers, Mudman?"

"Prayers are answered with faith, Little Muddy, not by others."

"Faith in the Creator or faith in God?"

"Faith in anything; so, take care where your faith is placed."

"That sounds like a riddle, Mudman."

"Well, then think about it Little Muddy and be careful where, or in whom, you place your faith."

"Mudman, is a created reality an illusion?"

"Aha! Young friend, you have asked a near ultimate question."

"Can a created reality be explained?"

"Yes and yes; however, all is based upon conjecture."

"C'mon Mudman, is that one of your 'made-up' words? What does 'conjecture' even mean?

"An opinion or conclusion formed on the basis of incomplete information, meaning no one knows."

"What do you believe about reality, Mudman?"

"I am not human, Little Muddy; faith does not apply to me."

"What is reality, Mudman?"

"God is reality."

"Talk about being frustrated, Mudman, 'God is reality' is a frustrating term!"

"God is 'frustration' itself, Little Muddy. To understand He is everything is ultimate."

"I don't understand, Mudman."

"That will not always be so, my young friend, but you have concerns; how can I help?"

"What happens to humans in this creation when they die, Mudman?"

"No one here knows the answer to that question, Little Muddy, and everyone desires to know." he answered.

"I'm pretty sure you have an idea, Mudman." I argued.

"Well Johnny, if your path is guided by reason, you will likely reach a reasonable destination." he stated and added, "Think about it this way,

#1 God is Everything,

#2 the Creator is a creation.

#3 the Creator created our reality.

Those are three ways one begins the journey. It is important to understand that our creation was **of** God, **by** the Creator. Yes Johnny, you were created **of** God; as such, you are an immortal part of Everything, meaning you are part of God and will always be part of God."

Mudman continued, "Something very important follows this conclusion Johnny, because all action results in consequences. All in this reality are created of God. What part of everything they will ultimately occupy is a consequence of their existence here. Understand this, every human is personally responsible for what happens to him in this existence and the next. Every human determines his own rightful place in Everything by the life he lives in this creation. That being the case, is it not evident that a life of goodness (ethics, morals, and kindness) should be taught, learned, and lived by every human? Think about this, terrible places are also included in Everything, meaning they are of God as well; however, they are miserable places to exist. That is the wonderful part of being a human; you choose your place in Everything by the choices you make here, in this reality. You choose!"

"Wow!" I exclaimed. "Mudman, you sure have a way about you. Who else can answer an unanswerable question and make an impossible answer sound reasonable? The destination reached with your reasonable explanation explains everything. Now you have me thinking that you do understand what happens to humans in this creation when they die. Thank you Mudman. You answered my question."

"You are welcome, Little Muddy." he replied. "Any other questions today?"

"Only a few hundred," I answered, "Nothing you can't handle."

He laughed and replied, "Shall we begin with one? What is on your mind?"

"Mudman, Thomas Jefferson wrote that all men are created equal, but that is not true; people are not created equal because some have more or less than others. Some are smart and some are stupid, some are pretty and some are not, some are strong and some are weak. There are many other examples of the inequality of humans, but you know what I mean. How can people be considered to be created equal when it is obvious they are not?"

I could see that Mudman was thinking how to answer in a way that I could understand. I have complained to him often that some of his explanations are 'over my head' and need to be brought down to my level. That very thing is evident when I talk to my brothers. I can tell by the blank look in their eyes that something I just told them did not register in their minds or was beyond their ability to understand. Mudman was now considering how to communicate at my level. Sometimes he assumes I am smarter than I am.

"Little Muddy, that is a relative question based entirely upon how one defines 'equal'. We have talked of this in another now. Equal is interpreted by many humans as being, 'the same as' something or someone else, which is well, stupid. Being 'equal to' and 'the same as' have different meanings that I do not plan to discuss at this time because it is my belief you are already aware of the difference."

Mudman continued, "Allow me to begin by saying emphatically that all humans **are** created equal because they are created of God, meaning they are a part of everything. A denial of that truth by any or all humans is foolish, unreasonable, and ridiculous."

I broke in, pointed at him and said, "Why don't you just say what you really mean, Mudman. Don't hold anything back!"

Mudman glared at me briefly, then smiled and stated, "I am trying to use words and definitions that are within the understanding of a young, aspiring comedian and with his permission, I shall continue."

And continue he did, "Anything judged by a creation as an example of inequality is the result of that creation's ignorance of creation and its creator."

Mudman explained, "Humans, generally, are unaware they are created beings; they are either ignorant of that fact or they are stupid and cannot know any better. Either way, very many humans seem not to be aware of their creator. It is important you understand a truth, Little Muddy: humans who are unaware of, or do not accept, the idea of creation are not necessarily good or bad people. Good or bad among humans is determined by something entirely different. I should mention this as well, all humans are stupid and ignorant to some extent. That is a created directive applied to human design by the Creator, as is learning. All creatures are created with a relative ability to learn, without which creation would have no reason for being; meaning, of course, that all creatures do not have the same ability to learn.

"Now, back to the question of equality. Little Muddy, I affirm that the written statement 'all men are created equal', is true. All humans are created equal is more fitting, as some of you humans are sensitive to gender designations. I can see by your expression that you question that declaration, but consider this truth before objecting: It cannot be stressed enough that humans are created of God, by the Creator, which makes all humans equal, not to each other, but 'in the eyes' of God. However, no two or more humans are created the same; there are many differences between individuals as well as between genders and races. All differences are judged by humans as to whether a particular difference is more advantageous to one than to another. It is important you realize the Creator does not create human judgment, He observes it, and very possibly learns from it. When a human observes differences between himself and another, he makes judgments based upon that observation. Those judgments result from created imperatives we have already discussed, along with teachings, and experience."

"Many common differences among humans are universally understood as good things and are accepted as such. Some uncommon differences are understood as existing and as a result, tolerated by most. Some differences are not tolerated, especially those between cultures. The human response to all differences existing among people in this creation is uniquely human and results from their personal prejudices and the created ability to choose."

"So, little Muddy, when you perceive that a person, or race, has qualities that result in an advantage over others lacking those qualities, you naturally believe something is wrong because people are not equal. You overlook the obvious because it is something of which you do not approve. People were not created to be equal to each other, Little Muddy; there is little to be learned from a creation where everyone is equal. Humans are created different from each other for the purpose of observing whether they will learn to live in harmony, despite their differences, or not. Presently humanity is failing, in a large part due to people's inability to adjust to the lack of equality among them. What is most destructive, is forced equality, which always results in division and often leads to violence. Because of their design, it is the human way."

"Something to understand is, the effort to achieve equality among humans is considered to be a noble quest; however, neither is it noble, nor is it smart or good. Such a quest is futile. As long as diversity exists, inequality exists. Harmony will only be achieved when humanity accepts and peacefully adapts to differences. A highly unlikely occurrence. Well, Little Muddy, are you keeping up? There is much to absorb here."

"Thank you Mudman," I said, "for explaining equality. The saying, 'All men are created equal' has recently become a problem for me to understand because it seems clear that all men are **not** created equal. Now, I understand. You know something else Mudman? Understanding that God is everything explains so many of my questions that I hardly know what to ask anymore. The thought that every human determines his own place in Everything by his own actions in this reality is outstanding in its fairness. That means that no one ever gets away with anything, good or bad, and each person is responsible for his choices. Everyone ultimately winds up where they belong in Everything."

"Mudman," I continued, "the 'Everything' concept answers questions about life, death, heaven, hell, and all in between. God, being everything, is all inclusive. A terrible person, after dying, will find himself in a terrible place in keeping with his choices and the life he lived. That terrible place is a part of God because God is everything, and that person is constantly reminded that he put himself there. Everyone receives a reward in keeping with his moral and ethical merits. That is justice. One's station in life counts for nothing, no matter how high or how low; rather, his place in Everything is determined by how he lived his life. A good or bad result in life means nothing; it is what you do that determines your value in Everything."

Mudman listened to me talk about what he had been teaching and sat there across from me, saying nothing. He stood up and, like he does sometimes, glided out into the swamp and stood there, blending with his surroundings. Always makes me believe that he is in deep thought about something. After a few minutes, Mudman returned and sat down in front of me again.

"Johnny," he began, "your way of explaining things told you is interesting, not only because of accuracy, but it indicates how well you listen. However, I have a question to ask you. Do you believe that which I tell you?"

"Yes." I answered.

"Well young Johnny," he said, "that concerns me, in that you may not be understanding what I teach, in the correct light."

"Correct light?" I questioned.

"You realize Johnny, all I have told you is an attempt to reasonably explain the unknowable based upon reasonable assumptions. No one **knows** anything in this created reality because knowledge is absent here. Faith and choice were created into our reality, though. Humans can and do choose to believe or not believe anything or everything. All created reality is most certainly an illusion. It is perceived as real by creations because they are in it. For creations, this reality is as real as anything can possibly be; however, from our Creator's point of view, our created reality is simply an experiment to determine how mankind, whom he created as sentient beings, will manage their existence, given the imperatives installed in his created world.

One can only imagine what such a creator thinks when observing the results of his creation; it is unlikely, though, that he thinks of us as anything other than insignificant objects of interest, created for the specific purpose of gaining an insight into probabilities regarding the future of his own reality, such as it might be. It is reasonable to wonder if our creator realizes that he too is likely a creation."

"Mudman," I replied, "The idea that this reality of ours may be an experiment to evaluate an unknown outcome is something acceptable to me. I have done such experiments myself with ants, snakes, and fish; but, I am struggling with the idea that no one in our world knows anything. How can that be true? Everyone believes they know something; many even believe they know more than others. The thought that knowledge is absent from our reality doesn't make sense."

"Did you hear what you just said, Johnny? You stated that everyone **believes** they know, not **knows** they know, something. That is because your belief in knowledge is relative, Johnny. "When you strongly believe something, you are convinced you know something and when you 'kind of' believe something, you think you 'kind of' know something. Knowledge, if such a thing exists somewhere, is not relative; 'kind of' knowing is not knowledge, nor is strongly believing something."

"Okay Mudman, let's suppose there is no knowledge in this reality; why would the creator not include the 'ability to know' in his creation?"

"Because it is not in a creator's best interests for his creation to have knowledge, Little Muddy." he replied. "You will recall, in your bible, that the Creator was so displeased with his two human creations for eating of the Tree of Knowledge of Good and Evil that He banished both of them from Paradise. Why did the Creator do that? 'The man has now become like one of us, knowing good and evil' is what the Creator said according to your biblical record. That could not be tolerated! The Creator then banished Adam and Eve from Eden and blocked their access to the Tree of Life. In that action, you see the Creator recognizing the danger in having his creations not only having knowledge, but also gaining access to immortality as well. He took steps to prevent that from happening."

"I still don't see what is wrong with my having knowledge, Mudman." I replied. "I want to know things. Heck, I want to know everything!"

"What is something you would like to know, Little Muddy?" he asked.

Well, I should have seen that coming. Mudman asked me a question I was not prepared to answer. I felt stupid, because he was only responding to my comments; so, the question was my fault. There was only one way for me to answer: truthfully.

I replied, "I don't know what I would like to know, Mudman; I need time to think about that. Anyway, if knowledge is not present in this reality, how am I supposed to know what I want to know?"

Mudman thought a moment and stated, "I wonder if you could repeat that if I asked? However, I will not ask. Anyway, I have an idea what it is you want to know."

Here we go again! Mudman is saying that he knows what I am thinking, even if I don't remember thinking it. He baited the hook and knows I'm going to snap at it.

"Okay Mudman," I muttered, "I'll bite. What is it you believe I want to know?"

He smiled and said, "Johnny, this is too easy; you must be getting tired. You have already asked what you want to know and I gave you a reasonable answer based upon available evidence and logic; but such an answer is not knowledge. You are curious about life and death, my young friend. 'Something' or 'nothing' is your concern. If you could know one thing, it would be this: What happens to humans in this reality when they die?"

I didn't say anything, but you know something? That is exactly what I want to know! Mudman is right; he understands me. I just remained quiet and waited for his explanation.

When he continued, he asked, "Johnny, what would humans do with knowledge? Let us suppose people found out that that all created humans go to heaven? No matter what they do in this reality, they go to heaven when they die. What would be the result of no one having any fear of dying? Everyone goes to heaven, no matter what. What would be the purpose of life? You think maybe people would just opt out and go to a better place than this without penalty? Millions of them? Billions? Do you believe that type of knowledge would make people more likely to resist their evil nature and embrace goodness? Or would they just accept evil? Why not? Both of those actions result in the same outcome; everyone goes to heaven."

Mudman went on supposing, "Suppose people found out that created humans were just illusions, like a mirage, and upon dying just ceased to exist? What would that do to religion in the world? Why would people need to be moral, ethical or even civilized? They were never real and never really existed in the first place. Do you actually believe people could handle such knowledge, or any knowledge, for that matter? Knowledge in the hands of a creation or creations is a threat to creators. That is why the Creator of the Old Testament banished and cursed his 'enlightened creations' from Eden and forbade them access to the Tree of Life. He pretty much said, 'Adam and Eve are a threat to us!' Us? Makes you wonder who 'us' is, does it not?"

"Consider this a truth, Little Muddy," he advised, 'to know' is not included in any creation, individual or reality, because 'to know' is the exclusive domain of God. Humans were given something truly remarkable, though. They were created with the ability to believe, in which very great power resides; power that all humans possess, but of which very few are aware. You are becoming aware, Johnny. See that you do not abuse it."

You may remember me mentioning that Mudman often gives me more credit for understanding than I deserve; this is another of those times. Besides, I'm not sure how this 'faith thing' works anyway. But his statement brought questions to my mind.

So I asked, "What about you, Mudman? Were you created with the ability to believe? Do you believe anything?" I threw what I thought were tough questions at him and was eager to hear his answers.

Mudman didn't even have to think about answers; he simply said, "No, Little Muddy; I was created 'to be'. Faith does not apply to me."

I have mentioned before that Mudman occasionally 'yanks my chain' to get my attention or divert me to another subject more appealing to him. His answer about being 'created to be' and 'faith does not apply' was tempting, but I was intent on keeping my focus on the current subject this time. So, I asked him, "Mudman, how long have you 'been'?"

He stood up and glanced out into the swamp for a moment before replying, "Little Muddy, you have guided our conversation into an area where answers to your questions cannot give you satisfaction. As an example, the answer to that question is, 'your question does not apply to me'. Are you satisfied?"

"No." I admitted. "I am interested in knowing how long you have existed, though. Do you know how long you have existed, Mudman?"

"No, my young friend; I know nothing about that. Your term 'existed' does not apply to me. Nothing you will ask applies to me. Are you satisfied?" he asked again.

"Not yet, Mudman." I replied. "When were you created?"

"Now." was his answer, and he again asked, "Are you satisfied?"

Mudman was right about his answers to my questions being unsatisfactory. This could go on for hours and wind up nowhere. I was not satisfied, but this conversation wasn't going anywhere and had to end now; pretty much the place where it started. I closed my eyes for a moment and realized I was mentally drained. It was time to go home, rest, and return in another now.

"No Mudman," I replied, "I'm not satisfied, but I accept what is, is. Grandma once said that talking with me tires her out. Sometimes you do that to me. I learned a lot today, more than could have been expected. I have more to think about than I can think about. Thank you for that, but I'm worn out now and need to go home and think."

He did not respond. "Mudman? Mudman!" He was gone. I figured he was ready to call it a day, too. "I'm never going to get the hang of this doggone 'now' thing." I said under my breath and turned for home. I heard laughter coming from the swamp, but wasn't going to give him the satisfaction of letting on that I did. I didn't look back, but I went home laughing, too.

Chapter 33 - Parfait's Eden

There is something about my swamp that is difficult for me to accurately describe. I have great love for my swamp. I often use the word "my" when talking about this swamp, but that is not accurate; it does not belong to me. So, why do I have such great affection for a place? I've not figured that out, yet. One explanation to consider is that I belong to the swamp. Is it reasonable for me, or anyone, to feel that they belong to a place? I don't know, but it sure isn't anything for me to talk about with anyone else.

When I consider the swamp in the most objective way possible, it is clear that the things I do here are not "normal" when considered from the perspective of everyone I know. All anyone has to do to understand the danger here is to visit, but very few do so. Why do you suppose that is? (Mudman would not approve of that sentence.) It is because the swamp looks, feels, smells, and sounds menacing right off the bat! Meaning as soon as you get here. Virtually no one feels comfortable here in the swamp. One experience with mosquitoes and deer flies in the swamp is enough to keep most people away for the rest of their lives. The humidity and suffocating heat eliminates a large part of the human population from visiting. Those things are problems to be suffered before even setting one foot into the black water and mud of the swamp! That is unfortunate, because the mystery and wonder of the remarkable beauty here cannot be seen or experienced from shore. Yeah, the places I go and things I do in the swamp are not "normal" from a certain point of view. It must be admitted though, I like the fact few people come here; I don't want them here. Humanity destroys.

A wondrous, abundant life exists in the deep swamp, particularly northwest of where I enter. Life exists there, which few people imagine. The various colors of birds, fish, and reptiles are majestic, so as to bring tears to your eyes when looked upon. My first visit to that place was the result of foolishness.

The danger of going into the swamp at night or on foggy days has been mentioned before in this story, but of the two, fog is the most confusing. Going out at night is not uncommon for alligator hunters or people who are hunting frogs. There are some huge bullfrogs in the swamp that are almost never seen during the day; they are my reason for going out at night. Bullfrogs make for a good meal; momma and grandma really like fried frog legs. But I have a headlight and stay close to shore when hunting frogs at night, maybe 20 yards out, or so. Plenty of good hunting there, with little to worry about except cottonmouths. The big gators seem to stay away from my part of the swamp; little ones are seen every now and then, but not often. However, anytime baby gators are seen, day or night, I leave; because, their mama is around somewhere and there is no sense taking chances with her. But like I said before, for some reason known only to them, gators pretty much stick to their part of the swamp and are seldom seen this close in. I sometimes wonder if Mudman has something to do with that.

Anyway, the swamp is somewhat spooky at night and can be dangerous, making it important to be familiar with the area being hunted when going there. The truth is, the same thing can be said about everywhere one goes in this world. Day or night, I am comfortable in the swamp; I feel safe there. No people about of which to be concerned, only creatures of the swamp. Dangerous? Sure, without a doubt; but, not created with an evil nature.

Fog in the swamp, like fog everywhere, has an effect on perception that is confusing. When inside a thick fog, reality is surreal; your senses give you information that your reason says is false. It is easy to make stupid decisions or panic in a foggy swamp because trees, logs, and places of which you are familiar show up where they are not supposed to be, causing your brain to fog up. It may seem crazy, but often the best thing to do, is nothing. Just lay down in your boat or find a sitting place and stay put until your brain fog, or the actual fog, clears; thereby allowing you to reason your way out, or back.

Okay, back to my discovery of 'Parfait's Eden', a self serving name given to a special place in the swamp as a tribute to my ego. Remember, I was only a teenager at the time and didn't know any better. Anyway, in the few the times I went there, no human life was ever seen; so, as far as I was concerned, Parfait's Eden was mine. Later, when I told Mudman about my discovery of Parfait's Eden, he was amused.

"So," he commented, "now there is another place in the swamp you consider yours! Before long, you will be taking over the whole place and naming it 'Little Muddy Swamp'. Your young ego knows no bounds!" Then he laughed and smudged my face with mud. I laughed, too. It was plain he knew about my secret place. He knows everything about the swamp.

As I was saying, I discovered that place in the swamp by accident through foolishness. I took my pirogue out one foggy Sunday morning in June, not really worried about the fog because that condition was common on swamp mornings and usually burned off by noon. I leaned back in my pirogue for a little while, thinking about waiting for the fog to clear. It had rained Saturday and fishing was expected to be productive; so, I pushed my boat into the water and paddled out past where I normally fish and decided to try my luck a little further west than usual. I rarely went that way and was curious about the area. The fog was thicker than expected and pretty soon it became evident that the tip of my boat could not be seen. That was not something to worry much about, since I was familiar with the swamp there and knew my way around blindfolded.

Well, I should have put on a blindfold, because everything my sight told me was wrong. I could not see trees, water, anything. Stupid things were happening, too! A blurred tree on my right, one moment, was on my left in the next moment. The water on one side of my pirogue was higher than on the other side. I knew in my mind that something like that could not be true, but my sight told me otherwise. Laying down in the boat right about then and taking a nap would have been wise, but I didn't. Believing my boat was about to tip one way, I leaned the other way and tumbled out of the darn thing, pushing it away from me in the process. When I came up out of the water, I had a serious problem; I couldn't see my pirogue, or anything else for that matter; all I had was the paddle which I was holding while falling out. The fog was too thick. I was standing in water up to my chest, looking around for my boat, having no idea in which direction it had been pushed, nor which direction was where. On top of that, this was snake and gator territory and fog did not limit them.

There was one good thing about falling into the water; my mind was clear. I had not yet moved because movement in water creates waves and waves are a form of descriptive communication, whether they be sound, light, or water waves and I didn't want to advertise my exact position to anything out here; besides, which way was the right way to go? "Think, Johnny." I told myself. "Mudman taught you to survive here."

While standing there, unmoving, I felt a current around my legs. Alligator! My heart began racing and I couldn't breathe right; panic was rising in my chest! I couldn't see or think and every instinct told me to run! Yeah right, run. Stupid! Then something Mudman told me more than a few times entered my mind,

"Panic kills in the swamp, Little Muddy." he often advised. That movement around my legs was likely just a large fish or turtle; the truth is, it might even have been my imagination running away with itself.

I realized thinking about alligators and cottonmouths being next to me right now was unproductive and only created panic. Mudman taught me many times about the wisdom of "Now". There was nothing I could do now about critters over which I had little control; I only had control over me. Right now it was necessary to focus on a plan to deal with my current problem. Getting out of the water and locating my boat was my goal, which begins by choosing a direction to move in this fog. Standing chest deep in this swamp until the fog cleared was out of the question; it might be hours before it cleared enough to see well and 'here' is dangerous. It occurred to me that my rising panic was gone; concentrating on what needed to be done had calmed my mind.

What to do first was running through my head. I was heading west when I fell from the right side of the boat, which didn't help because when I surfaced, there was no way of determining which way I was facing. A better perspective than the current one was necessary; I needed to get out of the water and a tree was my best option. Afterall, I was in a forest of sorts, with trees all around, probably even one close by. I couldn't see as far as two feet in front of me, but I could hear and feel. My paddle would allow me to increase my perimeter by holding it out and turning in a circle. I might not be able to see out, but I could feel out! While holding the paddle straight out in front of me, I slowly turned to the left in a complete circle. Nothing! The fog was getting into my brain again, filling my mind with a lot of things that could go wrong with my plan, but I pushed them away, slowly waded four steps forward and held the paddle out to my right. My intent was to move my paddle from my right in a semi-circle to my left. A few seconds after starting, the paddle hit what felt like a tree. I was excited and waded toward what turned out to be a cypress tree holding a present for me; my boat was lodged against it floating high in the water! My delight in finding my pirogue cannot be described! I put my paddle inside it, grabbed a limb of the tree and climbed in. Very few times in my life have I been as happy as I was at that moment, sitting there in my boat, surrounded by thick fog, lost in the swamp and feeling quite wonderful! Life is great.

Although it seemed longer, I was only in the water a little over ten minutes. Now a decision had to be made; should I continue looking for a new fishing hole or give up and go home? The fog was still very thick, making going back to shore a guess. It was still morning and the fog was sure to lessen as the day progressed, so I decided to just stay where I was and maybe try fishing there until the fog lifted. My usual supply of water and sandwiches were intact, along with my hatchet which I used to mark the tree.

While preparing to start fishing and thinking about being lost, I had a thought. Before I fell from the boat, I was paddling west. I fell out on the right side, pushing the boat away from me in the process. That means that I pushed the boat southward. When I found the boat, it was lodged against the cypress tree on what would be the north side. My boat was facing west when I found it, meaning that shore is to my left right now! All I had to do was paddle that direction, slow and steady, marking my way as I went. I didn't care where I came to shore, because finding my way back toward home would be easy once I was in the shallows. I was feeling confident again, but I had made a foolish mistake; actually, I made two foolish mistakes. Number #1 was not staying where I was until the fog lifted. Number #2 was not thinking my reasoning process through before taking action.

What actually happened when I fell from the boat and shoved it away from me was something I should have considered. I was sitting in the back of the boat and fell out from there, pushing on the back of it in the process of falling and turning my pirogue north. When I found it against the tree, it was facing north, not west. So when I slowly and steadily began paddling to my left, I was heading west instead of south. My saving grace was stopping and marking my way on trees as I paddled through the fog.

I must have continued on for at least 30 minutes before realizing something was wrong. Shore should have been reached by now. I stopped and laid the paddle down, wondering how I could have gotten my directions so wrong. There was a continuous singing of birds, but I couldn't see them. The fog was still heavy, but obviously beginning to clear; the nose of my boat was now visible and so was the water around it. Another thing noticeable was the clear water; I could see to the bottom of the swamp! "Where am I?" was the question running through my mind; I didn't have any idea. I sat there in my boat, watching the fog turn into a mist settling across the water. A small group of singing little birds were flitting in, out and among the branches of a tree growing in the water next to my boat. Some were even perching on my boat, completely unafraid! They were totally yellow, creating a beautiful contrast to the green leaves of the tree. "This is a paradise in the swamp." I thought to myself. Discovered by accident, through foolishness. That is the story of how I discovered "Parfait's Eden".

It was still early morning and I paddled around the place, seeing things I find difficult to talk about because, well, just because. I do not even today know how to write about Eden. The water was deep there and clear to the bottom. This sounds crazy, but flowering plants were randomly growing on the bottom of the swamp. The most colorful turtles and fish ever observed live there. I say that because it is difficult to imagine such uncommon beauty being anywhere else. A small flock of wild ducks flew in and settled on the water, then swam up to my boat as if wondering what I was doing there. I couldn't stand it any longer and slipped out of my clothes and into the cool water just to be a part of the place. After swimming and floating there for,

I don't know how long, I dove to the bottom, picked a flower from one of the plants, swam back, put it my pirogue and got in myself. Fishing there never crossed my mind. I was tired and leaned against the back of my boat, watching the sun flicker in and out of the leaves in the tree above me. There are few times in my life I have been so content and more at peace than at that moment. I wanted to stay there and drifted into a deep sleep. I woke up with Rex licking my face and momma calling me to come home. It was late afternoon and my was pirogue pulled to shore. What had happened?

I have to say, waking up only half awake, with Rex licking my face was a shock. Had I just been to a most wonderful place or did I dream it? I actually wasn't sure. I kind of remembered paddling there and back, but that memory was foggy and I was drunk with happiness. Anyway, momma had called and I needed to get home, but that place I found was real in my memory and I couldn't get it out of my mind. I thought about it when we were eating supper, trying to remember anything that would prove I was or was not there. Then I thought about the flower! I jumped up from the table, told momma that I left something in my boat, and ran back down to the swamp. Sure enough, the flower was in the boat. It was true! I was there! I scooped up the flower and ran back home. Momma wasn't pleased that I left the table without excusing myself, but cried when I gave her the flower and put it in a vase with water. That thing grew roots and lasted for months. I knew where to go to get more and intended to do just that.

I mentioned mystery before. The most wondrous life in Parfait's Eden are the creatures that give evidence of their presence, but are unseen. They have never been seen, at least by me, but they are in the swamp and I have been among them. Alligator hunters sometimes talk about them, describing various experiences, but their stories are considered urban swamp tales among the general population, mainly because there is no evidence of their existence. As I said before, a mystery, and probably one best left alone. Whatever they are, I have come to like them.

Chapter 34 - Definitions

"Mudman, in one of my classes at school this week, the teacher is focusing on definitions of words and instructing us how to use properly use a dictionary and an encyclopedia. Today was our first day and she asked the class for words we would like defined and showed us how to look them up in the Webster Dictionary and the school encyclopedia. Each of us had to turn in two words."

"That sounds like a good teacher you have, Johnny. How many students are in your class?"

"Yeah, she is; I kinda like her. There are 18 of us in the class. That means 36 words were turned in to be defined. Mrs. Edwards wrote them all down on the blackboard and there were a lot of the same words turned in. I guess kids our age think the same way."

"What were the most common words turned in, Johnny? Do you remember?"

"Well, 'money' was probably turned in the most, maybe 8 times. 'God' was turned in a lot and so was 'Beaumont'. 'Rock and roll' was used twice and it's not even a word. There was a bunch of others, Mudman."

"What words did you turn in, Little Muddy?"

"I turned in 'illusion' and 'grace' because I have never found a good answer for them, along with a few others."

"I assume no one else turned in those words?"

"Heck no! The other kids didn't know what they meant either."

"Well, in fairness to the other students, Johnny, very many grown humans cannot define those words. How did the dictionary define them?

"The teacher said that 'illusion' was defined as, *a thing that is or is likely to be wrongly perceived or interpreted by the senses*, but no one knew what that meant. When she asked me to explain what I thought that definition meant, I said that it meant something that seems real, but isn't.

"What about 'grace'? How was that word defined in the dictionary? The teacher said the word 'grace' has many different meanings, depending on how it is used. She said grace is a part of God's character and God's grace means, undeserved favor.

"Did you or the class understand what was 'undeserved favor', Little Muddy?"

"Actually Mudman, I think that went over everyone's heads, maybe even the teacher's head too." Mrs. Edwards explained that 'undeserved favor' meant that people do not deserve the good God does for them and He does it anyway; or something like that."

"Have you had time to think about what she said, Johnny? Favors given that are not deserved makes God out to be a really good guy, doesn't it?"

"Mudman, I think you are being sarcastic on purpose. I mean, no one says, 'God is a really good guy.' That just isn't done. It's not respectful and sounds like you are poking fun at God."

"You are right, my young friend, I guess it does look that way, but God is a big boy; He can take care of Himself. Right? I mean, afterall, He is God."

"Mudman, you have a reason . . . what you are saying means something . . . I just don't see it.

"Little Muddy, your teacher said grace has many different meanings. How many of those did she reveal from the dictionary?"

"Just the one about God's 'undeserved favor', Mudman."

"It is also interpreted by human scholars as meaning 'undeserved mercy' and is written as an example of God's love for mankind; you know, 'for God so loved the world', and so on. Johnny, we have spoken of this in another now; so, you **do** see it. What is God?"

With that question, I immediately understood the meaning of Mudman's sarcasm and answered, "God is everything, Mudman."

"Why do you suppose your teacher focused on that one definition of 'grace', Johnny?"

"She was teaching what she believes to be important and wanted us also to believe, Mudman."

"Why?"

"Because she wanted us to know that God loves us."

"How is it that she knows God loves you?"

I thought about that for a moment and concluded there were two answers to Mudman's question, 'Because God loves everyone.' and because . . . because, I understood and quietly said, "Because that is what she was taught to believe, Mudman."

"There! You have it. Remember two examples of 'teaching stupid' Johnny, where you learned:

1. When people are taught what to think, that is teaching stupid.

2. When people are taught what to believe, that is teaching stupid."

"Your teacher was teaching 'stupid' to her class, Johnny and now she has passed it forward to a class of young, impressionable students who, in all likelihood, learned to believe something stupid. A tragedy, of sorts. And interesting that it remains unrevealed."

"But it is revealed, Mudman, I understand."

"So you do, my young friend; so you do."

"Mudman, what **does** 'grace' mean?"

"Well, Johnny, there are two usual ways to use the word 'grace', noun and verb.

1. As a noun. Praying before a meal is often referred to as, grace or 'saying grace', meaning 'giving thanks' to one's deity for the food provided, or she moves with grace.

2. As a verb. The governor will grace us later with his presence.

3. A person's name is a 'proper noun'. (Grace)"

"Mudman! What about the Grace of God?"

"God is Everything, Little Muddy, everything including grace. Assigning grace to God is mankind's way of 'humanizing' God. God **is** grace. Anyway, when certain religions assign grace to God, they mean Jehovah and Jehovah was and is not God; he was a creation of the Creator. That was revealed in our discussion of Jehovah. Saying 'the Grace of God' is a complete misapplication of a term. It is unlikely that truth will be accepted by Jehovah's believers because their belief is millenniums old and entire civilizations have been built upon that belief. In any event, my young friend, there is no such thing as the grace of God. The terms 'undeserved favor' and 'undeserved mercy' are human terms given to an undeserving deity, and do not apply to God."

"What is the definition of 'undeserved', Mudman?"

"The word 'undeserved' is defined to mean, 'not warranted, merited, or earned', Johnny."

"Mudman, what you just said can never be told to people, at least anyone I know. Remember when you defined 'consequences'? The consequences of that information would be bad."

"Maybe, and that is a sad commentary on humanity, my young friend; very interesting to watch, though."

Chapter 35 - Love and Evil

It was a cold day in January, 1958 before Mudman and I met again. I don't really like cold and wondered how the cold affected him. I will turn sixteen this year and am a sophomore in high school, meaning after school activities are occupying a lot of my time. Baseball, basketball, and studies take up so much of my time that weekends are the only free time left, and some of that is spent with family obligations, not that I'm complaining, mind you; I love spending time with family. It's just that my swamp is where I recharge, learn, and feel free.

I waited until noon to take a walk along the water of the swamp. It was cold and I was comfortable wearing my coat. The swamp in winter has a different look than in spring and summer, mostly due to the cypress trees shedding their needlelike leaves. The hanging moss remains though, exhibiting a ghostly appearance during the shadows of the day. Some say the swamp in winter is gloomy or spooky; they are forgetting the good things, like no bugs and fewer snakes. Alligators are rarely seen in the winter as well. I was enjoying my walk in the quiet stillness when I spotted Mudman approaching from the deep swamp. The bare trees allowed for a deeper view into the outer regions. I waved a welcome to Mudman and was genuinely happy to see him.

"Well Johnny," he greeted, "you look comfortable in that coat of yours."

"I am, Mudman." I answered. "I've been wondering how cold weather affects you."

"I am slower and quieter than in warmer weather." my young friend. "Are you here for the exercise today or one of our famous discussions?"

"Heck Mudman, I've been walking here today, hoping to talk with you. I miss our conversations." I confessed.

"What is on your mind, Johnny? Have a seat there on your log and let us get started. Are you intending to ask a question with a simple answer that requires a complicated discussion? That seems to be your style." he stated and sat down in front of me.

"No, nothing complicated." I replied. "I have some words that need explaining from a point of view other than mine and the dictionary. I'm not really interested in a definition of the word; it's the meaning that is of interest to me."

"What is the word, Little Muddy? he asked.

I answered, "Love. Our home dictionary reveals a definition of love as, 'an intense feeling of deep affection' and I'm satisfied with that definition, but I wonder why 'love' does not have more of a positive effect on humanity? Jesus often advised his disciples and others to love one other, but love has not been and is not as effective as evil. Why is that?"

"Nothing complicated." he said and smiled. "Perhaps we should discuss the meaning of 'complicated' first." Mudman resumed, "Actually Little Muddy, it is surprising you have not before pursued this subject. Philosophers, authors, and poets have, through several millenniums, endeavored to unravel the mystery of love, without achieving an adequate solution."

He commented, "I noticed that you cleverly avoided asking, 'what is love?', my astute young friend. Could it be that you already knew the answer to that question?"

"God is love." I responded.

"Yes!" he exclaimed. "That is the only reasonable answer and would have concluded our discussion; however, you did not ask that question, making it necessary to carry on with your actual questions. The answer to your second question regarding why 'love' is less effective among humans than 'evil' is another one of your queries which has a simple answer that begs a complicated discussion.

"Actually though, that is not your question. Evil is not the opposite of love, as you insinuate; rather, hatred is the word. To compare love and evil is a far more difficult task than is love and hatred. You see, love can be evil and evil can love. However, since you asked, I will go with love and evil."

"Come on Mudman, don't make me beg." I laughed, "Just tell me the doggone answer!"

"Johnny! Johnny!" he exclaimed in fake shock. "Such language! What would your momma say?"

"She would say, 'answer the boy's question!', Mudman. What is the answer, my big friend, I'm busting with curiosity here."

"Busting with curiosity? Well, that comment certainly deserves a response!" he retorted.

"Actionable-Ease." he responded.

"Mudman," I said as kindly as possible, "I suspect that answer cannot be found anywhere in the history of the English language. Did you just now make that up? It's not that I don't like it because 'actionable ease' sounds impressive; but, I don't think it has ever been used before."

"What difference does that make, Little Muddy?" he countered.

"As long as 'actionable-ease' is a valid answer, why should the term be disqualified? Because it is new? Does that even sound reasonable?"

"Well," I admitted, "now that you put it that way, Mudman, I agree. Actionable-ease is a good answer, as long as you can explain what it means. Please explain what it means."

Mudman began his explanation, "Actionable means, 'able to be done or acted on'. Ease means, 'absence of difficulty or effort'. Therefore, actionable-ease means *'an action taken because it is absent of difficulty, or in a word, easy'*."

"This means that evil is very effective among humans because the effort required to commit evil acts is less difficult than the effort required to commit acts of goodness. On the other hand, love is difficult for humans; that is why there is so little evidence of love among humans. Your Jesus said to love your enemies and do good to those who hate you. That is near impossible among humans, Little Muddy."

Mudman went further and said, "Humans are generally more interested in hearing the worst of another human than the best, and are more inclined to believe the worst than the best, whether it is true or not. Where humans are concerned, evil is far more seductive than love."

After considering Mudman's comments, I began to understand what he was telling me. "It seems to me, Mudman, 'actionable-ease' is a short way of saying, 'taking the path of least resistance'. As you have pointed out in our discussions, humans must overcome their basic evil nature with ethical and moral decisions on the journey to goodness and love; a journey, by the way, heavily weighed down with difficulties."

Mudman was happy. "Little Muddy, you are an affirmation that my teaching ability is boundless! Let us now proceed to your first question while the iron is hot!"

Mudman was on a roll and seemed to be enjoying himself. I'm not sure how 'enjoy' applies to him, but it looked to me like he was having fun.

He hesitated a moment and stated, "As I recall, you were wondering why love does not have a more positive effect on humanity. The truth is, Little Muddy, love has always had, in every instance, a one hundred percent positive effect on every single thing, person, or collective where it has been generated. The reason love has not had and does not have a more positive effect on humanity is the lack of love in the world, caused by stupidity."

"Wait a minute Mudman," I objected, "you have already taught that stupidity is the cause of the downfall of nations! Now you're blaming it here as well; even stupid people have the ability to love, Mudman. Blaming stupid people for the lack of love in the world is not fair."

"Little Muddy, in my defense, nothing has yet been said about stupid people or the ability to love; however, that being said, the stupidity of the human collective **is** responsible for the lack of love in the world."

"Mudman, what are you trying to, uhh, aw heck! I mean, what is the stupidity of the human collective?" I finally asked.

Mudman was adamant in his answer. "When God is foremost in mankind's belief structure, Little Muddy, love is not only prevalent in their lives, but goodness itself is there as well, leaving little to no space for evil. Mankind's stupidity is their stubborn insistence on believing in creations instead of God. Creations are not love; God is love and as mankind's belief in God is reduced or eliminated, love and goodness is reduced in their existence as well, opening opportunities for evil to thrive. I will say it again so that you will not forget, Little Muddy: the reason love does not have a more positive effect on humanity is the lack of love in the world, a lack caused by stupidity."

I don't care what Mudman says about knowledge being absent in this reality, his understanding of how things work here is awesome. I stood up and walked around a bit to warm up, then sat back down, expectantly.

Mudman asked, "What are you thinking, Little Muddy? Are you keeping up? Our talks can get a little deep sometimes."

"Yeah, Mudman," I replied. "I'm keeping up. Your explanation regarding love was great and cleared up my questions about the effectiveness of love in our reality."

"Well, my young friend, have you another subject to discuss today or is the cool weather getting to you?" he inquired.

"It is pretty cool today, Mudman," I agreed, "but I'm just getting warmed up. I have a subject about which I am quite interested and should have asked you about before now; but, having never really been comfortable with this subject, I never brought it up. 'Evil' is what I want to discuss now, Mudman." I said.

Mudman thought a moment and then quietly inquired, "What exactly is it you want to understand about evil, Little Muddy?"

"Something!" I almost screamed. "I want to know something about evil! I don't know what it is, how it is, or why it is. I am almost afraid to talk about evil and don't know why. Then you go and tell me that I was created with an evil nature and I don't know how to fight it, much less defeat it!

"Wow, Little Muddy," he replied, "you are passionate about this subject. How did I miss seeing your interest here?"

"I avoid thinking about evil, Mudman," I confessed, "and when evil is talked about, I steer clear of discussing its meaning."

Mudman responded, "Okay then, let us see if we can get an understanding of evil. Have you noticed that very often when evil is presented to an audience of humans, an association with the supernatural is implied. In your picture shows, evil is equated with horror, spirits of the dead, or demons of the underworld; vampires, witches, werewolves, and demon possessed things are examples of evil on display."

"Just listening to you talking about such things brings scary images to my mind, Mudman. Even though those things do not exist, they are frightening to think about." was my comment on his explanation.

Mudman corrected me, "I never meant to imply those things do not exist, Johnny. My comment was about how they are used to demonstrate and explain how evil is displayed **to** people, **by** people."

"Wait a minute!" I exclaimed. "Are you telling me those things exist? Tell me you are not telling me that!"

"This is a created reality, Johnny; the Creator can create anything into his creation or remove anything. Why not those things? You created them in your mind from reading a story or watching a movie; how is the Creator any different?"

"That may be true, Mudman, but a story in a book or movie is not real." I argued.

"Johnny," he countered, "we have discussed this before; our created reality is an illusion, but is real to you because you are in it. From the outside looking in, it is only a movie, of sorts, providing certain entertainment and information to its creator."

I just had to make this comment, "There is something I have said before and I'm going to say it again, Mudman; what you are teaching here is far outside the ability of most, and maybe all, humans to understand and is certainly outside their willingness to consider."

"Which has nothing to do with the accuracy of the statement, my young friend." he objectively observed. "Humans, as a collective, will believe what they will, do as they choose, and generate results of their own making, fulfilling the purpose of their creation, whatever that may be. The desires and beliefs of the human collective are no concern of mine. On the other hand, to use one of your sayings, individual humans are of interest."

"Humans are interesting creatures." I affirmed.

"Yes. Well, as I was saying," Mudman continued, "evil is usually presented to human society as a supernatural entity and something of which they should fear. Your response to evil is typical and was created and shaped by such representations."

I was bothered by what he said, and responded accordingly, "Mudman, are you saying that evil should not be feared? I am afraid of evil; that is why I always try to avoid thinking or talking about it. I fear evil and I'm not even sure what it is."

"Young Johnny," he advised, "you are not afraid of evil, it is your learned perception of evil that creates your fear."

"Does that mean I should not be afraid of evil?" I asked.

"Little Muddy, the prime imperative of life is survival. Anything that threatens survival is feared on some level, meaning that both survival and fear are relative. The ultimate threat to life is death, creating great fear, resulting in almost any effort to assure survival. Less serious threats are met with less fear and a more appropriate response."

"Does evil threaten life, Mudman? Is that what causes my fear?" I persisted.

Mudman responded, "Johnny, you are hearing, but not listening to what I am saying. Listen! Your fear of evil is caused by your perception of evil, meaning your way of thinking about evil is that which must be addressed, not evil itself."

"For some reason, Mudman, it seems you are saying that evil is not all that bad and should not be feared. I am sure you don't mean it, but that is what it sounds like to me."

He hesitated a moment, then looked at me intensely and said, "You know something, Little Muddy? I take back what I once said about my being a great teacher. I am not getting through to you in a way required for you to understand. Let me see if I can do better."

First, let us consider bad and evil. Bad means wrong, wicked, immoral or all of those things. Evil means **profoundly** wicked and immoral, meaning that evil is leaps and bounds worse than bad. The word evil can be used as an adjective or a noun. Evil is part of everything and God, being everything, means that evil is of God. Are you still with me, Little Muddy; we are involved in a difficult subject."

"You have my mind racing with the thought that evil is of God, Mudman." I admitted, "But I am still of the opinion that evil should be feared. You know, Satan is to be feared and he is the personification of evil."

"Personification, is it?" he queried. "Your vocabulary is growing almost as fast as you. In regard to Satan, he is of God, but was not created by our Creator."

I had to laugh at Mudman's 'matter of fact' way of delivering that information. He glanced at me in surprise and demanded to know what was so funny, which resulted in my laughing harder. He watched and waited patiently for me to regain my composure and explain myself. Mudman really had no idea of the importance, to me, of his 'innocent' comment. In the bible creation story, Satan was not part of the creation of Eden or mankind; he was an intruder, a serpent placed there to test the fidelity of the created beings, Adam and Eve. I had to wonder about his involvement here, if he even existed.

I explained, "Mudman, you made me laugh by your calm way of saying that Satan is not created into this reality, making it seem like it is something everyone knows, when they don't! It was surprising to me. I have two questions. First, what is it that made you decide that Satan is not a creation? Second, how did he get into our created reality?"

Mudman's answer was surprising. "First, I did not say anything about Satan not being a creation. Second, I did not say he was in our reality. We have discussed hearing and not listening more than a few times, Little Muddy; were you not listening?"

"Mudman," I replied, "Nobody listens to everything they hear. I'm working at it, but that is a talent that takes a lot of practice." Then added, "Are you saying that Satan does not exist in our reality?"

Suddenly, a thought ran through my mind. "Wait a minute, Mudman!" I exclaimed, "in our reality"? That's what you said, 'in our reality'. Does that mean Satan can exist here as a type of visitor without actually being created here?"

"Well, well, well!" he retorted, "how about that! Little Muddy does listen to what he hears afterall." and then he answered, "Yes, my young friend, existing here without being created here is a possibility and seems to be the only way of explaining some of the things that happen here; not only regarding Satan, but others as well."

I made a point of emphasizing, "This is really big and interesting information, Mudman; how come you have not

talked about visitors to our reality before?"

"In this reality, order must be followed, young Johnny," he replied. "Some things cannot be learned without preliminary teaching or preparation for such learning. One must be taught simple arithmetic before learning about multiplying and dividing numbers, and so on. It was necessary that you learn about creation, creations, and the concept of a creator before moving on to higher things."

That made me curious. "How many 'higher things' are there to learn?"

"More than this now can hold, Little Muddy." he answered. "Understanding such a thing can be disappointing, as well as unsatisfying; however, being of God, your nows are not limited and what those nows come to be is totally dependent upon what you do in this one. You determine what you get, Johnny, not God, not the creator, or anyone else. **You**. That is true for every being anywhere and everywhere."

"Is that also true for you, Mudman?"

"No, Johnny, that does not apply to me."

"Why not? You make decisions, you make choices, you do things."

"I am not a being, Johnny."

"You are a being to me, Mudman."

"That is your perception, Johnny."

"If you are not a being, what are you?"

"I am a consciousness, Little Muddy."

"Mudman, you are difficult for me to understand."

"That is not what you meant to say, Johnny, but I understand what you mean."

"How do you know what I meant to say, anyway? What did I mean to say?"

"You meant say I am difficult for you to comprehend."

"Those words seem to have the same meaning, Mudman; what is the difference?

"The words are much like 'hearing' and 'listening', young Johnny. One can understand and read a language and not comprehend what was written or spoken. In our example, you have an understanding of me, but have not yet comprehended what it is that I am."

Well, I wasn't about to get into that right now. For some reason, Mudman was guiding our conversation away from the subject of evil. I was cold and needed time to consider what he had told me today. Something else was bothering me that needed thinking about as well, but I couldn't think what it was right now. My mind was too full and tired.

"Mudman, there is much more to ask you about evil," I said, "but the cold is getting to me and I have a lot to think about now; so, I need to go home."

"I understand," he replied, "but you never asked the question on your mind; it will lead to an interesting discussion, because it is a question that is not often asked."

"Come on, Mudman," I argued, "I don't even have another question to ask right now. I'm tired and cold and have no questions on my mind, except maybe what momma is fixing for supper. You've got me thinking, though. I'll bite, what do you suppose I want to ask?"

"He pointed at me and demanded, "What is it, concerning our subject, that you would like to know right now before leaving? Think, without trying."

Think without trying, he demanded. How the heck do I do that?

I just blurted out, "Mudman, is Satan evil?"

I stood there and watched as he turned, waded into the water and, without saying a word, glided off and disappeared into the swamp. I turned and headed home, thinking, "What a stupid question to ask of Mudman! Of course Satan is evil, everyone knows that. Don't they?"

Chapter 36 - Satan

As usual, my meeting and discussion with Mudman provoked questions and deep thoughts in my head. Normally, I can reason things out pretty well by writing them down and doing some book research, but the question about Satan being evil was difficult. Besides, I was not comfortable thinking about Satan; I mean, no one wants to think or talk about him, since he is thought to be totally evil, and thinking otherwise will send one straight to hell, which is a terrible thought in itself. But I wanted to know the 'whys' of the conventional thought that was influencing my beliefs. What that meant was, I needed to talk with someone about it before my next meeting with Mudman. It might help to understand a point of view other than my own. Anyway, that was my plan. Who do I talk to? Or rather, as Mudman would say, with whom do I talk? Well, grandma was available and she will not be as judgmental as most others. Might talk to momma as well, now that I think about it; however, momma is kinda leaning toward the Jehovah's Witness religion these days and after reading some of the books they gave her, I have some questions for them too. Momma wasn't too keen on my talking with them, though.

So, after school one evening I sat down on the couch next to grandma in the living room; she was watching wrestling on TV. My grandma loved watching wrestling. She loved Rito Romero and Ricky Starr and hated Mr. Moto and Bull Curry. My brothers were there too, laying on the floor practicing wrestling holds on each other. She complained about one of the combatants being a dirty wrestler and the referee letting him get away with 'eye gouging' or something like that. She looked over at me and asked if I was already done with my homework. After nodding yes, I mentioned there was something I wanted to talk about with her after wrestling was over. Well, grandma got right up off that couch and said there was no time like the present. "That dam refree don't know nuthin' 'bout rastlin' anyway, an' he's gonna let dat cheatin' crimnal win dis match." was her comment before we left for her room.

Grandma sat down in her rocker and asked, "Whatcha got on yur mind, son?"

"Grandma," I began, "You know about my bible reading? Well, some questions have come into my mind that need talking about."

Grandma, never being one to mince words said, "Ever time I seed-ya boy, ya got yer nose stuck in sum book nobody ne'er heerd of. Now dat ain't no bad talk! Jus sayin' how much ya like ta read an' all; I'm be proud o' ya fer dat too. Now gimme one o' dem questyuns in yer mind."

"I am interested in what you think of Satan, grandma." I said. "Is he a person and is he evil?"

"Land sakes alive, Johnny!" she exclaimed. "Whatcha doin' messin' about w'such thangs son? Satan, is it? Dat thang ain't nuthin' to think 'bout, much less talk of. Best ya clean yer mind o' dat serpent an' let it be."

"But grandma", I protested, "I don't really know anything about Satan, except what I read in the bible, and the bible doesn't mention anything really bad about Satan. The worst thing Satan seems to do is tempt people. He is mentioned in the bible, many times and I have not found where has he personally killed anyone or physically hurt anyone."

"Johnny boy," she cautioned, "yer not afixin' to say dat Satan feller ain't evil are ya? Dat serpent is a bad'un, ya know."

It had become evident that starting this discussion with grandma was a mistake. She is incapable of talking about Satan in any light other than the one fixed in her mind. She will stick to her guns without considering anything else. I learned something, though; the accepted reputation of Satan being an example of ultimate evil is solidly entrenched in humanity, very many of whom know little to nothing about the subject. They fear him.

I had to do something about grandma, though. Because of my statement about Satan, she is beginning to suspect that her grandson has fallen under the spell of evil, something untrue that must corrected. Leaving the conversation now seemed wrong; so, I decided to explain, as best as I could, my reason for investigating Satan.

"Grandma," I explained, "I'm not saying anything not written in the bible. You know that God created Satan and you have told me many times that God does not make mistakes, meaning that Satan was created to be the way he is, for a purpose. I don't know why God did that, but He did, and I have been wondering why."

"Lawd gudness, child," she replied, "I done tol' ya many times, der ain't nuthin' God cain't do and that He wurks in 'steerous ways. Sum things you ain't s'pose to know; ya just 'cept em. Dats the way things gotta be."

"I know, grandma." I admitted, "It's just that sometimes I wonder about things I don't understand."

"Well, der ain't nuthin' wrong wit wundrin', child," she advised. "Jus be careful where doz dreams take ya. Dang it boy, tawkin' witchya wears me out at times. Git on outa here and let an ol' woman get her rest!"

That worked out reasonably well, except grandma talked with momma and momma wanted to talk with me. One day, the lesson not to talk with some people about certain things will stick. Talking with Mudman has spoiled me because with him, everything goes. I am drawn to the freedom in our talks.

Momma caught me first thing the next morning before breakfast.

She didn't seem very concerned and simply said, "Grandma says you were asking some questions about Satan yesterday and has it in her mind that you don't think Satan is bad. She's worried about you. What is it you're wanting to know, son?"

"Aw momma," I answered, "grandma over reacted a little bit when I asked about Satan. I have been reading the bible lately, trying to figure out why Satan has a reputation for being so evil. I can't find anywhere in the bible where it says that Satan personally murdered anyone, stole anything, or physically hurt anybody. He does tempt people to sin, but a lot of people do that to other people in our society. People who give in to temptation have themselves to blame and should stop pointing their fingers at Satan or anybody else. Sin is a personal action. The way I see it, people like to sin; being bad seems to be more fun than being good. I just want to know why Satan is considered to be so evil. Now, he did rebel against God, his father, but many human kids rebel against their parents. Humans do a lot of really evil things to each other because they choose to do so. The thing is, Satan almost always gets blamed for the evil things humans do and I don't understand why. 'The devil made me do it' seems to be a sorry excuse for making bad decisions."

"Johnny," momma observed, "It is plain why grandma is worried about you. The way you explain the Devil makes him appear to be no worse than ordinary people and even better than some of them. I have never heard any adult talk about the Devil the way you just did, much less any child. Why are you so interested in Satan, son?"

"I am not interested in Satan, momma." I responded. "I'm interested in understanding why he is considered evil by everyone, because I don't see it, the evidence, I mean. It is my hope that grandma or you might be able to tell me why; afterall, y'all have been to church much more than me and know more about this stuff than I do."

"I'm not so sure about that, Johnny," she replied, "people don't think about the things you think about, especially kids, but that's not what I'm worried about. You just can't go around talking to people about Satan not being evil, son. People are not reasonable about that and might begin thinking you are possessed by demons, or worse. The devil is a very sensitive subject and some people get crazy when they hear someone defending him. You just can't trust people to be sensible about things like that."

Momma was hearing me, but she was not listening.

"Momma, I never said that Satan isn't evil and I'm not defending him." I argued. "I just don't see why everyone believes he is evil. Humans are evil, momma; they murder, rape, steal, maim, cheat, and hurt each other all the time. That is evil conduct. I don't see why all those things are Satan's fault. Maybe someone smarter than me can explain it."

"Listen to me, Johnny! Do not ever tell that to anyone." she demanded. "Besides, you cannot be be sure whether someone is smarter than you or not, but when it comes to talking about the devil, no one can be trusted. At least wait until you are older and have more experience with people. You may, or may not, eventually get a reasonable answer to your questions, but wait until you're older and develop a few friendships with people who have similar interests. Now is not the time. Do your research, but keep your ideas to yourself. You can always talk with me."

Momma didn't know about Mudman. 'Now is not the time' is what she said. "Now is all we have." I said to myself, then told momma, "I understand, momma. Humans seem to have

an evil nature, making them unworthy of trust."

"Good lord, son!" she exclaimed. "Do not ever say that out loud, even in private!" Then she commented to no one in particular, "Where in the world does that boy come up with such things?"

"Johnny, I'll smooth things over with grandma." she said and added, "don't you go getting her all upset with questions for a month or so; come to me when you have questions."

"Momma."

"What is it, son."

"I have a question."

"Really, Johnny?"

"Well, you just said to . . ."

"I know exactly what I said, son!" she interrupted. "Okay, ask away."

"Do you believe Satan is evil, momma?"

"Yes."

"Why?"

"Cause that is what I have been told all my life."

"Could you have been told wrong?"

"No, son. Satan is evil."

"Can you name one 'evil' Satan has committed, momma?"

"Johnny."

"Ma'am?"

"You realize I am your Mother, don't you?"

"Yes, ma'am."

"Have you completed your chores this morning?"

"No, ma'am."

"Then you best be getting to them."

"But, momma? . . ." She left and headed to the kitchen.

It is true, there are some things that cannot be discussed with some. It is more true, there are some things that should **not** be discussed with some. It is ultimately true, there are some things that are not discussed, period; apparently, Satan is such a thing. I wonder why?

Chapter 37 - Human Trash

The next Sunday was a nice day in the 70's. I went down to the water in late morning, paddled my pirogue out to the tree line and just floated there, listening to the swamp and wondering where the conversation with Mudman was likely to go today. I wasn't sure anymore whether Satan was a good subject to talk about, or not. His involvement here was a mystery that teased me, though.

It was beginning to look like Mudman had other things to do today; so, I paddled my boat a little further into the woods, picked up my rod and reel, and settled in for a few hours of fishing. I heard them before seeing them. As I turned to face the sound of voices, four canoes came into view being paddled in the shallows close to shore by eight people. I was about thirty yards from them and unseen in the shadows of the swamp. There were two adults and six boys about my age; they paddled near where my pirogue is usually hidden, got out and waded to shore. The boys split up and began walking along the edge of the water about a hundred yards in each direction. The two men opened a paper that looked like a map and sat down on my thinking log, talking and pointing at the map. They were acting strange, but were not breaking any laws as far as I knew.

"What do you think, Little Muddy?" quietly asked Mudman, "is our discussion duo turning into a group?"

Surprised, I looked around and he was leaning against the tree behind me up to his chest in the water. The truth is, I was really happy to see him. Maybe he could explain what was going on there at the edge of the swamp; so, I asked him.

Whispering, I said, "I have been watching them, but don't have any idea who they are or why they're here. They don't seem to be doing anything wrong, though."

"Do you recognize any of them, Johnny?" he asked.

"I can't see faces very well from this distance, Mudman." was my quiet response.

"Can you see what is in the last canoe?" he spoke softly.

I looked and whispered, "Two boxes and a rifle, but that doesn't mean anything; a lot of people bring guns when they go into the swamp."

Mudman smiled and stated, "Only the boxes are of interest, Johnny. Watch them. Remain quiet, still, and in the boat."

While we watched from the shadows, the boys came back. One of them spoke to the men, then walked to the last canoe and motioned the others to follow. They unloaded four boxes from the boat. They had been stacked side by side. I only saw two stacks and mistook them for two boxes from this distance and turned to tell Mudman, but he was gone. The boys stationed themselves facing outward about 20 feet apart, like they were guarding the area from intruders. What the heck was going on here? Mudman said that only the boxes were of interest, so I watched them. One of the men went to a box, cut the seal with a knife, opened it and removed a round metal container with a lid; it looked like half a garbage can.

Wouldn't you know it? I could hear my brothers calling me. It wasn't long before they showed up down the shore a-ways, hollering their lungs out. "Johhnnnyy! Johhnnnyy! Momma says come home!" Then they saw the boats and came running to see what was going on.

The boys keeping watch were surprised and two of them moved to stop Ricky and Rocky, but one of the men gave an order and all six boys went directly to the boxes and put them back in the boat. Then they got in their respective boats and waited. The two men greeted my brothers and said something to them. Rocky seemed happy and was jumping around like he had just found a puppy. The man gave them something and both brothers took off excited and running for home. Then the two men got in their boats and all of them paddled on down the swamp out of sight.

Mudman commented, "Well, that was interesting."

Startled, I turned and saw him standing next to my boat. "Where did you go?" I asked.

"I have been here all the time, Little Muddy." he replied. "Just watching, with you."

"You want to tell me what we were watching, Mudman?"

"Your mother wants you home, now."

"Mudman, do you know what that was all about?"

"I have seen it in another now."

"Here, in my part of the swamp?"

"No, they usually go in north of here."

"Why were they here now?"

"Do not know, but soon will."

"You're not going to tell me what they're doing, are you?"

"Not now. Your mother wants you. Go!"

"What was in the boxes, Mudman?"

"Your mother wants you. Go!" he ordered.

It was obvious that Mudman was not going to tell me anything today and momma did send the boys to get me; so, I paddled to shore and went home wondering what it was that took place in the swamp today. Another mystery to solve. I wanted to know what that man said to my brothers, anyway, and what he gave them. They have already told momma by now. What was in those boxes?

Just as I was getting home, the boys came running out the door, all excited. A man down in the swamp gave them each three silver dollars for telling him about the fishing around here. They told him that fishing wasn't good here because the water was too shallow, but fishing in the deep water further out in the swamp was good. The man was happy to hear that news and paid them for telling him. According to Rocky, the man was real nice and was just taking some boys on a fishing trip for the day. My brothers couldn't wait to go to the store and spend their money.

Momma wanted to know what I saw and I told the truth, such as it was. I saw two men and some boys paddle some canoes to shore and get out to rest. Ricky and Rocky came running down to the swamp, calling for me to come home. One man talked with them and then the men and boys got back in their canoes and paddled on down the swamp. Momma commented that they were probably boy scouts on an outing with their troop leaders and it was nice of the man to give my brothers some money.

Something else was going on there with those people, but I had no idea what it was. My thought was that Mudman would tell me the truth when next we met. The next day, after school, I walked to the swamp hoping to see him there. I had about an hour before dark, so there wasn't time for a long conversation. I sat down on my log and waited.

"What do you think, Johnny?" he asked. "You have any idea what those people were doing here?" Mudman settled in beside me on the log.

"No." I answered, "I was hoping you would tell me."

"I have watched them in other areas, Johnny. They have a business that requires the swamp and more places as well."

"A business? What business requires the swamp?"

"The swamp is where people sometimes dump their trash, Johnny."

"Trash? Since when does it take eight people to dump four boxes of trash?"

"Well, perhaps there were more boxes when they set out. Four boats, 4 boxes in each."

"What was in the boxes, Mudman? I saw a metal can in one box. What was in it?"

"Bodies."

"What? Bodies? What kind of bodies? Animals?"

"Babies, Johnny. Human babies."

"Mudman, you're telling me that human babies were being dumped in the swamp?"

"Are being dumped in the swamp. Little Muddy."

"Why? Why would anyone do that, Mudman?"

"They cannot dump trash like that just anywhere because people would object."

"Trash like that? Mudman, you know dead human babies are not trash!"

"Trash is discarded matter for which people no longer have any use, Little Muddy."

"That is wrong and immoral, Mudman!"

"The babies are not alive when disposed of, Johnny."

"That makes no difference, Mudman, someone killed them!"

"Are you aware of abortion, Johnny? Have you read of it?"

"Not much. It's when a girl gets pregnant and has the baby aborted before birth."

"Is the baby alive when aborted, Little Muddy?"

"I don't know anything about abortion, Mudman and I don't even like to think about it!"

"Remember, you asked what was in the boxes in the boat, Little Muddy."

"Yeah, but I never even thought that they might contain dead babies! That is evil!"

"Why, Little Muddy? Those people did not kill the babies."

"But they know what is in the boxes, Mudman! You don't dump dead babies like trash."

"Those aborted babies are unwanted human waste, Little Muddy. They **are** trash."

"Mudman, I know you don't believe that. Those babies were humans, created of God."

"What does that have to do with anything, Little Muddy? Their remains are still trash."

"I don't know! I don't know! It just seems wrong to treat them like trash!"

"What would you do with the bodies, my friend?"

"I would never take the job of collecting them in the first place."

"Someone must do it, Johnny. It is necessary that trash be disposed of; otherwise, a mess results."

"There can't be that many aborted babies, Mudman. Why not arrange to bury them?"

"There are many abortions every year, Johnny. Perhaps a million per year, or more."

"A million? How come nobody ever talks about that? I've never heard about that!"

"People don't generally like to talk about their trash, particularly illegal trash, Johnny."

"Illegal?"

"Abortion is illegal, Johnny, and the possession of human fetuses is a crime."

"So, those people in the swamp were breaking the law?"

"Yes, and they will go to evil lengths to avoid being caught. Be wary of them, Johnny."

"Are those people evil, Mudman?"

"Evil is resident in all humans, my young friend. Those who resist it have value."

"Why don't those men reject their illegal and immoral jobs? Others have."

"You already possess the answer; actionable-ease, Little Muddy, actionable-ease. They work for money, just like almost everyone else, Johnny," he stated, "however, they will resort to evil measures when threatened, pretty much like all humans. It is advisable, in your society, to avoid those who delve in illegal activities or consort with those who do. Leave them to their kind. Genuine happiness does not reside where evil abides."

"I still don't understand why those boys don't get a different job." I persisted. "They don't have to work for those men, doing an immoral job that could get them arrested and put in jail. There are lots companies they could work for."

"for which they could work, Little Muddy," he corrected. "Those young men are hired as guards who do the actual work, illegally disposing of the abortion remains. They feel an importance, an empowerment, the likes of which a regular job seldom offers. On top of that, illegal work usually pays better than a regular job. A dream come true."

"A dream come true." I mused. "Life is always about power and money, Mudman. . . power and money."

"Yes, my young friend," he said, "two of the lures with which Satan baits mankind. Many humans will do anything for a taste of them, always assuring a full stringer on every outing."

"Satan? What do you mean? I thought you said . . ."

"Johnny, have you noticed the darkness? It is past time for you to be home."

"It was dark. Time passed without my noticing. I really did need to go."

"There is only now, Little Muddy, but it is a big now and always present."

I stood up and hurried home. Momma was not going to be happy with me.

Later on that night in my room, Mudman's words came drifting back to me, "always assuring a full stringer on every outing." I made sure to write them down in my notebook. After the experience in the swamp and all the talking about abortion, fetuses, and illegal work, Mudman, with that phrase, revealed the answer to a question I earlier demanded, "Is Satan evil?" The answer seems to be no, but he is certainly a tempter who exploits mankind's basically evil nature.

Chapter 38 - The Great Truth

I discussed my conclusion with Mudman the next day. He stood, staring out into the swamp like always and finally said, "Your deduction is sensible, Johnny, but why do you suppose Satan tempts humans with their weakness? What is there for him to gain?"

"I'm not sure, Mudman, but where is the profit in doing it for nothing? I'm thinking Satan tempts people out of curiosity or meanness; but, the thing is, maybe this reality of ours is an examination of some sort to grade humans, with Satan doing the testing."

"You know, Little Muddy," he said, "your simplistic way of explaining your thoughts is engaging and your deductions are interesting. How long have you been thinking this way?"

"I told you about my study of Satan in the bible, Mudman, and wondering why some people are good and others aren't. I'm just now learning to make some reasonable sense of it all that I can believe. When you revealed our creator to me and explained the reasons creatures and people do the things they do, my way of seeing the world changed."

"Once again, young Johnny, it is incumbent upon me to remind you that knowledge does not exist in this reality. You must take care to remember that your deductions are opinions based upon reasonable assumptions."

"You know what, Mudman?" I countered, "Where there is no knowledge to be acquired, great faith just may be a superior replacement; afterall, no one can possibly know whether great faith is, or is not, knowledge itself, can they?"

"Okay smartypants," Mudman laughed and asked, "What is your conclusion regarding our Satan discussion? You have an idea in that head of yours, do you not?"

"An idea is a nice way to put it, Mudman," I remarked, "a complex idea based upon my limited understanding of the way things are in this reality and, of course, your teaching. Our creator placed us in what seems to be a balanced reality, held together by opposites. A huge mathematical equation, where even though they both look different, the left side always equals the right side. You simply cannot insert something in the left side without increasing the right side of the equation with something of equal value, indicating that something cannot be added or removed from a balanced reality if balance is to be maintained."

"Mudman, I know that I'm boring you with this simple stuff," I admitted, "but this is the way I see a closed reality like ours, and it helps me explain the existence of Satan and evil."

"Little Muddy," he exclaimed, "you have my attention." and added, "We might need to add to our list of topics a discussion of the term, 'simple stuff'; I am no longer certain I know what it means."

Mudman was teasing me; it is just his way of encouraging me to continue. I think he is interested in my point of view and that alone is inspiring.

I continued, "If evil is created into our reality, it follows that goodness must be created here as well. They differ, in that evil is inherent in humanity and goodness is learned by humanity. Evil, meaning profoundly immoral and wicked; Goodness, meaning profoundly moral and virtuous. Mankind, being created with an evil nature, does not have to strive for evil, for evil comes easy to them. Achieving goodness, on the other hand, requires two things of an individual human; he must resist his evil nature and embrace goodness. How is the sincerity of such a great achievement tested? Temptation! Of course, temptation requires a tempter, which is where Satan comes in; he is the perfect tempter."

"Like mankind," I continued, "Satan is created of God. His purpose seems to be that of an obstacle that examines and tests mankind's sincerity in their effort to choose goodness by tempting their basic evil nature with money, pleasure, and power. Three lures that always assure a full stringer on every outing."

"Each human determines his or her individual destiny." I reasoned. "Which will it be? Righteousness? Or the lures cast by Satan? There appears to be hope for some individual humans, but devastation for the human collective, a self-determined outcome, resulting from their choice of intelligent-stupid leaders and their faith in human creations."

"What do you think, Mudman?" I inquired. "This has been on my mind for a long time, but is my first attempt at trying to explain my thoughts. Everything is based upon my personal deductions, though; I have no proof and don't know anything for sure."

"No one knows anything for sure, Johnny. I have to say though, your deductions and conclusions are reasonable, so reasonable in fact, that you might want to keep them to yourself. The religions of this world are always looking for someone to crucify in the name of their particular deity, and your viewpoint has a taste of truth to it, making it dangerous to some."

I responded, "I doubt anyone is going to pay attention to the thoughts of a fifteen year old kid, Mudman. Anyway, I feel like I'm missing something important."

"I pay attention to you, Little Muddy. You add to my education regarding the study of humans."

"You know what, Mudman? That is the best compliment I have ever received. Thank you."

"Johnny," he then asked, gently, "did you give any thought to your question about how Satan was able to be in this reality without being created here?"

I thought a moment, and a light turned on in my mind! I stood up and shouted, "That's it! That's what is missing, Mudman! You said Satan was not created by the Creator and was not created into this reality!" I pondered that possibility, calmed myself down and quietly said, "Mudman, Satan is not here; he cannot be here and was never here. How did I miss that?"

Mudman replied, "No one is perfect, Johnny. You laid out a great explanation of what could have happened, but you're going to have to rethink your narrative. And we have still not explained Satan. Does he exist, or not?"

I was disappointed because I was so sure of myself. I began pacing and thinking.

"Mudman is correct, without the existence of Satan, my whole narrative falls apart!"

I thought, "What did Mudman say? We have still not explained Satan. Does he exist, or not? I am convinced Satan exists, he is mentioned several times in the bible; everyone in the world has heard of the 'evil one'. But how did he get into this reality without being created into this reality? Satan is not the creation of a creation; he is an original creation and many believe him to be the creator of evil."

My brain was spinning, "The legend of Satan being a fallen angel is created into our reality, meaning the legend was put here by the creator. Ours is a created reality; so, it follows that our creator exists. Satan exists, but not in this reality. How can that be? How can he be here and not exist here? Impossible!"

From somewhere, in my racing mind, an unimaginable, unthinkable thought occurred and gave birth to a shocking revelation.

"No! It can't be!" I exclaimed to myself.

I turned and looked at Mudman; he was sitting on the log, calmly watching me. I stammered, "Is Satan . . .? Mudman smiled and nodded.

I whispered, "Satan is our Creator!"

"That was pretty good, Little Muddy." he observed. "You worked it all out in your mind. I guess your idea of the way things are is still a solid observation. Satan is the obstacle, the tempter, and the tester of a sincere quest for goodness. He is also our Creator, apparently observing what humans will do with the freedom to choose their own path. Will people strive for goodness or submit to evil? Evil is the path of least resistance. Want to guess where to find the crowd?"

Mudman was talking as if everything was normal, pleased that his student had just realized that two plus two equaled four. I, on the other hand, was shocked by the thought of Satan being our Creator. Thinking the unbelievable made my legs weak. I went to the log and sat down beside Mudman, my mind a jumbled mess. I wanted to hear Mudman's thinking on my revelation, but could not seem to get the words started, so I began with one word.

"Mudman."

"What is on your mind, Johnny?"

"Satan is our Creator."

"That seems to be true, my young friend."

"I never thought of Satan being the Creator before."

"It is not a new idea, Johnny. In fact, it is ancient."

"You know, Mudman, Satan being the Creator makes sense."

"Well, it certainly answers many of your questions, Johnny."

"Mudman, have you always been aware who is Satan?"

"Yes."

"Why didn't you tell me?"

"There are some things in our reality require discovery, Little Muddy."

"Why not just teach those things?"

"There is magic in discovery, similar to creation, young friend."

"Mudman?"

"I understand, Little Muddy."

"Understand what? I haven't asked anything yet!"

"Everything in this reality here follows a progression, Johnny. I suspect you have a comment, not a question."

"Because of what I have learned today, I understand something that is too big to talk about."

"Another new discovery?"

"I don't know about 'new', but it is original with me."

"That being the case, Johnny, it belongs to you."

"You know, don't you Mudman? You have always known."

"Little Muddy, I observe and absorb. Human affairs are theirs."

"You are interested in humans, though. You study us."

"All things interest me, Johnny; however, the swamp is my concern, not humans."

"I don't believe that, Mudman. You are concerned about me ."

"That I am, my young friend. That I am."

"Why?"

"You give the swamp affection, your love. The swamp does not forget."

"Mudman, my new discovery seems unimportant, now."

"It is an important truth, though, young friend."

"Another untold truth, Mudman?"

"Perhaps. Certainly beyond human acceptance."

"What do I do with it, Mudman?"

"That truth belongs to you now. You decide."

"You also know the truth, Mudman."

"I am not human, Little Muddy; truth does not apply."

"What about humanity? Do they deserve the truth?"

"Humanity chose its truth long ago and followed a creation instead of God. Perhaps the next collective will be smarter. It will be interesting to watch."

"What about God, Mudman? I wonder what God thinks of the truth?"

Those last two questions were met with deafening silence. No wind, no birds, no movement in the swamp, nothing. I just sat there on the log, waiting.

Mudman stood up from the log, looked at me, then turned and glided into the swamp. It took awhile, but he returned and sat down beside me.

"Johnny," he began, "your discovered truth is not a secret. You can reveal it to anyone. It is a truth, a dangerous truth, but a truth nevertheless. It is one of many truths, hidden within the symbols, books, structures, and rituals of mankind; some truths you have already discovered, so many more await your discovery. That is how truths are absorbed; they must first be discovered. I know what you are eager to ask right now. You want to ask why truths are hidden? You already know why, my friend, because your truth is in you now and you are reluctant to tell it, even though you believe it to be something mankind should know. You will work it out, just follow your learnings. There now, see what you have done? You have affected my way of talking!" We both laughed.

Mudman continued, "Nothing happens in this reality without a reason, Little Muddy, meaning there was a reason for your discovery. It is yours to do with as you please. Why have I told you all this? Your last question caused me to reflect on why I exist. Your query regarding what God thinks of the truth remains a great question. The only answer I have is this: God **is** truth and you are in possession of an important truth. Do not allow that understanding to overwhelm you, Johnny, because few, if any, will accept that truth. Too much money, too much power, and too much shame is at risk in such an admission. I will watch, with great interest, your decision and suspect it will wait until another now."

"Mudman, why do you exist?"

"That is my truth, young Johnny."

"I know why you exist, Mudman."

"Really? This should be good. Why, Johnny?"

"God wants you to exist, Mudman."

He was silent for a few minutes, thinking; then he smiled, pointed at me and ordered, "Little Muddy, you go home now.

Your brothers are coming to get you and are excited about something. Guess you are about go on another of those outings, of which your family is so fond. Remember now, everything happens for a reason in this reality."

Then he reached down, pinched some mud, smeared it on my cheek and stood, looking at me.

This had been quite a day.

Chapter 39 - The Farewell

Sure enough, my brothers came running, excited about something momma wanted to tell us and urging me to come home, now. Interesting, how things happen, is it not? I wondered about that 'everything happens for a reason' saying and had some arguments to give Mudman about it next time we met. My brothers hurriedly rushed home and I slowly followed them.

I turned around like I usually do to watch Mudman glide into the swamp, but something was different. There were very many alligators now in the swamp and mosquito hawks were everywhere! Some were even landing on me! Mudman was gliding into the swamp alright, but he was gliding backwards, facing me! I had never seen him do that before. I waved to him; he waved back and held his hand high as the swamp slowly absorbed him. The water thing followed, its wave herding the alligators back to the deep. I thought to myself, "Mudman sure has a way about him."

"Wow!" I thought. "That was impressive. Wonder what that was all about?" When I got home, I found out. Momma was in the kitchen, all excited. She took one look at me, grabbed a washrag, wiped the mud off my face, and commented that it will be easier to keep clean in the city without all the mud around. Momma had found a buyer for our house and a steady job in Dallas. We were moving to Dallas and I would finish high school there. Momma started her new job in a week. We had a week to move. Everyone but me was excited about starting a new life in Dallas. I expected to live here the rest of my life. Everything was perfect. Momma straightened me out on that. Her hours had been cut, making the family income inadequate to cover our cost of living, including grandma's social security. Selling the house will give us enough money to pay off the car and have enough left over to live on for at least six months. Dallas was our salvation.

It was plain now what that demonstration in the swamp was about; Mudman was saying goodbye to me. Somehow, he knew. I ran back down to the swamp to look for him, but saw nothing. I bent down, took off my socks and shoes, and walked into the muddy shallows, where I stood in silence, perhaps for the last time. I love this swamp. The feeling of the mud between my toes made me happy. I was alone and pleased with the solitude, for there was I, a fifteen year old boy, barefoot, standing in the shallows, staring out into the deep swamp with tears running down my face. I stood tall and said out loud,

"Goodbye, Mudman. . . until another now."

Suddenly, the swamp came alive with all of its sounds of birds, frogs, crickets and creatures. I knew he was there with me. I love this swamp and hate goodbyes. I stood there and listened to the music of the swamp in a now I will never forget, then slowly turned and waded to shore and walked home barefoot, carrying my shoes. I never saw Mudman again. He is still there. Mudman is the swamp.

Chapter 40 - Epilogue

My life changed drastically, afterwards. We moved to an old crowded neighborhood in Oak Cliff, just south of Dallas, where parking your car in front of your house was sometimes a problem and your neighbor's house was spitting distance from yours. In other words, culture shock. I adapted though and began High School in Dallas, where I found the curriculum there to be at least a year behind that of my Beaumont school. Now that made classes boring, but it also gave me a reputation of being a math and physics whiz there; I wasn't. The subjects studied there were just easier because I had already seen them before. Shop class and art were more difficult. Classrooms had more students and the teachers were more interested in grades than teaching, at least from where I stood. Worst of all, I lost all eligibility in sports. In the fifties, a student had to attend a school for one year before becoming eligible to compete. I joined the Army soon after graduating.

I hated the military. In the early 60's, the Army was a boiling pot of racial discord. I met Negroes for the first time in the Army. It was not cordial. Because of time spent with Mudman, the results of forced integration imposed upon a diverse captive society were well within my understanding; however, the Army is run by drones who do not listen to inferiors. No luck there, I was on my own. Again, I disliked the military and was very happy to be honorably discharged in 1963. Looking back, I have to admit that my military years were of benefit; I needed them. Joining was one of my best life decisions.

Marriage, college, children, and career followed suit, in proper order. Sounds great, right? That's because it is. But, I learned more useful information in six years with Mudman

than in all the time since. I missed my swamp.

I went back for a visit, you know, thirty-five years later. I was fifty years old at that time and visiting a relative who lived near Beaumont. I parked on the street and walked to the house where I once lived. There was an old woman at the side of the house on her knees, working in a flower bed. She asked why I walked down there instead of driving. I explained that I lived here back in the fifties and just wanted to walk around and visit some of my old memories. She stood up, shaded her eyes with a gloved hand, and took a long look at me.

"What's yur name, mister?" she asked.

I apologized for not introducing myself, told her my name and asked if it would be alright to walk down to the swamp behind her house.

"She looked intensely at me, grinned and said, "So, yur Johnny Parfait. Yur him!"

"Him?" I said, wondering.

"Yep, 'him', dat local legend 'round heah."

"Legend?" I laughed, unbelieving. "What legend?"

She replied by saying, "Da one bin tol' by sum folks 'bout a swamp boy who tol' stories 'bout seeing dat Bigfoot thing 'n talked wit snakes 'n gators. Da boy who swum naked, not afraid, in dat deep swamp, and paddle a pirogue by his self to dark places no one dare go. Dem gator hunters tell ole tales 'bout a swamp boy wit p'tection, a beest under de water that looks out for 'em. Dat be you!"

Then she laughed and stated, "Course, all dat be bullshit, but makes fur a good story. Thang is, dat legend gets bigger sum time. Good stories do dat, ya know. Dey git a life o' der own, don't cha know. What did ya really do in dat swamp when ya lived here, anyways?"

I told her about my fishing for perch and crawfish and that I did not really spend much time in the swamp.

"Well, dat figgers." she commented and asked, "Didya really have a snake and turtle zoo that you charged kids for lookin'?"

"Yes." I admitted. "That much is true. There were rabbits and flying squirrels there, as well."

"Well," she said, "shur is gud to meetcha. I'll go on down to dat swamp witcha, if'n you don't mind; ain't bin down der in a gud while, 'n ain't ne'er gone alone. Folks don't go to da swamp deez days, much. Might want to be on the lookout fur snakes and such, bin rainin' sum here lately and dem copperheads be out and about."

We walked to the swamp; I sat down on a dead tree and just looked around. The water had risen from when I lived there. There was less shore. The water was clear, but looked black because of the mud.

"Mr. Parfait," she said urgently, slapping at her arms, "we best be gittin' on back. Deez dam skeeters'll drain us dry afore long."

"You go on back, ma'am," I replied, "I'll be right behind you in a few minutes."

I love this swamp, the way it smells and feels. I bent down, took off my socks and shoes, rolled my pants above my knees and walked into the muddy shallows. I reached into the water, pinched some mud from the bottom and smeared it on my cheek. The feel of the mud between my toes filled an emptiness within me. I saw small perch, darting through the water, chasing and feeding on bugs, and listened as birds and frogs chirped their songs in bass and soprano. I felt great happiness; I was where I was supposed to be. While gazing into the shadows of the deep swamp, a compulsion urged me to just start wading there and stay, but I couldn't; there were obligations, and secrets still held a firm grip. Mudman told me long ago there are truths yet to be discovered, truths for me to find.

I was alone here now, actually pleased with the solitude. There was I, a fifty year old man, standing in the muddy shallows, barefoot with his pants rolled up, and staring into the deep swamp, reminiscing, with tears rolling down his face. While I stood there, the swamp erupted with its unique music of countless voices. "Mudman is here," I thought, "he has ever been." Long ago, I came to realize that this swamp is an original creation, conscious of itself and has existed for millenniums. Mudman is that consciousness personified. He observed and absorbed those things about which he talked. The swamp was, is, and will be here as long as this reality persists.

A final question was begging for an answer. Why me? Why did he choose that ten year old Johnny? I don't know for sure, but it may be that he saw my love of the swamp back then, or absorbed it. In any event, because of Mudman, I saw and learned things few, if any, people have seen or even thought about in their lives. I still carried discovered secrets of untold truths that cannot be told to the stupid, which eliminates the 'blissfully ignorant herd', their drovers and owners. This book reveals a few, enough for you to see why some truths cannot, or should not, be told. I suspect that you, the reader, might be better off basking in your "blissful ignorance".

Many thoughts and more flooded my mind as I slowly waded out of the swamp and walked back to the house, still barefoot, and carrying my shoes.

The old woman saw me return and commented, "Dem skeeters dun drove you back, I sees; reckoned dey wud. Ya got sum mud on your face, too."

I thanked her for allowing me to cross her property and answered, "Mosquitoes don't bother me much, ma'am and one always gets a little muddy in the swamp."

"Dat be sump'n else to add to da legend," she laughed, "dat swamp boy has de power to skeer off bugs! Nice meet'n ya, Johnny. I'm be tellin' fo'ks ya cum to visit. They ain't bleevin' me none, tho." Then she laughed again. I laughed too, and wondered if she knew my grandma, back in the day.

I faced the swamp, raised my hand high, and held it there a moment.

"Watcha doin', mister? Who you be wavin' at?

"No one, ma'am. Just saying goodbye. . . until another now."

"Nuther now? Whut's dat mean? Best not talk lak dat out loud, cuz fo'ks 'll think yur a bit tetched in the noggin'." Then she laughed and said, "Lak me." and laughed again.

"I heered the noise ya steered up out der. Ain't ne'er heered sump'n lak dat afore 'n spect I ain't bout to agin."

Then she added, "I bin seein'. Ya done went an' tol me a story 'bout dat boy not spendin' time in dat der swamp, didn't 'cha? Yur him, I see'd it; but ya don't lak fo'ks to know. I done figgered it, cuz I see's thangs."

I squeezed her hand softly, kissed her cheek, said goodbye, and walked back to my car, barefooted and carrying my shoes. I have never been back. I know, you have a question and I know what it is. Yes, I saw Mudman. Mudman is the swamp.

Until another now. . .

John D. Parfait, Jr.